BIG BANGS

Howard Goodall is a composer and broadcaster. In addition to a number of choral works and music for the theatre, he has written the theme tunes to many TV programmes including Blackadder, Mr Bean, Red Dwarf and The Vicar of Dibley. He has won great acclaim for his own programmes shown on Channel Four, Howard Goodall's Organ Works, Choir Works and, most recently the series, Big Bangs on which this book is based. He also presents BBC TV's annual Choir of the Year competition and hosts Channel Four's Glyndebourne programmes.

Howard Goodall

BIG BANGS

The Story of
Five Discoveries
that changed
Musical History

_v_

VINTAGE

Published by Vintage 2001

4 6 8 10 9 7 5

Copyright © Howard Goodall 2000

First published in Great Britain in 2000 by
Chatto & Windus

Vintage
Random House, 20 Vauxhall Bridge Road,
London SW1V 2SA

Random House Australia (Pty) Limited
20 Alfred Street, Milsons Point, Sydney,
New South Wales 2061, Australia

Random House New Zealand Limited
18 Poland Road, Glenfield, Auckland 10, New Zealand

Random House (Pty) Limited
Endulini, 5A Jubilee Road, Parktown 2193, South Africa

The Random House Group Limited Reg. No. 954009
www.randomhouse.co.uk

A CIP catalogue record for this book
is available from the British Library

ISBN 0 09 928354 9

Printed and bound in Great Britain by
Cox & Wyman Ltd, Reading, Berkshire

Frontispiece:
With Zulu children, filming 'Howard Goodall's Choir Works'

CONTENTS

FOR VAL
AND MY MUM AND DAD
WITH LOVE

PREFACE

In September 1995, I was hosting a live radio quiz show called *Key Questions* in the English city of Lichfield. The idea of the programme was that listeners and members of the studio audience posed musical questions to an expert panel, and on this occasion a man asked the panel what they thought was the most important event in the history of Western music. The panel members that evening were the jazz composer and bandleader John Dankworth, music journalist Annette Morreau and young composer Julian Phillips. All three panellists gave the same response: Bach's 48 Preludes and Fugues and the invention of Equal Temperament. We all tried heroically to summarise for the audience in under two minutes what this invention was and what it meant, but I think we knew that we had not done it justice. How could something that was so important be so difficult to explain?

Three years later I was in the office of Michael Jackson (the controller of Britain's Channel 4 Television, not the llama-fancying entertainer) discussing the possibility of a series of TV programmes that might look afresh at the great sweep of Western classical music, when I mentioned the invention of Equal Temperament again. I said that it was an event of seminal importance to Western music, and yet few people had a clue what it was. Well, what is it, then? Jackson asked. I replied that he'd have to commission a series to find out, and so he did.

What grew from that conversation was the idea of a series of films to examine the five critical turning points in European musical history, *Howard Goodall's Big Bangs*. In the months that followed, I tried my five chosen big bangs out on various musicians to see if their own lists would differ radically from mine. I qualified my choice by saying that I was interested in changes to music that happened in one place at one time: one day the invention wasn't there, the next it was. This ruled out the symphony, which emerged gradually over several decades, and though we often say Joseph Haydn was the 'father' of the symphony, what we mean is that he was the first composer to write a lot of them obeying one particular, much-imitated formula. The thing itself had been around in various guises well before Herr Haydn. It also ruled out the violin, which had evolved slowly for centuries, and the cello (Julian Lloyd Webber's and Steven Isserlis's suggestions). Moreover, my brief was confined to classical music, so inventions like the electric guitar or the synthesiser would not count.

I was relieved to learn that my musician friends mostly agreed with the list. In the year that it took to make the TV series, I never once regretted the five choices, nor wished we could have had ten of them rather than five. Though ordered roughly in the chronological sequence that the 'inventions' occurred, each of the programmes (and each of the corresponding chapters in this book) reaches back and forward across history to tell their own stories. This is not an old-fashioned History of Western Music, starting with African tribal chant and trawling through to Andrew Lloyd Webber. And this is more than the usual 'book of the series', too.

I had discovered when researching my previous TV projects that much of the most fascinating detail that one unearthed along the way had to be left out when it came to filming and editing the final programmes. Writing a book would allow me to include and elaborate upon these details: to say more about the incredible, hidden room we were shown in Mantua, which has only been revealed in the last eighteen months after nearly 400 years, or to look more fully at the extraordinary process of transferring a 90-year-old recording onto a modern CD. The book gave me the opportunity to cover aspects of music's journey that I could not in the series: to consider the immense contribution of Jews in the twentieth century, for example – not a 'Big Bang' as such, but a significant phenomenon nonetheless. But I also wanted to put all these facts and particulars into context, to make this a personal statement. So between the pillars of the big events I have reflected on some of the issues raised. Why does music have an effect on us? Where does it come from? Does it have a meaning? Spending a year travelling the world, making a TV series like this has been an amazing experience. I have read so many books, met so many people, and visited so many historic places, that it would be strange if I had not come to some conclusions about the subject in which I have been immersed. Every so often the mad pace of it would be halted mid-flow for the recording of some music along the way. I am thinking of the eerie calm one late summer evening that came over a completely empty, darkened Canterbury Cathedral during the filming of a performance of Dunstaple's *Veni Sancte Spiritus*. In this same place the very first performance of the motet had been given, in 1416, for Henry V after Agincourt. The hush and concentration required for filming makes one hear music in an unusually focused frame of mind. Dunstaple's work has a strange, unfamiliar beauty. It is music written during the savagery of the Hundred Years War, yet it is totally devoid of aggression, jingoism or pomposity. It was impossible not to be moved.

Recording excerpts from Monteverdi's opera *Orfeo* at a studio in North London, using reproduction ancient instruments and boys' voices, was another thrilling experience. Though I have been a professional musician for over twenty years I have never seen and

A horn-player,
11th-century
French treatise

heard, close-up, the bizarre Renaissance instruments called cornetti. These look like bent ebony tubes of about two feet long and sound like a cross between an oboe and a trumpet. They are famously difficult to play well and there are only a handful of players in Britain who can wield them with any degree of confidence. We had two of these players, magnificently taming their cornetti, producing the most magical, haunting noise to accompany Orpheus's descent into the Underworld. The whole studio watched in wonder as they weaved expertly in and out of the voice's troubled utterances. Monteverdi would have been proud.

On another, frozen February day, thanks to persistence and inspired negotiation by our Associate Producer, we were finally allowed inside the ruined hulk of the Venice opera house, La Fenice. Hard-hatted, we clambered up the burnt-out stairways front of house, almost as if we were en route to our seats in the dress circle, suddenly turning a corner into the auditorium that was destroyed by arson in 1996. I do not know if it was the shattered remains of the walls and proscenium arch, or the sight of builders beginning restoration work that most hit me, standing there on that precarious ledge in the blinding sunlight. But my voice caught in my throat. The startling fact is that for Venetians the fate of La Fenice *really* matters. I was standing in the hollow shell of a place built for classical music, and it was too important, too precious, too meaningful to knock down. The music that flooded into my head was the gorgeous, melancholic tune from Verdi's *La Forza del destino*, known by many as the music for the film *Jean de Florette*:

> *Le minaccie, i fieri accenti*
> *Portin seco in preda i venti . . .*
> (Let threats and violent words
> be carried away by the winds).

Moments like these made me want to assess the emotional impact of classical music, which is what I have attempted in this book.

I am adamant that the understanding of classical music does not need to belong to a club of people with specialist knowledge. Everyone who enjoys music should be able to fathom the content of this book. No one need fear the use of jargon like hemi-demisemiquaver, *coloratura*, or *Gesamtkunstwerk*. If I have to use technical words I explain them. I do not pretend that all the concepts in this book are easy, but I have tried to show that music is really no more intimidating than any other art form or science.

I made the TV series with a team of intelligent professionals, none of whom would describe themselves as musically well informed. If I could explain an idea successfully to them, the logic ran, then it would work for the public in general. Perhaps the gentleman from Lichfield who asked that original question about Western music will finally get his answer.

Howard Goodall
London, November 1999

OVERTURE

We are sitting at one end of a time corridor, over a thousand years long. We, that is you and I, are trying to concentrate on the dark remoteness at the other end – the Dark Ages of Europe. They, the foreigners at the other end, are almost silent. Whilst we are bathed in light and colour, they are hiding from the harsh glare of the sun in what looks like a cell or a tunnel. To us they seem like children in many ways, with their Nativity stories, ghosts and miracles, their unquestioning beliefs and their Gardens of Eden. If they could see us, they would think us indescribably rich and exotic.

At our end of the corridor there is a musical cacophony, at theirs a profound and disheartening silence. At our end of the corridor there are a thousand different voices demanding to be heard, demanding our attention. Music has become more than a backdrop – it has become a blaring soundtrack for practically every event in our lives, whether we are travelling, eating, shopping, exercising, making love or being cremated. We are even given music to 'listen to' in the womb. Knowledge and information overwhelm us. At their cold and gloomy end of the corridor, however, only a trickle of learning and culture survives from classical times, mainly through hearsay and deduction. An almost dried-up riverbed of cultural information stretches from the fiefdom of Northumbria to the heel of Italy, by way of a few scribes and harassed librarians. The Roman Empire has disintegrated in all but name and every settlement and community is fending for itself.

They have all but lost the flow of the blood of music. It has become for them a distant, heartbreaking echo, surviving only in the keening lamentation of what will one day be known as 'Gregorian' plainsong. This, the mother of our music, inherited rough-edged from the Jews then smoothed into a musical marble, a last mournful relic of centuries of joyful exuberance, is their solace in the medieval gloom.

They do not use the word with familiarity or ease, but they are the first peoples of a new confederated race: Europeans. Sacred plainsong, with its attendant frescoes and Romanesque temples, is the only thing that says to them 'This is Us and *not* the Byzantine East, This is Us and *not* the Muslim South, This is Us and *not* the Barbarian North. We haven't the libraries and learning of Islam, nor the opulent sophistication of the Empire that fans out from Constantinople, all we have that is truly ours is this tentative and haunting song.'

Gregorian chant's most characteristic musical shape is that it continually turns in on itself, like a shell. Its melodies don't stretch outwards expansively, they fold inwards. Its parameters are restricted to the comfortable vocal range of an average singer, never exploiting the giddy potential lying at the strained, higher end of the voice – a technique so familiar in Middle Eastern, Asian or African chanting. Is its lack of daring and bravado something to do with Christianity's birth as a secretive, persecuted, underground movement? Or is it the first sign of a 'different' Western European approach to music, more reflective and insinuating? Its note-patterns are clustered into 'modes', half-remembered rules and theories from the lost music of the ancient Greeks.

Every single note of the music of Imperial Rome, in the absence of any form of notation, has been lost. The survival of something quite so delicate as Gregorian chant for hundreds of years through war, invasion and pestilence is nothing short of miraculous. A millennium and a half later we treat this sacred music as if it is merely wallpaper for the ear. 'New Age' aural incense – a soothing, mildly hypnotic balm, antique and unthreatening, stripped of all context and intention. The *faith*

David composing the Psalms, from the 8th-century Canterbury Psalter.
Surrounded by trumpeters and clapping dancers, David plays a lyre-like harp,
while notaries take down his song, trumpeters play and dancers clap.

and purpose of it is irrelevant. Its Christianity is ignored, or
rather conveniently lost, thanks to the CD's super-reverberant
acoustic and an indecipherably dead language. At our end of
the millennium corridor there isn't much space for *meaning*.

The 'Gregorian Experience' is just a nice sound now, no more. Our medieval ancestors' most precious, fragile gift, centuries in the making, whisked to the top of the 'classical' charts on a whim.

I am a composer. Not an important one, but one who feels nevertheless part of some kind of ancient, almost mystical tradition, and who feels he owes a debt of gratitude to a humble monk at the other end of this millennial corridor. Only we are afforded the luxury of time-travel back down the wormhole, since they are forever trapped back there, in an age of violence and instability, these thousand-year-old foreigners.

I am embarking on a journey at the turn of the twentieth century to find the man who gave Western European music the wherewithal to begin its staggering history. He wouldn't have used the words Western or European about himself, at least in the sense we use them. He was a jobbing musical director at a cathedral church in what is now called Tuscany, in the first twenty years of the eleventh century, charged with the task of teaching the choristers Charlemagne's chants. These chants formed the backbone of the worship of the period, replacing the earlier Gregorian collection.

If you visit Arezzo, the town where Guido 'the monk' spent much of his life, you become aware quite quickly that he is an elusive and mysterious man. For a town whose other famous sons – Francesco Petrarch, Piero della Francesca and Giorgio Vasari – compete for the visitor's attention, it's hardly surprising the guidebooks are so lamentably sketchy on the life of Guido Monaco (*c.* 990–after 1033). In a fit of nineteenth-century civic pride, the town put up an imposing statue to him in its own Guido Monaco square, and one or two bars and trattorias remember him in their names. A small plaque is embedded in the wall of a house near the Duomo telling the conscientious passer-by that Guido lived and worked there. In fact, it's the wrong house next to the wrong cathedral and he certainly wasn't born in Arezzo – the nearby village of Talla claims, equally hopefully, to be his *actual* birthplace.

The cathedral he did work in is now a fenced-off hilltop ruin and the home of a dozen or so feral cats. It was demol-

The plaque celebrating Guido in Arezzo

ished by Cosimo de Medici in the sixteenth century to punish the people of Arezzo, nominally his subjects at the time, for their persistently rebellious behaviour. The 'Duomo Vecchio', as it is known affectionately, had in any case been superseded in the twelfth century by an imposing *new* cathedral on the opposite hill. This latter building still stands, magnificently, but the original 'master' copies of Guido's own textbooks – the *mappa mundi* of Western music, have long since disappeared.

Guido of Arezzo is an odd choice of hero, I know – a musician no one's ever heard of – a donnish Benedictine pedagogue from Northern Italy, but to my mind he's no less important than Beethoven or Presley, Wagner or Stockhausen. He is their *sine qua non*. He is the father and facilitator of every note they wrote. Guido of Arezzo gave us, among other things, our system of musical notation.

What writing is to language, notation is to music. Guido taught us how we might write our music down. His solution – worried out of a bewildering chaos of possibilities, like precious metal from ore – has served us unswervingly for a thousand years. Mostly we do not know his name. Mostly we take for granted his inestimable gift to us. There was no notational system before him, and there have been no serious alternatives since. None of the world's other musical cultures have ever developed a comparable notation. European music took his rules and ideas and began a soaring flight, unmatched anywhere in its sophistication and ambition. So I can't let him slip away into obscurity.

He isn't the only musical alchemist I am looking for. There are others, great facilitators, like Claudio Monteverdi (1567–1643) or Bartolomeo Cristofori (1655–1731), who are the Darwins or Einsteins of music, the brilliance of whose discoveries and contributions set in motion tidal waves of creativity in the years that followed. It's curious that their achievements are so anonymous, considering the role music plays in everyone's lives. It's as if we had learnt about $e = MC^2$, but had forgotten who first figured it out, or had had the experience of psychoanalysis but had never heard of Sigmund Freud.

Even at the beginning of my quest to know these ingenious and inventive people better, I am struck by the fact that their ideas are part of a system of music that is being eclipsed as I write. I did not intend there to be a valedictory flavour to my journey, but it is unavoidable: the music of the next thousand years will not be dominated by the unique and complex European musical language of the last. New priorities and tastes will prevail. Improvisation as a means of composition is already much more widespread than the older written form and will continue to develop. The blurring of distinctions between performer and composer, the clamour and energy of the ethnic and spontaneous, and above all the flight from counterpoint (the layering of more than one tune or line upon another) are early-warning signs of a massive sea-change.

Guido, in the early eleventh century, was fascinated and challenged by the growing possibility of the then radically new ideas of 'harmony' and 'counterpoint'. Now, most college music students are absolved from grappling with his ancient theories on these subjects: they are no longer really relevant to the overwhelming bulk of modern musicians. So it does seem right to take one last look at the system we have inherited before Guido's clever codes are replaced by those of the computer, the sequencer and the optical fibre.

I am going in search of a shy and distant genius. From our crowded, cacophonous end of the time corridor, I am peering into his empty room, his silent, almost-musicless world, at the place and time of the birth of Western Europe. He is an age away, and yet he is my brother.

ONE

The Thin Red Line

*Guido of Arezzo and the
Invention of Notation*

If you're a non-musician there are a few very basic facts you
may need to get the full value out of what I'm about to unveil.
Here they are:

1 Everyone knows that since our hunter-gatherer days we,
   Homo sapiens, have had music for our rituals, ceremonies,
   dances and amusement. What is less well known is that the
   fundamental raw materials of music are pretty well the
   same now as they have always been, albeit in rather more
   sophisticated modern forms. You can sing; you can strike a
   piece of skin strapped tightly over a gourd and make a
   drum; you can hit different lengths of wood; you can blow
   into a hollowed-out tube of some kind like a flute; you can
   make a shell or horn resonate; or you can pluck a piece of
   cord as in the guitar or harp. You could, for variety, slide a
   piece of catgut across the guitar strings instead of plucking
   them, as is the case with the violin family. You can mix 'n'
   match these ideas – like stretching your piece of cord over
   your hollowed-out bit of wooden tube, and so on, but that's
   basically it. Every musical instrument we have now is developed one way or another from one of these starting points.

2 All the ancient civilisations – Chinese, Indian, Inca, Aztec,
   Egyptian, Greek, Roman – had more or less sophisticated
   versions of this motley collection. What they all did was to
   divide the different sounds they could make into higher or
   lower pitches, so tunes could go up or down. They made

higher notes by shortening the piece of cord, for example, or striking a smaller bit of wood or blowing down a shorter piece of tubing, because little things make higher sounds than big things. The contrast between the higher and lower sounds was thought to be most creative and melodious, so they started to make the steps between the highs and lows closer together, in order to provide a wider range of possible contrasts and places for the tunes to go. These steps of pitch later became 'scales'.

3 Our music derives a good deal of its basic theory and science from the Greeks, in particular Pythagoras (fifth century BC). The Greeks made crucial decisions about the distance between musical steps, for instance, which we in Europe broadly went along with (see chapter 5 on Equal Temperament). It was the Greeks who started calling the notes by letters of their alphabet (ΑΒΧΔΕΦΓ etc.), an idea we adopted. The Greeks also, tantalisingly, had a primitive form of notation for musical notes that we have identified in modern times. Fragments of this system, whereby the note names were placed above a sung text with various dashes and dots to indicate rhythm, have been found on a tombstone from Asia Minor (now in Copenhagen's National Museum of Denmark) and on some Euripides play scripts. But their notation system wasn't widespread and it was lost to the generations that followed. As far as even the Romans were concerned, it hadn't existed.

4 Until the Roman Catholic Church set about codifying music in earnest in the early Middle Ages, virtually all music was part of a handed-down, oral tradition – most of it was improvised on the spot and never heard of again. If we didn't have tape recorders, that is how popular and ethnic music would still be performed and enjoyed nowadays. Sooner or later someone somewhere was going to attempt to capture this improvised music so it could be reproduced again and again. The Chinese, although very good at music and possessed of many sophisticated and

subtle musical instruments, never got further than a crude system of notation known as 'tablature' (which I will describe in a moment). In fact, no one in the world had any luck with notation, except a few inventive and inquisitive monks in Western Europe.

Suppose you have composed or retained in your head a collection of tunes that you want others to reproduce at will without the help of a notation system, what do you do?

Well, you could teach them to a few other musicians with good recall, and they could teach them to a few more, and so on, until quite a lot of people could memorise your tunes – rather like chain letters or pyramid selling. There are several drawbacks to this method. The musician you teach it to might decide he or she had an improvement to the tune and modified it before passing it on to musician number three. If these Chinese whispers went on down the line, it wouldn't be long before your original tune was unrecognisable. I have experimented along these lines and found that the passed-on melodies begin to diversify after only one or two people in the chain. Or again, the musicians might memorise the tune initially, but over a period of days or weeks the chances of their forgetting it irretrievably multiply alarmingly.

Drawbacks aside, though, it was the best that was on offer to a musician in the days before notation came along. This was the state of affairs for hundreds of years with respect to the chants sung by monks all over Christendom in the first millennium AD. There were hundreds of these sacred chants – the words those of the Mass, the psalms, the hymns, the scriptures. What they constituted was a vast mental library of melodies to cover every service for every day of the year.

In the seventh century Pope Gregory the Great (c. 540–604) ordered a compilation and standardisation of the entire chant repertoire, so that the whole territory of Christian Europe should sing from the same hymn book, as it were. This sounds a lot easier than it was in practice. Though they had the *words* written down, these poor monks had to keep in their heads *all* the tunes. This meant that every note of every chant had to be

'The Procession of Lictors', engraving by Fantuzzi, the 1540s

taught, parrot-fashion: 118 Graduals (about 3–4 minutes each), 70 Introits (3 minutes each), 100 Alleluias (2 minutes), 18 Tracts (5 minutes), 107 Offertories (8 minutes), 150 Communions (3 minutes), 600 Greater Responsories and several thousand Office Antiphons. Some time-on-his-hands scholar has estimated that this repertoire amounts to the equivalent of memorising the total output of Beethoven and Wagner put together (roughly 80 hours of continuous music), without the help of music notation: an incredible accomplishment.

What other comparable feats of musical memory are there to put this into some kind of perspective? Well, there are the

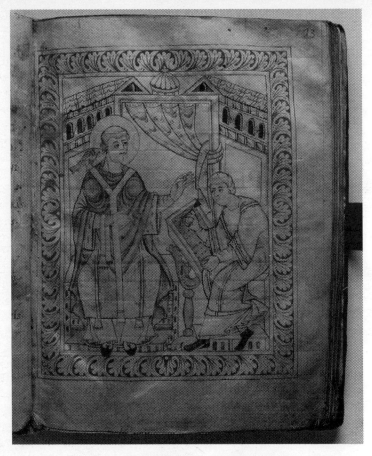

Pope Gregory the Great listening to a bird and directing a monk
to take down its song, 12th century

Aboriginal 'songlines', introduced to many in the West by
Bruce Chatwin in his book, *The Songlines*. The concept here
is that song melodies, not dissimilar to chants in many
respects, stretched across Australia's vast outback from one
end to the other: the song being, in effect, a musical map of the
terrain, passed on from song keeper to song keeper, from generation to generation. The thought of nomadic musical orien-

teering – songs that covered journeys, and the details within them, over thousands of miles – is staggering.

It is clear, though, that this was a shared memorising task – i.e. they all undertook one section each. At any one time, individual Aborigines would know their own sections of the songline but they were not expected to know the *whole* route. European monks of the first Christian millennium, by contrast, were each expected to know the entire chant repertoire.

There are resonances here with African melodies too. One way of conceiving, memorising or recreating an African melody was to treat it as a description of a journey, a place, or an event. If you could imagine yourself ambling, walking, running, staggering, climbing, darting, swimming, ducking or weaving along, you had an idea of the pace and 'feel' of the rhythm. If you knew the contours of the landscape you could describe or reproduce the shape of the melody, and so on. However, individual African musicians, like story-tellers, were expected to have 'their' set of songs, not to regurgitate the entire collection of tunes belonging to every tribe in the region. Thus the Gregorian collection of tunes appears to be almost unique in its scale and in the enormous and exacting demands it made upon the monks' memories.

In the tenth century, someone estimated that it took over ten painful years to teach a young boy chorister the chants he would need to know by adulthood for the singing of services in abbeys, cathedrals and churches. Suppose, though, you have managed to teach some poor lad the entire repertoire from memory. Isn't there another big question? If *one* singer knew the tune he was about to sing, how would he coordinate with *another* singer standing next to him to agree on the melody in the same place at the same time? How would you get a whole choir to sing together? These conundrums plagued the musical directors of all the abbeys and churches across Europe.

As part of his attempt to clarify and unify the practice of chanting across the continent, Pope Gregory set up a 'master choir' in Rome (the Schola Cantorum – 'school of singers') and ordered that all the different chants in use be codified and streamlined into his one definitive collection. It was a hideously ambitious undertaking, because not only were there all the different chants, there were also any number of monastic settlements who had their own highly idiosyncratic methods of performing or memorising them. But the great codification was embarked upon, and the Schola Cantorum acted as a kind of taste-monitoring unit, trying out sections of chant to see what worked best. Then, at roughly the same time as St Augustine was dispatched to Britain to re-convert the Celts and Angles, experts were sent forth from Rome to fan out across Christendom humming all the new 'official' tunes. John 'the Deacon' Hymonides, a ninth-century historian and monk, reported Gregory's achievements in a Vatican-commissioned survey with lofty pride:

> At this time . . . cantors of the Roman school were dispersed throughout the West and instructed the barbarians with distinction. After they died the Western churches so corrupted the received body of chant that a certain John, a Roman cantor . . . was sent . . . to Britain by way of Gaul; and John recalled the children of the churches in every place to the pristine sweetness of the chant, and preserved for many years . . . the rule of Roman doctrine.

Towards the end of the eighth century, ecclesiastical reforms were under way throughout Europe and plainchant began a major revision. On the initiative of his father King Pepin the Short (ruled 752–68), the Emperor Charlemagne (ruled 768–814) commissioned an authoritative anthology of the Gregorian chants, suppressing the regional chant 'dialects' such as the German or Celtic versions. It is Charlemagne's collection that we have inherited in the modern age, which is why this chant should probably be called 'Carolingian' (in the period of Charlemagne) rather than 'Gregorian'.

How was this massive job of codification and streamlining possible if there was no way of *writing down* the melody of the chants?

All over Europe, a system had developed of writing squiggles and lines above the words of the appropriate text (the psalm or hymn or canticle of the day), rather like acute, grave and circumflex accents, or the signs you see in phonetic dictionaries. These squiggles and accents were known as 'neumes'. Neumes indicated when your singing pitch went up or down and roughly speaking whether it was short or long. They attached themselves to each syllable of the text, and so in theory you could potter along with the words in front of you, following the neumes, letting your voice go up a step or down a step, or up three and down two or whatever, whilst singing – like complicated reading, really. This wasn't as helpful as it sounds, because these neumes didn't for some reason think to give you a *reference* pitch for where you were in the chant, just in what direction to go.

This is the fatal flaw of neumatic notation. The neumes give you the *shape* of the tune you're singing but they don't tell you from *where* you're starting. Neumes are like a map with just the shape of the roads on them, no names, no numbers, no bearings – no north, south, east or west. Hopeless. Unless, of course, you know the tune already and all you're doing is jogging your memory. Which is precisely what neumes were for – jogging the memory. There isn't enough information in a neume to tell you how to sing the thing totally from scratch.

To make matters worse, hardly any two musical monasteries across Europe used the same dots, squiggles and accent marks. Recent scholarship has identified about a dozen *species* of neume-types, covering large areas by distinct region – Aquitainian, Breton, Frankish, Northern Italian, and so on, and within each region or species there would be scores of variations and permutations. I have seen a chant book from one monastery that has the work of five different scribes over several decades, with each scribe developing his own idiosyncratic version of the neumes. All this was a recipe for confusion.

However, by the end of the first millennium AD the neumes of certain leading musical centres, like St Gallen in Switzer-

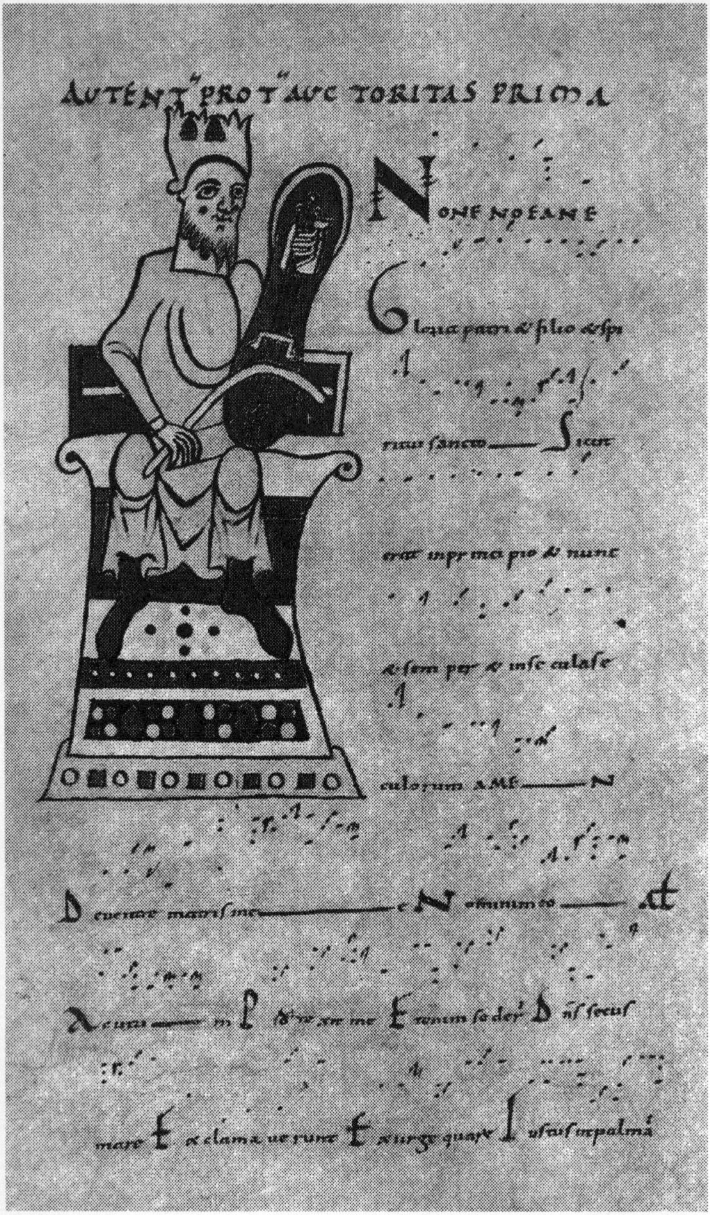

land, were approaching some kind of agreed pattern. They even had names. The basic note unit, not too long not too short, about the length of your average syllable, was called a *Virga* or *Punctum*. If you lengthened this a bit it was a *Punctum mora*. If your syllable had two notes instead of one, and they made a little step from one up to the other, it was called a *pes* ('feet'), and so on. There are much more complicated 'compound' neumes for show-off singers, called things like *Virga subtripunctis* and *Virga praetripunctis*, and ones with enormous potential for sexual innuendo, like *pressus*, *oriscus*, *quilisma* and *climacus*.

One way of side-stepping potential disagreement about the correct interpretation of the neumes was to have one leader, or cantor, who read the signs, and all the others would copy slavishly what he did. They followed his intentions by watching his hands. He would indicate the movement of the tune by gesturing his hand about into various positions like a one-armed bookie at the races. In Coptic Egyptian churches there are still some cantors who direct their choirs this way, a skill that has remained virtually unchanged in two thousand years. It isn't bad, this method, but it's still handicapped by the reliance on one singer knowing his chant, successfully transmitting it a split-second in advance to his colleagues, and in his memorising the whole repertoire and not dropping dead before an assistant can be trained up. You may at this point be thinking that what I am talking about is a conductor, but I'm not: a conductor may indicate how to phrase your notes, true, but always assumes you have your notes clearly written down in front of you. A conductor doesn't tell you which notes to sing or play. This ancient wrist-manipulator does.

Another reason why neumes are unsatisfactory is to do with *modes*, and it goes back to the Greeks. Modes are a sort of government of notes; they are what came before 'keys' in later music. Like the laws that govern us humans, they arose

Opposite: Neumatic notation: a player with a 'crwth' (a Celtic cittern played with a bow), mid-11th century

as a result of observing behaviour. The Greeks found that if you played or sang notes in particular sequences up and down the steps, the combination of notes created certain moods (hence 'modes') or feelings.

To modern listeners of music this shouldn't be especially difficult to grasp. The sequence of notes employed in, say, George Michael's song 'Careless Whisper', has a sadder effect than the sequence in his 'Wake Me Up Before You Go Go'. Even non-musicians are aware that 'minor' key music is more melancholic or thoughtful than 'major' key music. 'Greensleeves' sounds a lot more woebegone than 'We Wish You a Merry Christmas', the 'Moonlight' Sonata a lot more gloomy than 'Land of Hope and Glory'. Strictly speaking, the modern concept of 'major' and 'minor' came along centuries after medieval 'modes', but elements of the major–minor contrast exist in the modal system all the same. For example, the 'Hypolydian' mode is an ancestor of the modern key of 'C major' (which you will know from 'Can't Buy Me Love' or 'Love is the Sweetest Thing') and the 'Aeolian' mode is the ancient equivalent of the modern 'A minor' (as heard in Bacharach and David's 'Anyone Who Had a Heart' or Mary Hopkins's 60s hit 'Those Were the Days').

You can think of the ancient modes, if you like, as signs of the zodiac for musical melodies. Notes clustered together in the arrangement of a particular mode will exhibit certain tendencies and characteristics, depending on their position in that mode's layout – early, middle or late. Not only that, but other modes (as in astrology) may exert a secondary bearing or influence on the notes. An 'authentic' version of a given mode treats one note as the governor, a 'plagal' version of the same mode will treat another of the notes as its centre of gravity. You may think that the signs of the zodiac are enthusiastically promoted only by those with a commercial interest in them – that is, newspaper proprietors – but an intelligent defence of them might begin with the notion that the 'characteristics' of the signs have emerged as a result of centuries of careful socio-anthropological observation. So it is with the 'characteristics' of the musical modes.

The Greeks also thought that you could organise notes ('pitches') into a ladder of steps from the bottom of your instrument to the top. A piano keyboard illustrates this notion fairly clearly, with each note a rung on the ladder.

However, the decision as to how many rungs there would be (in other words, how close together the steps might be) was a cause of immense controversy and debate for centuries. It only really became standardised in the eighteenth century (see chapter 5 on Equal Temperament). But in the Middle Ages there was a kind of 'Approved List' of acceptable rungs, some a little closer together than others. The section of the ladder that was germane to the performance of chant was the section that covered the singing range of a normal adult male.

So hold in your mind's eye this section of ladder, if you will. Now arrange the rungs so that the steps aren't *exactly* the same distance apart. This is what the creaky medieval musical ladder was like – the spaces between the notes were uneven. You could still walk up and down it but some rungs would require delicate placement of the foot so as not to fall. If you were going to sing up and down this ladder, you might need a navigational aid of some kind, a guide to the rung formation. This is what a mode could do for you: it was a guide to the layout of notes.

What a mode did, in crude terms, was to tell you that if you were starting from, say, rung number 25, the first two rungs upwards were an average distance apart (a 'tone') but the two after that were much closer together (a 'semitone'). The upward journey from one rung, it was found, might be rather morose in character, whereas the journey from another rung had an altogether more cheery disposition. They gave these routes names, like the Phrygian, the Dorian, or the Lydian mode.

There are two other things about modes you should know. The first is this. The medieval Church, once it realised you could arrange notes into modal ladders, soon became dictatorial and effectively ruled that you *had* to use these arrangements, you couldn't wander off on your own improvised version. Folk musicians were blissfully free of this kind of

Guido of Arezzo working on his treatise 'Regulae rhythmicae',
11th-century miniature from an edition of his *Micrologus*

dogma, and indulged in all sorts of promiscuous behaviour with their rungs, but they weren't under the jurisdiction of the Pope. Ironically, these days folksters are rather more attached to modes than anyone else: this is because they are true anarchists and stick up for anything that's out of favour or antiquated. But in the first millennium church musicians never strayed off the official modal routes.

And in that case, knowing *which* mode you're supposed to be in is nothing short of essential. A neume is no help at all in telling you, either. Prior to the arrival of a decent signpost to tell you which mode you should follow, choirmasters had to work out the modes for themselves by painstaking trial and error – singing through the chants in all the possible modes until one sounded more correct than another. This was a procedure fraught with risk, as they couldn't always be sure they'd picked the right one, since taste, mood and personal preference played an influential part in the selection process, as you can well imagine. The only other option, available late on in the history of Gregorian chant, was to purchase a complicated tome from the Vatican which listed the chants (by their first-line titles) and gave you their official modes.

What was needed was a sign at the start of the piece which says what rung you start on and what mode you're following. It may seem obvious to us, because we take this sort of thing for granted, but in AD 1000 this idea was totally baffling. Until Guido of Arezzo.

The second other thing you need to know about modes is that inside a modal ladder there is a hierarchy of notes. The note you end on is called the 'final'. This note is the top-dog note, because it acts as 'home' to the mode, but there are other notes with secondary pulling power. The relative pulling power of notes within a mode is all to do with natural harmonics and the intrinsic resonance of different materials, like the different susceptibility of materials to electrical conductivity, or the magnetic forces of some metals as opposed to others. In short, certain rungs on the musical ladder exert pressure on others, like planets in orbit around the same sun. Medieval musicians became obsessed with these hidden powers, as if there was a kind of undiscovered alchemy behind it. Theorist after theorist tried to unlock the secrets of the modes, drawing up elaborate and bewildering diagrams and graphs to explain the meaning of it all. Most of them were trying to find hard evidence of the hand of the Almighty in the mystery of music. They were attempting the same thing in all areas of science and mathematics, of course, but with science and maths there was a system available to them to articulate and illustrate their theories: numbers and letters.

Since the hierarchy of notes in a mode seemed to be an immutable rule of nature, theorists and scholars thought it essential to employ these rules both in the teaching of music and in their books on music's hidden meaning. However, the whole discipline was embedded in fog and uncertainty, on account of the fact that you couldn't *look* at the notes you were talking about. Imagine teaching maths without numbers and equations, or geology without relief maps. This is what medieval music theory was like. Musical notes existed as sounds, as things you could reproduce with your vocal chords or on an instrument, but you couldn't *observe* their behaviour on a page in any meaningful way. Until Guido.

Not only did Guido provide a map for musical notes, a visual representation of an aural phenomenon, he also devised a totally reliable system for instant recognition of the relative power of notes in modal sequences. Darwin didn't *invent* evolution, of course, all he did was demonstrate clearly how he believed it worked, and how one might find the evidence for it in the natural world. Likewise, Guido didn't *invent* the way notes in a modal ladder exerted power over each other, but he came up with a rock-solid guide to these properties which any musician could use as a compass. His method was called 'sol-fa', and it made its most memorable appearance into ordinary folks' lives thanks to Julie Andrews and *The Sound of Music*.

You will no doubt recall the song, 'Do Re Mi', where headstrong ex-nun-turned-governess Maria ('a flibbertigibbet, a will-o'-the-wisp, a clown!') teaches her cute Tyrolean rugrats their musical scale with the aid of, as it turns out, Guido's sol-fa system. The only modifications that had been made to his prototype between 1020 and 1960 were the addition of one more step in the ladder ('Tee, a drink with jam and bread') and the naming of the first step 'Doh', instead of Guido's 'Ut'. The French went on using 'Ut' to mean the note 'C' for centuries after Guido, which is touching. At any rate, 'Ut, a deer, a female deer' doesn't have quite the same ring to it somehow.

Guido's tune, called 'Ut Queant Laxis', wasn't as catchy as hers but the idea was the same. Guido ('a jack-of-all-trades, a helluva guy, a Mensch!') wanted his pupils to be able to 'hear' in their heads the relative pitch of notes, to develop an instinct as to how high or low a given note would be. You see, before you can sing a tune properly you have to be able to recognise instantly the distance between notes. For example, when we sing 'Should auld acquaintance be forgot . . .' we know that the first leap is up four notes: 'Should ⇒ auld . . .'. The distance between two notes is called an interval, and Guido came up with a novel way of recognising intervals. First, he taught his choristers a hymn tune ('Ut Queant Laxis') that he'd made up for the purpose.

The names 'Ut Re Mi Fa So La' are the first syllables of each phrase of this hymn. Each line of the song began with a different note and the notes were arranged into a neat ladder from low to high. So if he'd wanted his boys to hear in their heads instantly the four-step interval that begins '*Should ⇒ auld* acquaintance be forgot . . .' he'd have told them to think of '*Ut ⇒ Fa* . . .'; if he'd wanted them to sing the chimes of Big Ben he'd have said 'La Fa So Ut, Ut So La Fa'. The advantage of calling the notes Ut Re Mi instead of A B C is that Ut Re Mi as a system works universally for *all* modes and keys. The Westminster chimes are always 'La Fa So Ut, Ut So La Fa' but in the modern key of C major they are: E C D G, G D E C, whereas in the key of G major they are: B G A D, D A B G. In A♭ major they are: C A♭ B♭ E♭, E♭ B♭ C A♭. In F# major they are: A# F# G# C#, C# G# A# F#. See what I mean?

But how did Guido choose the mini-words 'Ut Re Mi Fa So La'? The text of the tune he taught his choristers was the Vesper hymn for the feast of John the Baptist. He'd cunningly made sure that each line of this hymn began with the six notes

of his 'master' modal ladder and so he made each first syllable
of the words the sol-fa mnemonic, thus:

> *Ut queant laxis*
> *Resonare fibris*
> *Mira gestorum*
> *Famuli thorum*
> *Solve polluti*
> *Labii reatum, Sancte Johannes.*

The meaning of these Latin words is rather appropriate too:
'That your servants may with relaxed throats sing the won-
ders of your deeds; take away sin from their unclean lips, O
Saint John.'

The curious amongst you will want to know why 'Ut'
became 'Doh' at some point in the nineteenth century. I have
looked into this matter and all I can come up with is that one
or two other theorists tried alternative naming systems over
the years and the only thing that survived of one of them is
their use of 'Doh', absorbed into the mainstream of Guido's
method by evolution. It's not much of an explanation but it's
the best I can do, I'm afraid, and anyway think how dull life
would be without one or two unsolved mysteries.

Now we've sauntered down sol-fa lane, we can find the
main highway again and investigate Guido's other great gift to
posterity.

Guido Monaco had the laborious and thankless task of
teaching the cathedral choristers of Arezzo all the hundreds of
chants in the Christian calendar. His monumental contribution to the development of Western music was to come up
with a system of notation that allowed his choristers to read
the notes of the chants directly off the page: to *read music*. He
demonstrated this radical new idea in two publications, *Aliae
Regulae* (some time before 1030) and *Micrologus* (some time
after 1030), and he lived long enough to be aware that his
ingenious jottings had made an immediate and powerful
impact. His fame had him summoned, probably in 1028,
before Pope John XIX to demonstrate his theories, and to

show off the wondrous party trick of boys singing a melody they'd never seen before by following the notes above the text.

Were there any other early systems of notation in circulation at around the time of Guido, in AD 1000?

First of all, we should deal with *tablature*. Tablature is, simply, playing information for musical instruments. The ancient Chinese had tablature, as did the Indians and other ancients, in varying degrees of sophistication. Tablature even exists today in Western music, in the form of 'guitar symbols' which are ubiquitous in popular music.

Whereas musical notation tells you what notes it wants you to play, in what order, with what rhythm, and for how long, it doesn't give you any help as to *how* you are expected to make your sounds. Tablature, on the other hand, gives *only* this information. Tablature tells you where to put your fingers on the instrument to make the sound but it doesn't give you the order, rhythm or length of the intended notes. Tablature is for players who already know the style and tune they're going to perform, but who don't have the detailed instrumental hints and tips on how to reproduce it. All 'guitar chord symbols' (modern tablature) can do is tell you where to put your fingers on the strings – nothing else. Modern sheet music of popular songs with these symbols assumes you already know the song, the style, the speed, the rhythm, the groove – and so does ancient Chinese tablature. Consequently, tablature leaves the performer in charge of the majority of musical decisions; while notation shifts the emphasis dramatically towards the composer.

Tablature progressed independently of score notation for quite a while, reaching a high-watermark in the seventeenth century with immensely complicated lute music. Then it suddenly seemed unwieldy and inefficient, and disappeared. Its reappearance in the twentieth century in the transcription of popular songs is indicative of a trend whereby performers once again were becoming the creators of songs, not just their interpreters. Many of these performer–composers did not read music notation and so took to a method of indicating at least some of the information through non-musical symbols

Lute tablature

(none of which would have been possible without the invention of recorded sound to show what the style, rhythm, melody, speed and groove of the song actually was).

Tablature, needless to say, is totally useless when it comes to singing; I doubt therefore whether Guido of Arezzo gave it a moment's consideration when he developed his method of notation. What he must have caught a glimpse of, though, was a halfway-house type of neumatic notation, popular in the Frankish north and Aquitainian west, that had attempted some kind of vertical arrangement of the neumes on the page to imply their relative positions.

Meanwhile, other scribes had experimented with the idea that the words of the text themselves would move up and

down the page to illustrate what the sung notes should be
doing,
so the   out
    words   leapt ab-   the
        suddenly   page   this.
                             like
It may look absurd to us now as a method of showing the tune,
but you must admit there is a certain compelling logic to it.

I am sure Guido had done his research into the state of the
art vis-à-vis neumes when he was devising his tutorial for
reading chant. Though he lived and worked in the northern
half of Italy at a time when communications were distinctly
patchy, he would have been familiar with the predominant
Frankish schools of neumatic notation. The influence of
scribes from Aquitaine, in particular, can be seen in his work.

What Guido did was to draw a straight thin red line along
the top of the text which he said was the pitch F (he was using
the medieval system inherited from the Greeks of calling notes
by the first seven letters of the alphabet). If a neume (the signs
like acute and grave accents above the syllables) sat plonk on
the line, like a starling on a telegraph wire, it was always an F,
no quibbling, no messing about. He wrote a small 'f' on the
start of every red line to be absolutely unequivocal about it,
and thereby invented the 'clef' – the modern 'bass' or 'f' clef
is a direct descendant of Guido's prototype. Why did he
choose F as his master pitch? Well, two reasons. Firstly, it is
the note slap-bang in the middle of a man's natural singing
range, so used probably more than any other note and therefore a good line to draw through the middle of your notation.
Secondly, Guido knew that if you sing up the scale of rungs on
your musical ladder it's nearly all full steps, or tones, but there
are two half-steps, or semitones, in the pattern. One of these
is the step leading from E to F. By choosing F, Guido was being
as helpful as possible – giving the unwary singer every opportunity going of seeing the semitone step clearly. He might have
written MIND THE STEP instead.

When he added a second line, in fetching yellow, for the
note C, his logic was impeccable because the step from B to C

Guido's original red line

is the one *other* semitone pitch-step in the scale. Guido was no fool. His 'C' clef survives in the modern 'C' clef used by violas. The clef we use most of all in the modern era, the treble or 'G' clef was a later addition to the clef family but flows logically from Guido's original idea. Oh, and why is it called 'clef'? It's the French word for *key*, isn't it? Who told you music was difficult?

The simplicity of this approach may seem obvious but it had taken a few thousand years of music to get to that point.

It was a gigantic breakthrough. Now you always knew what note to start on, and what mode you were in. You had a fix, a grid reference, a Pole Star.

If a neume sat directly above the thin red line it was G, directly below, E, and so on. Devastatingly simple. Shortly after inventing the red line, as I was saying, Guido came up with a yellow line above it for C, five steps higher. This grid of pitch lines with spaces between them soon became known as the 'stave' (or 'staff' in America). On your stave you could hang your notes in any order you liked – it was a washing line of musical pitches – and as Guido soon saw, the boy choristers found it incredibly easy to master. They were the first human beings on planet Earth to *read* music. Sounds had become ink.

This is what he wrote about his system to a friend (in the prologue to his *Antiphoner*, a collection of chants, in about 1030):

Therefore I have decided, with God's help, to write this antiphoner in such a way that any intelligent and studious person may learn the chant by means of it; after he has thoroughly learned a part of it through a master, he will unhesitatingly understand the rest of it by himself without one. Should anyone doubt that I am telling the truth, let him come to learn and see that small boys can do this under our direction, boys who until now have been beaten for their gross ignorance of the Psalms and vulgar letters. Often they do not know how to pronounce the words and syllables of the very antiphon which they sing correctly by themselves without a master . . .*

He didn't let it rest there. Cast your mind back to Wrist Man, or pseudo-conductor. Guido thought that the manual method of indicating musical pitch might yet come in handy (so to speak) – the fact is, he didn't really know which of his

---

*Translated by Oliver Strunk revised by James McKinnon, quoted in *Source Readings in Music History*, Vol. 2. Revised edition, W. W. Norton & Company, New York & London, © 1950, 1978, 1998.

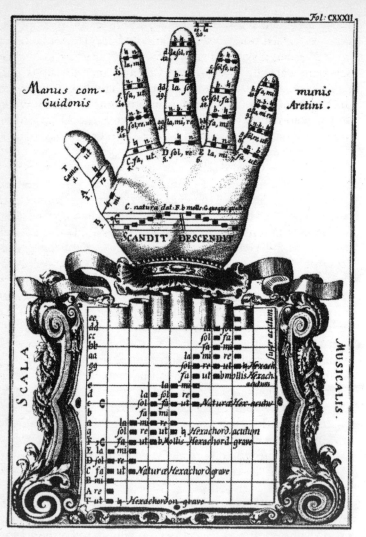

The Guidonian Hand, Guido's device for showing the notes of the scale

innovations would be the bigger success – and he attempted to revise that too. His technique of hand signals, which we now call the Guidonian Hand, became a standard, and was rigorously taught to music students for hundreds of years thereafter (as indeed was the rest of Guido's theory). If you look at your own hand you will see the fingers divided up into three segments each by creases, and various other divisions and sub-divisions elsewhere on your palm. The finger segments and other parts of the palm were given a note each, as it were, so you could point to that segment and imagine the appropriate note as a kind of visual table of the pitches. It was a pocket calculator for musical notes.

Remember, all this was happening before piano or harpsichord keyboards were readily available to present the singer with a graphic layout of the musical ladder in their mind's eye. The Guidonian Hand was a shortcut to identifying your notes and their relationship to each other. Although Guido's hand system has fallen out of usage, the *idea* of such a thing was remarkably persistent, and as time went by others took over the Wrist Man concept and adapted it to different needs. In particular, a method of teaching songs to infants developed in Eastern Europe using a hand-manipulating technique. The Hungarian composer Zoltán Kodály perfected and disseminated it at the turn of the twentieth century and it is still widely popular today among enlightened singing teachers.

You may remember the Steven Spielberg movie *Close Encounters of the Third Kind*. In it, there is a memorable scene near the end where François Truffaut attempts to make contact with the friendly aliens by means of hand signals denoting musical pitches; eventually the aliens' Mother Ship responds to the musical notes by copying the pattern. The hand signals used were none other than Kodály's, who himself had been inspired by Guido.

So, to recap, Guido of Arezzo presented a convincing and workable system of writing music down, clarified and streamlined the neumes, and created sol-fa. He offered a model for the modern 'scale', or musical ladder, made modes easy to identify and follow, and threw in some helpful hand signals for good measure.

But what he didn't foresee was quite how dramatically successful his methods would prove in the long run. In particular,

'Sumer is icumen in', English square-note notation
from the 13th-14th century

he could not have guessed that his clear stave notation would
change the course of musical history. Because it could now be
written down, a more sophisticated variety of music could
exist that didn't rely on one person's memory. In other words,
Guido paved the way for the emergence of a new, distinct
species of musician: *composers*.

What is so striking about what happened next, the creation
of the conceptual artist – someone who made up new musical
ideas in their head, not just by improvising with an instrument
– is that the responsibility for the making of new music shifted
from performers to thinkers. The Western music that issued
forth after Guido's description of notation is characterised by
the existence of composing specialists. These dreamers
thought up music that couldn't possibly have been conceived
by spontaneous playing; what's more they were able to con-
struct forms and structures for long pieces of music that were
way beyond the capabilities of a normal person's short-term
memory. Notation paved the way for great feats of musical
architecture.

Composers didn't need long to start experimenting and expanding on the forms they could now see in front of their eyes. Guido himself, having made available the world's most effective composing tool, was also far-sighted enough to spot that the composition of new tunes would be a big growth industry. A fair amount of his theory involves advice and tips to budding composers. Within a hundred or so years following the publication of his notation system, we see for the first time the actual names of composers attached to music – the first 'named' composer is generally thought to be the Frenchman Pérotin (*c.* 1170–*c.* 1236). For better or worse music began to *belong* to certain people. Before, it had been a shared, common currency, an endlessly recycled and repackaged commodity. Now it could become a permanent record, a one-off, a work of art.

Needless to say, this psychological transition was to have a powerful impact on performers: in effect this was the moment when their role began to diminish. This was a purely Western European phenomenon. Music now belonged to its creators, not its re-creators, and for the first time in human history they could be, and often were, different people. Armed with their new toy, composers tried all sorts of elaborate techniques that had been too difficult to attempt in the player–improviser days. One of these was the notion of *counterpoint*.

Counterpoint is the trick of playing two or more tunes at once, fitting them together neatly like Across and Down clues in a crossword. Making a tune sound nice is quite difficult. Making two sound nice that are happening at exactly the same time is more than twice as difficult, believe you me. Making three or four or – in the case of Mahler or Stravinsky – ten or eleven work on top of each other is mental Olympics of the most spectacular kind. To achieve this feat, you need to see the notes laid out in front of you like the figures and lines on a mathematical graph. Without notation, making two tunes fit together is like trying to play Scrabble without the board *or* the plastic letters.

In Guido's time, church musicians were experimenting for the first time with the idea of combining two voice lines to make a primitive form of harmony. This crude layering of notes was sometimes called 'organum' and there were strict rules as to what notes you could or could not combine. The first counterpoint pioneers found successful note combination incredibly hard, and struggled to make the things work. Guido's writing is full of soothing and comforting words to these grimly determined but challenged musical engineers. He offers many possible avenues for experiment and gives a list of 'nice' or acceptable-sounding combinations, studiously avoiding the horrid or ungodly.

Now, *accidental* counterpoint is of course possible when a group of musicians are playing and improvising together, as in jazz, and the latter can be fiendishly complex. Accidental, improvised counterpoint is a feature of Indian and many other forms of music too. But it is necessarily limited to what can be imagined and played there and then: what one's hands are capable of doing without too much interference from the brain at any one time. The players in improvisations like these typically limit the parameters and variables to some extent in order to make it feasible. For example, the harmony is set beforehand to an agreed, slow-moving, repeated pattern. This means in jazz or rock that a round-robin of, say, twenty-four chords will form the basis of all the improvising. To some extent the rhythmic pattern will be similarly prescribed at the outset.

If you're furrowing your brow at this, think of what it would be like to make up a limerick with a group of people, one line each at a time. Imagine doing it slowly at first, to give you time to think of the rhymes. Now imagine doing it at high speed, and each of you doing it in a different accent or language. It still sounds vaguely feasible, doesn't it (even if the quality might suffer somewhat)? All the time, though, you are allowed to keep the metre of the limerick, its pattern and shape, as a constant, invariable given. This gives you a bit of time to plan ahead. The minute you started to change the metre *as well*, while maintaining the rhyming, the narrative and the meaning, the game would become virtually impossible. If, on the other hand, you were allowed to write it all down in advance, consult a rhyming dictionary, and give yourself plenty of time to devise complicated metre changes, the game becomes possible again. Notation did this for music: it allowed a far greater degree of complexity and imagination than was possible with the limitations of making something up, with a bunch of mates, at full performance speed.

Let me give you a practical example. I'm improvising at the piano, something I do for pleasure from time to time. Whilst my brain is working at breakneck speed to stay ahead of my fingers and give me new ideas of a tune to play, new ideas of chords that will accompany it, and a rhythm to generate at the same time, what my hands keep wanting to do is return to all their favourite nooks and crannies. Familiar and easy chords and styles by me are one thing, but they will also want to include familiar or recent musical ideas by other people. If I have just been playing some Bach or some Gershwin, the chances are that echoes and riffs from these composers will leak into the improvisation. It just can't be helped, since the brain is already overloaded with tasks to perform at top speed. Consequently, my improvised music is much less layered and detailed, and much less original, than the music I make up in my head when I have a visual map of it available to me in the form of notation.

By and large, the structure of an improvised piece, whoever is creating it, is going to be necessarily much simpler than that of a written work. You may, as a listener, of course, *prefer* the simpler forms that emanate from improvised music: the overwhelming bulk of popular music is made this way, after all. I'm not making a qualitative judgement here at all, merely talking about form and structure. If buildings were built by trial and error rather than by reference to an architect's plan, you could have a perfectly lovely mud hut or garden shed, or even a house, but you couldn't do a pyramid, an Aztec temple, St Paul's Cathedral or the Kremlin.

Fitting two tunes together led to harmony. The chords that miraculously fit together and create warm, life-enhancing sonorities and that we take for granted in modern life were painstakingly constructed and argued over for hundreds of years. Sounds we hear and think are gorgeous would to the ear of a medieval bishop have sounded like the dreadful howling of the dogs of hell. The first 'chords' were no more complicated than two notes together, and even then, in Guido's time, there were only about five possible combinations they thought sounded even passable. It took ages to expand this to three simultaneous notes, then four, then more. When you hear your average electric organist playing 'My Way' you may be hearing chords made up of eight, nine or ten separate coordinating notes at any one time, and yet even *three* simultaneous notes took the finest brains in Europe centuries to handle with ease.

Quite often, in medieval music, one constant, rooted-to-the-spot note droned on and on unchangingly (it was called, amazingly, a 'drone') and above that the main tune meandered around, thus creating lots of consecutive harmonies as the tune found itself in varying positions against it. This type of harmony still chugs happily on today, for instance in bagpipe music. That bagpipe music is practically the same as it was many centuries ago gives some indication of the speed at which 'classical' music has developed in the same period. The concept that the droney bottom bit might *also* move around took a giant step closer to realisation with the arrival of notation. Guido even gave specific instructions to his colleagues across Christendom about the   satisfactory movement of the drone to make it sound more pleasing.

Between the year 1000 and, say, 1400, European musicians learnt from scratch a whole vocabulary and grammar of music, making a language where previously there had been very limited communication. If the complexities and nuances of spoken and written language had also been lost between the end of the Roman Empire and the reign of Charlemagne, the process of rediscovering the possibilities of language would also have taken a great deal of time. For language there was a viable written version that preserved the Romans' linguistic sophistication but this was denied to music; the richness of Roman music-making is lost to us because it was never transcribed. If they had chordal harmony there's no way we'd know now, and there certainly wasn't a way Guido's contemporaries knew either. They pieced music together, note by note.

In the 3,000 years from Moses to the time of Charlemagne, music basically consisted of a tune and some rhythmic accompaniment. From the arrival of notation, the speed of change and development of music up to our own century was in comparison dizzyingly fast. To Guido, counterpoint was as daringly new an issue as digital broadcasting technology is to us. I don't think he realised quite what a genie he was letting out of his lamp, giving music a grid to work on, and thereby making billions of new harmonic combinations possible.

So Guido unleashed the power of counterpoint onto European music. His system paved the way for the composition of music with a vastly expanded architecture, for the emergence of specialist composers, and for music that was wholly independent of a performer. Music could finally be preserved on the page in more or less the form the originator intended; it was no longer hostage to the unreliability of someone's short-term memory.

Music could now transcend the moment, the person, the country or the language and be transported all by itself to another person, another country, another place and time – and still be that same piece of music. We can only guess what music sounded like to the ears of Antony and Cleopatra or Pharaoh Rameses II, but we can actually hold in our hand and perform the music composed during the reign of Richard the Lionheart or Napoleon Bonaparte, thanks to Guido.

A thousand years from now, though, I doubt that the music of *our* time will be preserved in so simple and resilient a form of reproduction. The vast bulk of it will be kept as recordings on digital media. On the surface, this appears infinitely more resilient and long-lasting than paper and ink. Unless you have no electrical power, in which case you have no music preserved at all. None. Or unless it turns out that time corrodes

Overleaf: Frontispiece to *Encomium Musices,* c. 1590, showing a Motet for six voices by Pevernage

the information stored digitally in a way we have no way of predicting. But let's say, for the sake of the argument, our millions and millions of recordings are stored perfectly for hundreds of years. Would that it were as straightforward as that.

Let's go back to languages for a moment. Suppose you want to speak to a man in Albania and you don't speak Albanian. You find a translator, don't you? Someone who can speak *both* languages. Or you develop cutting-edge computer software that can hear Albanian and translate it into English. Whatever anyone claims, this sort of error-free program doesn't exist at the moment, but I concede that it might one day. If such a program existed, the need for someone to learn English *and* Albanian would, in theory, gradually disappear. When the program then developed a bug or an error the interpreter, unfortunately, wouldn't be around to sort it out, but the new *incorrect* translation would probably be treated as acceptable usage. The computer would eventually be the only party in the transaction that knew *why* it was doing what it was doing. The logic of the problem would not be that of Albanian grammar or English grammar, but the logic of the computer.

Now let's look at modern solutions. The easiest and quickest way to preserve your music is to record it with the latest digital technology. The drawback with this method is that only *your* recording of it is saved – the piece itself, independent of you the performer, is not (at least in a form easily readable by another musician at another time). There needs to be a way of preserving the *music only* if others are to be able to play it at some future date. Up till now we have used a modernised version of Guido's stave.

The most recent development along these lines is software that allows you to input your music into a computer and turn it into printed sheet music. For composers like me it is a time-saving boon, as word-processing is for journalists or novelists. I can input the notes onto the 'virtual' score by using a typewriter keyboard or an electric piano keyboard. The ability of computer software to translate the playing on a piano keyboard almost instantaneously into printed music is a wonder to behold and also a great liberation for composers and musicians who can't read music.

There is a problem, though. Music is an extraordinarily subtle form of shorthand. Writing it down is a process full of suggestion and ambiguity. There are many reasons for this. One is that we are all writing our music in the context of a time and place where an awful lot of musical style is simply *understood*. For example, I do not have to explain to a modern musician that the pitch of 'A' in my music is set electronically at a frequency of 440 hertz, that there are 12 semitone steps between each octave, that the chord C's constituent parts are C, E and G, and that the expression 'crotchet equals 120' means that the basic pulse of the piece is cantering along at 120 beats per minute. All of these things are important ingredients in the music but they are all *assumed*, and only one (the last) is indicated at all. The printed copies of my music will not contain them, but they are there nonetheless. These kinds of assumptions have been part of music ever since Guido's invention of notation, making the 'authentic' performance of very old music a subject of great debate and scholarship (all of the above list would have been more or less alien concepts to a medieval musician).

This is just one reason why music is a shorthand, not a full and complete graph of instructions. Computers, on the other hand, hate shorthands and ambiguities. They are precise, on–off creatures. If Shakespeare had used a word-processor, a spell-check alarm would have gone crazy trying to keep up with his new words and expressions; it would have loathed his multiple-choice approach to spelling and his uncontrollably imaginative invention of new vocabulary. Lewis Carroll and his portmanteau words wouldn't have been much better off.

When I play music into my computer it has to *guess* what it *thinks* I mean, and I have to spend a good deal of time afterwards editing the incorrect guesses into correct musical information. The *real* complexity of what I'm playing was always in the past thinned down into a shorthand version on the page, but the computer wants to write down the *actual*, not the *implied* information. Anyone who has ever used a scanner

Teaching the Guidonian hand, from the *Day's Whole Book of Psalms*, 1563

to read and reproduce a printed document will be familiar with this syndrome.

While there are still plenty of musicians with the old music-reading skills around, computer scores can still be made to make sense. But the skills required to read and write multi-layered musical scores are dying out. They are not needed for many music courses in schools and even university students have much less need for and familiarity with these techniques. A tiny minority of non-classical musicians has what one might describe as advanced music-reading skills. With all our amazing sophistication and technology, we are in danger of reverting to the situation in the Dark Ages when only a minute number of clerics and scribes really knew how to decode musical knowledge.

Let me go back to the Albanian-translating software. The danger is not so much that Albanians and Britons won't be able to communicate with each other but that the immense subtlety and nuance of their inherited languages would have to be made acceptable to the logic and certitude of the computer. The internal subtlety of regional dialects within languages, the tiny inflexions and tones that enrich meaning would give way to the yes–no logic of the software. The machine would do to the assumptions and ambiguities of spoken language what it already does to musical language. Detailed language would be replaced by Phrase Book language, rich poetic vocabulary replaced by Business Vocabulary.

Lest you think I'm being a Jeremiah here, I should point out emphatically that I am not being judgemental about the music created with computers *per se*. Pop music doesn't suffer artistically from being scribbled on the back of an envelope or being made up by composers who do not read music. Nor is the complexity of a 'serious' orchestral concert work necessarily jeopardised by the arrival of mechanical notating devices. In the short term, in fact, the existence of easy-to-use notators will probably produce a greater amount of printed music than ever before. However, the *psychology* of writing music will without doubt be transformed alongside the technology.

Guido of Arezzo would have loved the 'Sibelius' music software I have in my studio. It would have made the job of codifying and filing the great repertoire of chants he managed every day of his life much, much easier. But instead he had to develop a handwritten system of wonderful flexibility and subtlety, a system that ultimately made possible the *Saint Matthew Passion*, *The Marriage of Figaro* and *The Rite of Spring*. I believe it was our great good fortune that he did, for whatever happens next, written music's first millennium has been a fantastic adventure.

TWO

VATICAN SECRETS

Around 1640, the Italian composer Gregorio Allegri wrote a piece for a nine-part choir. *Miserere Mei, Deus* is justifiably one of the most famous and beautiful of all sacred vocal works. This is why:

It is a setting of the Ash Wednesday Psalm ('Have mercy upon me, O God, according to Thy loving kindness'), and was written while Allegri was an employee at the papal chapel in Rome under Pope Urban VIII, during the heyday of the Counter-Reformation. The choir divides into a main group and a mini-choir (usually placed at a distance from the rest), who sing alternating verses of the psalm. The mini-choir is notable for its two solo treble parts ('treble' is a boy soprano) one of whom soars high up into the stratosphere touching a top C – this particular phrase is what makes the piece so distinctive. Even if you think you don't know it, you probably do.

The top Cs, however, spectacular and awesome to hear though they undoubtedly are, aren't the real reason this piece has earned a place in musical legend. The truth is, this divine and ethereal work was considered so spiritually powerful, so close to a sense of the Almighty, that the Pope insisted that only his personal choir at the Sistine Chapel should be able to sing it, and even they would only perform it once a year, during Holy Week. The performances were surrounded by an atmosphere of ritual and mysticism. The copies of the music were locked in the Vatican's vaults for the rest of the year, kept jealously away from the prying eyes of the musical directors of Europe. We are so world-weary these days that we may find it

44

hard to imagine a world in which a piece of sacred music might be considered dangerous or intoxicating, but this was indeed the case with Allegri's *Miserere*.

Composers and musicians travelled to Rome every year to hear this legendary piece and few were disappointed. All were impressed by the high theatre that led up to its opening bars, with candles extinguished one by one and the entire clergy kneeling in darkness and – certainly in its first hundred years of performance – they were equally impressed by the virtuoso embellishments of the high castrati on the top lines. In 1788 Goethe wrote about it in his *Italian Journey*: 'The music in the Sistine Chapel is unimaginably beautiful, especially the *Miserere . . .*', and in June 1831, two hundred years after its composition Mendelssohn described it like this:

> . . . at each verse, a candle is extinguished . . . the whole choir . . . intones, *fortissimo* a new psalm melody: the canticle of Zachariah in D minor . . . then the last candles are put out, the Pope leaves his throne and prostrates himself on his knees before the altar; everyone kneels with him and says what is called a *Pater noster sub silentio* . . . Immediately afterwards, the *Miserere* begins, *pianissimo*. For me, this is the most beautiful moment of the whole ceremony . . . the *Miserere* begins with the singing of a quiet chord of voices and then the music unfolds in the two choirs. It was this opening, and in particular the very first sound, that made the greatest impression on me. After an hour and a half in which one has heard nothing but unison singing, and almost without modulation, the silence is suddenly broken by a magnificent chord: it is striking, and one feels a deep sense of the power of music . . .

Although the Pope allowed two personal copies to be made as special gifts, one to the Emperor Leopold I and the other to the King of Portugal in the eighteenth century, the prohibition on the dissemination of the piece was thorough and meticulously observed. Until 1770, that is, when a precocious four-

teen-year-old boy shocked the musical and ecclesiastical world by memorising the entire piece (it's about 13 minutes long) on hearing it (once!) and duly copied it out for all to see. The *Miserere* thus escaped into the repertoire and was enthusiastically embraced and widely performed thereafter. The precocious boy, in case you hadn't guessed, was Wolfgang Amadeus Mozart.

It is worth reading the letter that Mozart's father Leopold wrote to his wife about the whole affair:

> You have often heard of the famous *Miserere* in Rome, which is so greatly prized that the performers in the chapel are forbidden on pain of excommunication to take away a single part of it, to copy it or to give it to anyone. *But we have it already!* Wolfgang has written it down and we would have sent it to Salzburg in this letter, if it were not necessary for us to be there to perform it – the manner of performance contributes more to its effect than the composition itself. So we shall bring it home with us. Moreover, as it is one of the secrets of Rome, we do not wish to let it fall into other hands, *ut non incurramus mediate vel immediate in censuram Ecclesiae* [so that we shall not incur the censure of the Church now or later].

Mozart, the music smuggler. He seems to have charmed all the cardinals with his pretty Austrian curls and his miraculous playing so no one took him to task about it. You can hear this piece at concerts occasionally, but the best time and place to hear it is on Ash Wednesday in an English cathedral, sung by boys (women can, of course, sing those incredible high notes, but I think even the most brilliant professional singers would admit the sound doesn't go right through you in quite the thrilling way the boys' voices do). Why an *English* cathedral? I hear you ask. Well, it would be lovely if you could hear it in the Catholic cathedrals and chapels on the Continent that it

Opposite: The Sistine Chapel, showing the choir gallery on the right

was intended for, but sadly they don't have choirs any more, not professional ones who do the old-fashioned stuff like this anyway. You need to hear this piece for yourself because only you will know if you think it has the spiritual power Pope Urban VIII claimed it had when he banned its publication.

My view is that the *Miserere* is indeed a work of rare beauty and subtlety, but the moment, the ritual, the drama of it has to be there for it to have its full impact. Many people have been profoundly moved by music on certain occasions and I am convinced that the overwhelming majority of these experiences are 'live' ones. The performers, the time, the place, the context are as important as the piece itself – both Leopold Mozart and Mendelssohn identified this aspect of the famous Ash Wednesday service.

I can offer you one or two special musical moments that I have witnessed.

I am judging a music competition in a small mixed school near Rugby. It is five o'clock on a wet June afternoon, and I have been listening, marking, encouraging, advising and adjudicating since nine o'clock that morning in a tiny hall the size of a big classroom. A twelve-year-old girl is shyly pushed forward to sing a song of her own choosing, unaccompanied, so that her House might attain a few more points by her entering, no matter what her individual effort might score. The omens are not good; the hall is almost empty with indifference, the other children have gone home or are playing on the lawn outside. Even more worryingly, the music teacher hasn't a clue what the girl is about to do.

When the delightful but nervy youngster announces she is to sing one of my favourite songs, the English folk ballad 'O Waly, Waly', which her mother taught her when she was younger, my heart sinks. But what comes from the mouth of this girl is a miracle. She is not Kiri Te Kanawa, Cecilia Bartoli or Whitney Houston. She isn't trained to sing, doesn't breathe in all the correct places nor stand with perfect posture and pose, but she is singing from her heart with the gift of an ordinary child. She means it. She cares about the jilted lover in the song. She knows all seven verses by heart.

48

It is as if the sound of children playing football outside, the summer evening chorus of birds, the creaking of the wooden chairs pivoting back on their spindly legs, the distant tractor mower, the drawing up of parents' cars, the high-pitched whine of fluorescent overhead lights and the humming drone of the nearby road have all been suspended in thin air, not silenced, but rendered insignificant by the voice inside the room. You rarely hear children of this age or over singing old English songs now, either. They're too antique, too quaint, too rustic and, well, uncool. So when she sings this timeless traditional plaint it is, for me, as if some echoing cry has come back to life again. Generations of forlorn lovers somehow find a voice through this girl's gentle, melancholy performance.

> For love is handsome and love is fine,
> And love is charming when it is true
> As it grows older it groweth colder
> And fades away like morning dew . . .

The song ended and the moment passed. The music teacher was speechless. The young contestant sang it again later that night at the prizewinners' concert and though it was beautiful again, it wasn't the same thing. It was the hour of day, the position of the sun in the sky, the background ambience of the exterior sounds, the unassuming expression on the girl's face not at all expecting praise or success, the spontaneous utterance of a song passed from mother to daughter. It was a magical five minutes. And it touched something deep inside me – it was 'spiritual' in its innocent way.

Another moment. We are in the north transept of Oxford's small and intimate Christ Church Cathedral. It is Holy Week. The choir are giving a complete performance of Bach's *Saint John Passion*, not as a concert, not as a service as such, but as an 'act of devotion'. There are no tickets, no programmes, no interval coffee and no final applause. The choir are in plain crimson cassocks, all the solos will be sung from within its ranks and the orchestra replicates the forces available to Bach himself in Leipzig, playing 'period' instruments. It isn't as long as the *Saint Matthew Passion*, but it's over two hours all the same. It is the story of Christ's trial, execution and resurrection, told like an opera without costumes, sets or actions. The choir consists of sixteen boy trebles (aged seven to thirteen) and fourteen men, mostly the right side of twenty-five, and they stand calmly for the duration. This type of music-making wouldn't suit the indolent or the impatient. The assembled non-performers (I can't really describe us as either 'audience' or 'congregation') are still and quiet. The performance is indescribably moving. Three snap-shots:

The young man who sings Jesus' friend Peter is a friend of the man who takes the part of Jesus. They have sung together many times. In the story, Peter betrays his friend. Suddenly, instead of two far-off Nazarenes in beards and sandals, this point in the story comes across as the disappointing, weak, everyday betrayal that it is in the original. Bach was writing about people, it occurs to me, not gods.

When Christ finally gives up the ghost on the Cross, the piece comes to a standstill. In concerts and recordings, of course, it never does, because time marches inexorably on. Here, the performers stand silently frozen for three or four uninterrupted minutes. It is dramatic and shocking, and seems agonisingly long. When the music begins again, the full weight and pain of this axis in the narrative sinks in. We *need* the music to breathe life back into us again.

Later on, one of the followers of Jesus of Nazareth who has come to witness the execution, sings a lament at his passing – 'Zerfliesse, mein Herze' ('Melt, my heart'). Tonight, as in Bach's time, this fiendishly tricky aria is sung by a twelve-year-old boy. This one is called Jonathan and the day before he has broken his arm falling from a tree. His arm is in a sling that restricts his breathing and he is demonstrably pale and fragile. When he starts, we can hardly hear him. His voice wavers and cracks, failing to reach the highest notes with confidence or stamina. He stands there, the notes not soaring but trembling. As the aria builds he manages to extract more sound for the longer phrases, but the effort seems to exhaust him. Because he sings in one of the finest choirs on earth, he is definitely swimming, not drowning, but the character of the song sounds, I think, *traumatised*.

I do not believe there was a single person present that night who was not held motionless to their seat by the sight of Jonathan's courage delivering this aria. A great stage soprano would undoubtedly make the song sound exquisite by her experienced interpretation and tone quality, but I doubt I will ever hear a performance that more poignantly revealed the truth of the musical setting.

> *Zerfliesse, mein Herze,*
> *in Fluten der Zähren,*
> *Den Höchsten zu Ehren.*
> *Erzähle der Welt*
> *und dem Himmel die Not,*
> *dein Jesus is tot.*

> (Melt, my heart,
> in floods of tears,
> To honour the Highest.
> Report to the world
> and to heaven our distress:
> thy Jesus is dead.)

Finally, a story about a Special Needs School in the Greater Manchester area. I am visiting the school as representative of the sponsors (Sainsbury's) of a series of musical workshops and therapy sessions run by the Hallé Orchestra's percussion department.

The children are severely mentally and physically handicapped, with one carer per child. Some of the children make no identifiable response at all. There is the usual special school atmosphere of affectionate firmness, and the percussion man proceeds with his turn, which involves much clowning and banging around. The kids are enjoying it enormously.

The climax to the workshop, which lasts about twenty minutes, is where percussion man, joined now by guitar man, hands out a percussion instrument to every single child and carer. He teaches everyone a rhythm to contribute to the overall orchestra of crashes and bangs, and those that can move do a sort of Brazilian carnival conga around the room with their guiros, maracas, cabasas and tambourines.

During this joyous cacophony I am watching a little boy of five or six, who can barely hold the drum he has been given – his carer keeps picking up the beater off the floor for him – but has, after considerable effort, mastered the simple rhythm everyone is whacking out. He isn't smiling or watching the other children, he's too autistic to focus his eyes, but he is hitting the drum rat-tat-tat in unison with everyone else. Not particularly remarkable, a child playing a drum, you might say. My gaze wanders to his right and I notice that his carer has tears streaming down her face. As she is embarrassed to be caught weeping, I look away. At the end of the session, though, I seek her out, telling her that I couldn't help noticing she had been crying and was there anything wrong?

She says, 'You don't understand. I have been working with this little boy since he came here four years ago. When he imitated the rhythm of the music just then it was the first time *ever* he had responded to something another human being had done. It is his first communication with another person. I was overcome by it, that's all.'

A child reaches across the abyss separating him from the rest of humanity – a journey for him as awesome and terrifying as you or I crossing the North Pole in winter. His lifeline not a word, not a glance, not a cuddle, not a smile, not a kiss, not a book, not a painting, not a film, not a TV programme, not a play, not a computer, not a person even, but a musical rhythm. This is the alchemy of music. It is deep, deep within us and always has been since the African bush and the Nile delta. It is a tiny indication, in the high-tech modern world, of 'where we are coming from', us *Homo sapiens*. Is this internal capsule containing music a spiritual thing, or a physical thing?

You had to be there. To trigger a response in us, music has to be 3-D, it has to be happening *to* us and we have to be reacting to it, we cannot be impartial. People who have had this kind of experience know that potentially it can change a

To all Lovers of Sciences,

THE greatest Prodigy that Europe, or that even Human Nature has to boast of, is, without Contradiction, the little German Boy WOLFGANG MOZART; a Boy, Eight Years old, who has, and indeed very justly, raised the Admiration not only of the greatest Men, but also of the greatest Musicians in Europe. It is hard to say, whether his Execution upon the Harpsichord and his playing and singing at Sight, or his own Caprice, Fancy, and Compositions for all Instruments, are most astonishing. The Father of this Miracle, being obliged by Desire of several Ladies and Gentlemen to postpone, for a very short Time, his Departure from England, will give an Opportunity to hear this little Composer and his Sister, whose musical Knowledge wants not Apology. Performs every Day in the Week, from Twelve to Three o'Clock in the Great Room, at the Swan and Hoop, Cornhil. Admittance 2s. 6d. each Person.

The two Children will play also together with four Hands upon the same Harpsichord, and put upon it a Handkerchief, without seeing the Keys.

A Notice in the *Publick Advertiser*, London, June 1765,
and Mozart, aged 7

person's life, that music is much more powerful than we care to admit. That is why the Pope locked Allegri's *Miserere* away in his Vatican vaults. He had witnessed the power of it and he wanted to control it. He probably would have held onto the fourteen-year-old Mozart and locked him up too, if he had known what unbelievable forces *that* child was going to unleash.

THREE

The Inventing of Opera

Of all music's forms, opera generates most rage, excitement and passion. It is the one musical form that has no meaning without the oxygen of performance: it lives and breathes in the charged atmosphere of public debate and politics. Opera did not emerge gradually, like the symphony or the concerto, it burst explosively onto the scene in the sixteenth century in a flurry of invention and controversy. Today, four hundred years later, in London, one of the world's great cultural centres, you can't even *re*build a new opera house without the whole country having an opinion about it. The building of an opera house has always been seen as a political act, one that confirms the status or power of a ruler, a city or a nation. The political furore that accompanies the erection of an opera house isn't just because of its expense; it is also because people are well aware that it is a statement, too, of the values and priorities of the society or clique that builds it.

Opera fuses music with universal stories and ideas, a combination that has always had an irresistible attraction. Opera has a unique role within music – it is the arena where music is linked most overtly with the real world, with real issues and real debates. It has become inextricably intertwined with political intrigue, revolution and nationalism, particularly in the country of its birth, Italy. Elsewhere it has thrived in cities of great importance, patronised by rulers of great power. What opera is not, whatever current thinking would have us believe, is a marginal or irrelevant art form – sought after only by the cognoscenti, extravagantly expensive and 'elitist'.

We applaud and encourage elitism in sport. So why are we so uneasy with the notion when it comes to the arts? This is a new phenomenon. For most of opera's history it has been music's most successfully populist product, often appealing to people who wouldn't dream of spending an evening in a concert hall or patiently sitting through a song recital at a local church. It still is classical music's biggest 'seller' – millions of people have access to and enjoy opera's greatest hits. It is just as expensive to see a Broadway or West End musical as it is to visit an opera house, yet you don't hear complaints that such musicals are 'elitist'. If opera had always been reserved for a privileged few, the days of its influence and cultural impact would be long over.

> Where should this music be? I'th'air or th'earth?
> It sounds no more; and sure it waits upon
> Some god o'th'island. Sitting on a bank,
> Weeping again the King my father's wreck,
> This music crept by me upon the waters,
> Allaying both their fury and my passion
> With its sweet air. Thence I have followed it –
> Or it hath drawn me rather. But 'tis gone.
> No, it begins again.

In *The Tempest* (1611), a young man finds himself shipwrecked on a deserted, magical island, lost and distraught, fearing his beloved father is dead. There is music everywhere.

We know that there was incidental music and song in Shakespeare's plays, many of which, like *The Tempest*, refer to the magical or mystical power of music. You could describe the Shakespearean monologue as the closest thing to a sung aria that the spoken theatre has to offer. It is a highly stylised solo moment during which the audience accepts the convention that internal thoughts are being brought to the surface. It isn't *real* in the sense that people speak like that in normal life. They don't, obviously. But within its convention of unreality it does nevertheless contain *truth*. This distinction between reality and truth is central to the debate about opera. Clearly, people don't sing aloud their thoughts or conversations in 'real' life, but opera adopts, like Shakespeare, the convention that despite its unreality an aria may indeed express great truth or poignancy.

Shakespeare was writing his extraordinary poetic dramas at exactly the time that opera was born. Like the Italian inventors of opera, he was influenced by classical drama, borrowing Greek and Roman plots and appropriating their political history for his own ends. What *The Tempest* also reveals, intriguingly, is a shifting attitude to music itself. It was written at a moment when the Pythagorean concept of music – that it is a representation of a greater 'cosmic harmony', or an earthly version of a music 'of the spheres' – was competing with a more modern 'Classical' notion of music as a vehicle for reproducing and touching the human emotions. Shakespeare's contemporaries called these emotions 'affects', and found music's ability to convey love, jealousy, rage, and so on, potent and irresistible. It was as if music's task was being rethought; where once it had tried to convey God's creative omnipotence, it was now attempting to conjure up Man's state of mind. Throughout Shakespeare's plays and sonnets music is seen as both a cosmic, supernatural force (as in *The Tempest*) and as an 'emotional' force (as in *Twelfth Night*'s 'If music be the food of love, play on').

For its inventors, opera was to be the perfect vehicle to demonstrate music's power over the human 'affects'. Believing they were re-creating the theatre of Ancient Greece, they held firmly to the view that Greek drama had been sung, not spoken. Their aim was to find a way that music could move swiftly and effectively through plot to allow space and time for more lingering, climactic moments of maximum expression and emotion.

The idea for a completely sung form of drama was conceived in one street, the Via de' Benci, in Florence. In two houses on either side of the street in the late sixteenth century, a sort of intellectual club met regularly to put the world to rights, talk earnestly about the arts and sciences and generally aspire to the artistic heights attained by the Greeks. They called themselves the Camerata.

DISEGNO DEL GRANDE ET MARAVIGLIOSO APPARATO DE FVOCHI TRIONFALI

The Piazza S. Pietro, Mantua. On the right is The Palazzo Ducale, where Monteverdi's early operas were performed; the fireworks celebrate the wedding of Eleonora Gonzaga and Emperor Ferdinand II, 1622

Two enthusiastic patrons hosted the meetings. One was a thrusting young silk merchant called Jacopo Corsi, the other a crusty old nobleman–songwriter by the name of Giovanni de' Bardi. The Camerata were a mixed bunch: poets, composers, artists, scientists and dilettantes. One of them was Vincenzo Galilei, father of Galileo, who wrote about the meetings that the members 'were in the habit of going to Bardi's house and there to pass the time in honourable recreation, with delightful singing and praiseworthy discussions'. Astrology, literature and philosophy were favourite topics, but the issue that dominated the proceedings time and time again was 'what was the music of the Greeks?'.

The Camerata talked about the creation of an 'ultimate' art form that would combine music, poetry, drama, dance and design, and after twenty-odd years of chit-chat and debate they put on their first collaborative show in 1598: *Dafne*. The poet Ottavio Rinuccini wrote the words, and Jacopo Peri

wrote the music, though none of it survives today. Rumour
has it that it owed a great deal to the popular court entertainments known as *intermedii* – a hybrid form extravagantly
crossing ballet, song recital, fashion show and poetry reading.
What the Camerata really needed, however, was a big showcase for their new form, and two years later a spectacular
opportunity arose in the shape of a royal wedding.

In 1600 Maria de' Medici of Florence married Henri IV of
France, and as part of the festivities, Peri's second experimental opera *Euridice* was performed in the Medicis' Pitti Palace.
However, this fledgeling opera, with its emphasis on doomed
love and man's arrogance, its half-spoken, half-sung declama-
tions and its pious sentiments, may not have been the ideal
choice for the climax of a riotous wedding feast. It was not a
success. Even the supportive Count Bardi commented that the
writers 'should not have gone into tragic texts and objection-
able subjects'. The Medicis probably found being lectured by
a bunch of well-intentioned dilettantes a bit much and sent
opera off for an early bath, reverting to camp comedy spec-
taculars for their next royal wedding.

After two false starts, opera looked dead in the water and
there might never have been an operatic 'big bang' were it not
for a lucky twist of fate. Two of the Medicis' wedding guests
in 1600 thought that the operatic after-dinner entertainment
might after all have some potential and they returned home,
their heads dizzy with the possibilities of the new form. They
were called Alessandro Striggio and Vincenzo Gonzaga, and
they came from Mantua. Vincenzo Gonzaga, brother-in-law
of the bride in Florence, was the head of one of the most powerful families in Europe, presiding over his mini-empire from
the splendour of a spectacular ducal palace in the heart of that
rich, proud city in northern Italy. Striggio was his friend and
secretary, a writer and composer.

Duke Vincenzo was an inveterate gambler and philanderer.
In his debauched youth he had murdered both the Mantuan
court organist, Detroffeis, and his Scottish interpreter, the
'Admirable' James Crichton, in duels over women, or so we
are led to believe. The Gonzagas had lived and ruled in

Mantua since 1328, turning it into a major centre of Renaissance art under Duke Ludovico II (ruled 1444–78) and the Marchesa Isabella d'Este (ruled 1490–1539). Duke Vincenzo (ruled 1587–1612) was the last in the family to take a serious interest in collecting art, his successors selling off a large portion of the family collection in 1627 to the King of England, Charles I. His ducal palace can still be visited today in all its glory, as can the other Gonzaga palace at the other end of town, the Palazzo Te, and in both you will see some of the most stunning Renaissance and Baroque frescos in Europe (by Andrea Mantegna and Giulio Romano, among others). Gonzaga narrowly failed to persuade the mathematician Galileo Galilei to leave his permanent post at the University of Padua to join his court in Mantua, but he did entice many others, including the influential writer Torquato Tasso.

Gonzaga and Striggio thought they might like to commission their own opera like the one they had seen in Florence. In the event, the piece that was finally composed was dedicated to Vincenzo's son and heir Ferdinand, but the Duke was undoubtedly a powerful influence in its inception. The big difference between the Medicis in Florence and the Gonzagas in Mantua, though, was that while the former had the innovative but uninspired Peri as their composer-in-residence, the latter had the greatest genius of the age, a consummate master of heartbreaking love songs and dramatic sacred music: Claudio Monteverdi.

The opera that Monteverdi and his librettist Striggio wrote, *Orfeo*, relaunched the form after its shaky start. It is to this beautiful piece, more than to the previous experiments *Dafne* and *Euridice*, that we owe the existence of opera today. Why was Monteverdi so well qualified for the job?

Born in nearby Cremona in 1567, Monteverdi came as a young man to Mantua to work for the Gonzagas, writing and performing madrigals for the Duke. Every Friday evening there would be a musical soirée presenting Monteverdi's latest songs for the Duke and a few close friends. We know that these private concerts took place in a mirrored, trapezoid salon, a room that was thought to be completely lost until the autumn of 1998, when palace scholars, led by musicologist Paula Bezzutti, discovered, to their amazement, in an attic void above a private (remodelled) ducal apartment, this very same room, bricked away in silence for 350 years. Its frescos on musical themes, dating from the late sixteenth century, are preserved untouched. The floor is so fragile two people must stand four feet away from each other in the chamber. Rubble and builder's waste lie all about, the hefty oak beams of the terracotta-tiled roof creak in the wind and the temporary lights that illuminate the abandoned cherubs and putti give it a haunted air. I was lucky enough to be granted access to this breathtaking find, and have rarely felt so acutely the hovering presence of a long-dead composer and his world than in that dusty, historic loft. Here the greatest composer of his day sat at a harpsichord with one or two other musicians, giving the first performances of madrigals that would later be heard in salons and courts throughout the Italian peninsula.

I know the word 'madrigal' inspires some unhappy associations in the modern mind: red-faced women or twerps in polo-neck sweaters going 'Fa la la la' and 'merry merry month of May'. Well, the English glee club and their dainty part-songs may well have developed out of the early madrigal, but that's about as far as the similarity goes. The 'late' madrigals of Monteverdi and Gesualdo had more of the steamy Mediterranean about them.

Red-blooded songs of love, betrayal and despair, struggle and passion, sometimes sung in groups, but eventually as accompanied solos, were more their thing. The lyrics of their songs are uncompromisingly erotic, bordering on the obscene, laced through with double-entendre and innuendo, the melodies wild and tortured, whilst extravagant effects and ornate word-painting were *de rigueur*. The harmonies are so daringly dissonant that they sound as if they could have been written amidst the decadence and exoticism of the Paris of 1899 or the Berlin of 1925 as much as the Mantua or Venice of 1600. Indeed, the history of harmony treats the madrigals of Gesualdo and Monteverdi (the Cole Porter and George Gershwin of the form) as something of an aberration, a hideous mutation of the natural order of things, experimenting with ideas that were about 300 years ahead of their time. The composers that followed withdrew in alarm from their harmonic perversity and simplified harmony again, a process of reaction that Monteverdi himself began in his own later career.

During his time in Gonzaga's employ at the Mantuan court, Monteverdi's madrigal collections were published to great acclaim and popularity, but they also underwent a thorough stylistic overhaul. Not only did he start reversing the harmonic mischief, he began developing a more fluid, less rum-ti-tum form of the song, less enslaved to a strict poetic metre, one that could adapt itself more easily to a narrative flow. This turned out to be a critical factor.

Like every other composer of his era, he also made a living writing church music. On the surface of it, writing liturgical settings would not seem a good apprenticeship for the inventing of secular music drama but in fact the relationship between the two has always been uncannily close. For a start, the annual dramatisation of the Passion story with music and acting had accustomed many church composers to the idea of music as a narrative tool. Medieval mystery plays, like those at York or Oberammergau, developed into the highly sophisticated and theatrical *Passions* of the brilliant Heinrich Schütz (a young contemporary of Monteverdi's) and of course J. S. Bach a century later. Schütz and Bach, however, wrote their Passion dramas for performance by choirs in churches without any staging, whilst Monteverdi and his successors like Cavalli and Vivaldi composed for the more flamboyant and secular medium of the theatre. The reason for this is probably connected with the fact the former were living and working in the Lutheran zone of post-Reformation Europe (which took a dim view of things bawdy or theatrical) while the latter were in Catholic Italy. Bach's great contemporary and fellow German, Handel, might be considered an exception as he wrote secular operas *and* biblical oratorios. However, he had emigrated to England, where the established Church was neither strictly speaking Lutheran nor Catholic. Indeed, England's Church was then, as now, more concerned with monarchy than deity, a state of affairs that at least had the virtue of allowing excellent Catholic composers a more or less free hand so long as they kept in favour at court.

Whether church music lent its drama and spectacle to opera, or vice versa, is something of a chicken and egg conundrum. What is undoubtedly true is that the music Monteverdi wrote for the church, like that of Handel, Vivaldi, Haydn, Mozart, Rossini, Verdi or Berlioz, is stylistically virtually identical to the music he wrote for the theatre. In some cases it is even exactly the same music: the opening bars of both *Orfeo* and his 1610 *Vespers* are such twins.

Monteverdi's primary motivation in composing his pioneer operas was to harness the power of music to focus on *human* feeling. Although gods and the supernatural feature prominently in the plot of *Orfeo*, it is Orfeo's emotions that really interest the authors. As with Shakespeare, the idea of music as part of some kind of universal magic co-exists with the more modern concept of its ability to invoke and touch the sensitivities of mere mortals. It is this that marks the point of departure from sacred music, not the choice of harmonies, the shape of the melodies or the constitution of the orchestra. God's celestial music is being replaced, in front of our eyes, with mankind's frail and troubled song. Not surprisingly, Bach's unbearably powerful and moving Passion oratorios concentrate overwhelmingly on the human story at the end of Christ's life, with God sidelined as a silent participant in the grim drama. By Bach's time, opera's *humanistic* priorities had become the norm for all sung music. It took until Olivier Messiaen in the mid-twentieth century for the notion of music as a mystical, quasi-religious power to begin anything like a respectable fight back.

With respect to Monteverdi, we know from his letters that he thought there was almost no point at all in sung drama if it wasn't solely concerned with human emotions. Time and again he objected either to spectacle for spectacle's sake or any attempt to give voice to non-human entities, believing it to be quite beyond the capabilities of the form. In one letter he complains, one assumes without irony or intentional hilarity, that he is having difficulty setting a scene in which the librettist asks for the North Wind to sing. How do *I* know, he wails, what the North Wind feels, for heaven's sake? What he would have made of singing trains (*Starlight Express*), singing crockery (*Beauty and the Beast*) or singing cats is anyone's guess.

So what was the classical legend he and Striggio chose for their plot? *Orfeo*, a story proclaiming the supernatural power of music – a gift so powerful that even death would be tamed. Of the first three operas to be written, *Dafne*, *Euridice*, and *Orfeo*, two chose this, the opera plot *par excellence*. Moreover, the archetype of Orpheus and his lyre would crop up constantly in works by Charpentier, Gluck, Haydn, Offenbach, Birtwistle – to name but five. The story tells how Orfeo, a musician, travels to the Underworld to win back his wife Euridice, who has recently died. Orfeo sings and plays so beautifully that he persuades the King of the Underworld to let him have Euridice back, a request that the King, also in love with her, grants on condition that Orfeo doesn't look back at Euridice on the journey back from Hades – a condition he fails to keep.

This was a plot infused with neo-platonic Christian thinking, very much in vogue at the time. Its writers knew what they were doing in choosing this allegorical fable, given that its first audience would include one of the most powerful men in Europe. The libretto of *Orfeo* has been described as a humanist manifesto, Monteverdi himself hoped it would be a 'true prayer'. Its sentiment is that music, the arts and learning could have a genuinely positive, civilising effect on humanity. The near-perfect cyclical, unified structure of *Orfeo* is itself part of the philosophy: Monteverdi, Striggio and other artists and intellectuals of the time thought that at best a work of art might be a mirror of the perfection of Divine Creation (indeed, the concept of a 'Universal Harmony' is actually referred to during the climactic Act 3 of the opera). What better metaphor for music's own role in society could there be than the tale of a man, heartbroken by the death of his beloved, who descends into Hades with only the beauty of his song to protect him? At his moment of greatest vulnerability and fragility the music of the opera becomes almost surreally delicate and gentle. No explosion of melodrama or rampaging Wagnerian storm, here, but a still small voice of calm echoing across the deathly straits of the river Styx. This weird, dream-like passage is the true beginning of opera as a passionate and dramatic form.

The first performance was given, not in front of a drunken gathering of aristocratics after a wedding breakfast, but to a cultured group, an intellectual academy of sorts brought together for the occasion in a mirrored hall inside the ducal complex. It was an immediate, unprecedented success, revived later that first month in the court theatre and thereafter in Cremona, Turin, Florence and Milan. It was published in two printed editions, 1609 and 1615, which for the period would have been an astonishing feat. And then, after this extraordinary first year, it was abandoned until the twentieth century. It is in some ways miraculous that it has survived at all, given its obscurity during the centuries after Monteverdi's death. When I spent an hour or two with one of the few surviving scores of *Orfeo*, in the library of Christ Church College, Oxford, what struck me was how easily comprehensible to the modern eye it appears. Had the score been in sturdy enough condition I would have been tempted to sit the copy on a piano and start playing it then and there. Monteverdi's musical intentions were surprisingly clear and unfussy, even if many of the details (what the instruments were, and what they should play, for example) are less obvious. For modern performance editions, divining what the composer intended is a veritable minefield, as so much of the relevant information would have been *understood* by Monteverdi's ensemble. Mind you, there never had been a published opera score before, so no one knew what exactly *should* be put into one.

Some things, though, emerge loud and clear. From the outset, Monteverdi insisted that this was a drama *through*

Opposite: Orfeo, published in Venice in 1609, two years after its first performance at Mantua: the title page and score

music. In other words, every event, thought, emotion, action or dialogue should as far as possible be expressed through the singing and playing; the songs shouldn't just be an opportunity for the singers to show off (a tendency that became almost epidemic in later years, unfortunately). He also realised that to stun his audience into alert silence, he could do a lot worse than borrow the grandeur and magnificence of church music. This was, after all, a story about Love, God and the Afterlife. The arrival into the theatre of brass and drums (cornetti, valveless trumpets, sackbuts and timpani) must have seemed extremely exciting (and loud!) to audiences who were more used to these instruments as trappings of royal or ecclesiastical ceremonies in big spaces. Monteverdi added them to a colourful array of 'continuo' instruments. The 'continuo' is a player or group of players who act as a kind of bedrock to the singing accompaniment, like guitar, bass and drums in a jazz or rock combo. It covers the basic material of harmony and rhythm, allowing the 'melody' instruments of recorders, trumpets, violins etc., to float more freely above the musical foundations.

Continuo instruments of Monteverdi's time were harpsichord, chamber organ, cello, viola da gamba (a Renaissance stringed instrument played between the knees – *gamba* in Italian), harp, theorbo (a type of guitar or lute), chitarrone (another long-necked type of guitar or lute), archlute (ditto) and lute itself. Normally you would pick one or two of this assortment, but in *Orfeo* Monteverdi went for the jugular and threw in the whole lot. It must have sounded amazing to a contemporary ear. Claudio's Palace Pluckers, you might have said, or the Incredible Mantovani String Band. When Glenn Miller was forced to replace his saxes and horns with extra clarinets in the late 1930s (I think some players failed to turn up for the gig, or something) he created a new, unusual sound we all recognise. Likewise, the Monteverdi mega-continuo-band must have sounded bizarre and wonderful, never mind the fact he had the local brass band contingent in there as well.

With so many different types of sound competing for the ear's attention plus a chorus of men and boys (borrowed, one assumes, from the Duke's St Bartholomew Chapel at the palace, Mantua's St Peter's Cathedral, or the equally impressive St Andrew Basilica) and all the soloists, there needed to be a firm master-plan for orchestral performance. The score itself was clearly such a plan, but Monteverdi also used a trick developed in his madrigal days to speed up the writing of parts and simultaneously give the players more individual freedom. This was known as Figured Bass.

Figured Bass means you only have to write out the bass notes for the cello and violone (the pre-double-bass double-bass) *once*. All the continuo players have it in front of them. Above the notes are a series of shorthand numbers that show the chord to play with each bass note. As long as you play that chord, you can play it any way you like, in effect. So the lute and the harpsichord and the theorbo and the chitarrone will all be looking at exactly the same information but they will all be playing different versions of it, thus creating a rich, orchestral blend, different every single time it's played. A modern version of 'figured bass' is alive and kicking in jazz and rock music to this very day. To Monteverdi it meant that he could have his cake and eat it: he could have lots of subtly different sounds playing together, but he only had to write the part out once. Neat!

Another technique he fine-tuned in *Orfeo* was a solution to the problem of moving text along at high speed (as an alternative to straight song) through a style known as *recitative*. To some extent, this technique had been road-tested, as it were, in Monteverdi's madrigals, but it came into its own with an involved plot and characters.

In a narrative story, you can't have metrically rigid, rum-ti-tum songs, duets and choruses all the time; you have to be able to say more mundane things like 'I am the Messenger who's come to tell you some very bad news . . .' In a modern musical, this line would probably be spoken. So why not speak it? Well, firstly, singing the whole piece from start to finish creates a stylistic unity and cohesion. Although Shakespeare jumps from verse to prose, we happily accept his convention of a heightened form of speech because it is consistent and poetic. Similarly, a good opera libretto will attempt to give the composer a text style that doesn't seem jumpy and fragmented. Secondly, opera singers tend to be less comfortable delivering straight speech than singing, which is difficult enough to do in itself, never mind adding character and motivation. Thirdly, there's no doubt that you can express much stronger, more daring thoughts through the 'filtered' medium of singing than you can through the raw candour of speech.

When I was a (much) younger man back in the mists of time, I used to write the songs for a scurrilous satirical TV comedy series called *Not the Nine O'Clock News*. In the songs we were able to say things that would have been totally unacceptable on network TV at the time if spoken in a sketch (we had, for example, a song about the Ayatollah Khomeini during Iran's embassy siege in London). From its very beginnings, opera found that singing allowed, ironically, a much greater freedom of expression than was possible in a play or a recitation. Moreover, when the language of the text becomes *highly* emotional, spoken delivery can sound melodramatic or precious. Through singing, the highest highs and lowest lows actually seem *more* plausible. The wailing and keening of Middle Eastern women who have lost their sons in some terrorist attack, the cry of anguish of a soul in pain, the shout of joy at some amazing piece of good news, all these are closer to the sound of singing than speech.

While Monteverdi's skill and brilliant innovations are of interest to the musician and the opera buff, *Orfeo* has a much greater significance in the wider history of music altogether. There had always been music that depicted things (battle-scene pieces for organ, love songs for lute and voice, choral motets expressing the sorrow and pain of the Crucifixion, and so on), but in *Orfeo* the *whole work* conspires to tell a story, to make a point, to convince an audience of its meaning. This piece of music is making direct, unselfconscious contact with the real, physical, non-musical world. It is music *about* something, music with an attitude and an argument. It is as if it has liberated itself from the purely musical bounds of its previous existence. Music, even portrayed as a *character* in this opera, has begun an interface with the rest of society, a connection

A commemoration of Monteverdi: the title page
of Marinoni's *Fiori Poetici*, 1644

that would single opera out from all other musical forms and return over the centuries to inspire and invigorate it. From *Orfeo* onwards, operas tackled politics, social behaviour, sexuality, power, race and class. Its appetite for the controversial, taboo or forbidden has been almost insatiable.

Although *Orfeo* was not the first opera – more like the third – it was without doubt the first *good* opera. Not just good but brilliant. Monteverdi's vision brought opera to life in no uncertain terms. His triumphant follow-up, *Arianna*, performed *al fresco* in a temporary wooden theatre within the Duke's grand equestrian enclosure to an alleged audience of 5,000 people, has been lost entirely (except for one popular lament). After these successes, both Monteverdi and opera moved to Venice, where by the end of his life there were a staggering nineteen opera houses in full flow. Indeed, the world's first commercial opera house opened there in 1637. Every composer in Italy got in on the act and before long opera's popularity had spread throughout Europe.

On the eve of the French Revolution, in 1784, the Comédie-Française performed a subversive new farce by Pierre Augustin Beaumarchais called *Le Mariage de Figaro*. It was an overnight sensation. A contemporary described it as 'the end of the old order' and Napoleon later said it was 'the revolution already in action'. The ruling houses of Europe reacted by having it banned. The man who ruled the largest slice of central Europe, the Habsburg Emperor Joseph II, was no exception. So imagine his alarm and consternation when he discovered that one of his court composers, young Herr Mozart, was presenting the now illegal play as an opera under his very nose in his own Viennese theatre. Being a great opera lover he couldn't resist it, of course, and Mozart's masterwork was allowed access to the royal ears in a way that was denied the play. Opera's dangerous liaison with power politics was reignited.

The Marriage of Figaro is about a count who is trying to use his position to deflower a young internee – sorry, maid – in his household. The girl in question, Susanna, is about to get married to the count's valet, Figaro. She is also the countess's maid and closest confidante. On the surface of it, it's a merry roister-doister of a sexual farce. But beneath the skin this is about the rich and powerful treating their employees like slaves and playthings, and no one who saw it at the end of the eighteenth century, with Europe on the brink of political implosion, would have been in any doubt of its message, including the Emperor Joseph, shifting uneasily in his royal box. What is doubly significant, though, is that the servants ultimately outwit and humiliate their master, and at the end of the opera this once omnipotent count is forced to kneel in humble apology to his wife in front of his whole household. At this moment of sublime music ('*Contessa, perdono . . .*'), it is as if the *ancien régime* itself is bowing to the inevitable and submitting to the greater will of its subjects.

Three years after the première of *The Marriage of Figaro*, in 1789, Camille Desmoulins leapt onto a café table in Paris and called on all French patriots to liberate themselves from the slavery of monarchy. One of the first acts of the mob was to storm the prison that had become a potent symbol of repression, the Bastille. That famous landmark has long since gone, but in its place now stands the new Opéra de la Bastille. The storming of the Bastille, which lit the fuse for the revolution, also inspired a wave of populist operas in which escape or deliverance from unjust imprisonment was the recurring theme, like Cherubini's *Lodoïska* and *Les Deux Journées*, or Grétry's *Richard Coeur-de-Lion*. Composers and their librettists, who had been the conscience of the ruling aristocratic elite *before* the revolution, soon became the conscience of the new bourgeois rulers with these so-called 'rescue operas'. As in Dickens's *A Tale of Two Cities*, they call for a universal compassion across the classes, with many of their heroes and heroines being good aristocrats caught up in a general terror. The most famous of all these rescue operas is Beethoven's *Fidelio*.

Fidelio, Beethoven's only opera, was premièred in 1806 in the same week as Napoleon's troops were occupying his home

Herbert's engraving of the excited audience at Auber's *La Muette de Portici*,
which fired the revolution in Brussels on 25 August 1830

town of Vienna. It is set in a prison, and though the action nominally takes place in Spain the allusion to Revolutionary Paris is unambiguous. The plot concerns the successful release from unjust imprisonment of a good man, but what really interests Beethoven is the generalised theme of liberation and deliverance. The opera ends with a passionate hymn to freedom, and ever since the piece has been associated with the overthrowing of tyranny (after the end of hostilities in 1945 opera houses all over Europe reopened with *Fidelio*).

France's Revolution may have begun with the storming of the Bastille, but Belgium's Revolution of 1830 was actually triggered by the playing of an opera. During the opening performance of *La Muette de Portici* by Daniel Auber, an epic and heroic tale of rebellious Neapolitan fishermen, the audience were so stirred by a duet calling for the casting off of the shackles of foreign oppression that they swept out of the theatre and began rioting, not even bothering to hear the rest of the piece. The theatre they were in at the time, the Théâtre de la Monnaie, still stands today as a permanent reminder to the Belgians of their moment of liberation. Crowds had been gathering outside in the square all week in expectation of some kind of showdown with the Dutch authorities controlling Belgium at the time. The appearance of the opera goers, fired with patriotic zeal, acted as a catalyst and the whole throng stormed up the hill to lay siege to the nearby courthouse, thereby beginning the Belgian Revolution. Within a few weeks the Dutch administration had left (after a modest amount of bloodshed) and been replaced with Belgium's first independent government. This is the duet that inspired the audience that night:

'L'Amour sacré de la patrie'

Better to die than live so abject!
A slave must not a greater evil fear!
Let us break the bonds that keep us subject!
Let us expel the stranger from our land!
Wilt go with me?

I will thy footsteps follow,
I'll go with thee to death!
With me to glory!
Either united in eternal sleep,
Or both with laurel crowned!
Love for our country gives us strength
And in the struggle gives us new vigour
If to this land we owe our lives
Let it to us its freedom owe!

Throughout the century that followed, opera continued its flirtation with, and exploitation by, the forces of revolutionary Nationalism. A great admirer of *La Muette de Portici* was the Czech (Bohemian) composer Bedřich Smetana (1824–84). Bohemia was in the nineteenth century a small part, politically and culturally, of the Austro-Hungarian Empire, and had had German imposed as its official language since the 1780s. The Czechs resented the authority of Vienna, and the continued use of their language in defiance of Imperial regulations was widespread. It had not, however, been heard in the theatres and opera houses of Prague. Smetana's first opera *The Brandenburgers in Bohemia* (1866), was written in the official German but its plot was unashamedly provocative. It tells of the thirteenth-century occupation of Bohemia by overbearing and brutal German troops, and the armed resistance the peasants mounted against them. The piece was an unexpected success and as a result Smetana was appointed director of the Provincial Theatre in Prague where it had had its première. Not so surprisingly, the Czechs were quick to revive *The Brandenburgers in Bohemia* after the expulsion of the occupying Nazis in 1945, and again in the build-up to the Soviet invasion of 1968.

The librettist of this opera, Karel Sabina, a spokesman for the Czech nationalist movement of the 1860s, also wrote the text of Smetana's second opera, *The Bartered Bride*. Significantly, with political self-determination so much in the air, the language this time was Czech. Seemingly powerless to prevent its production by the country's leading composer, the collaborationist authorities saw *The Bartered Bride* gather momentum as a popular work until it attained a status second to none in Czech culture. In the fifty years following its first performance it was seen over a thousand times in Prague alone. The music is suffused with Bohemian folk melody, the contour of the vocal lines carved out by the rhythms and shapes of the people's language. But there are two factors at play here: the need of a subject people for works of art that can voice their suppressed feelings through allegory, and the fact that something with as high a cultural profile as a new opera could raise the aspirations of a community beyond the particular political objectives of the moment. For supposedly provincial, unsophisticated Bohemians in 1870, an opera to rival anything presented in Vienna, Berlin or Paris was a statement of national pride.

Much the same can be said of the operas of Leoš Janáček (1854–1928), whose relationship with his native Moravia was comparable with that of Smetana in neighbouring Bohemia. But whereas Smetana received considerable popular support for his operas during his lifetime, Janáček's masterpieces (*Jenůfa*, *Kát'a Kabanová*, *The Cunning Little Vixen*, *The Makropoulos Case* and *From the House of the Dead*) came to prominence on the world stage after his death. There are other examples of the nationalistic aspirations of a people finding expression in allegorical operas, but the country in which opera spoke with the greatest power and relevance was that of its birth, Italy.

Though it was written by two Frenchmen and an Italian living in Paris, based on a German play about Swiss peasants and their Austrian rulers, Rossini's magnificent *Guillaume Tell* (1829) was a sign that trends in Italy were moving away from light comedy towards a more confrontational style of opera. It is quite different in tone and scale from anything Rossini had produced before in his prolific career (forty operas in twenty years). Gone is the knockabout farce embodied by *The Barber of Seville*: in its place there is an epic struggle about oppressed Swiss farmers attempting to overthrow an arrogant army of occupation. It has all the ingredients that

Smetana exploited from similar material – torn loyalties, compromised love, bitter internecine feuding and the stench of collaboration. Though many countries in Europe, Rossini's native Italy for one, would have identified strongly with the plucky Swiss canton folk marching through the mountains to overthrow the yoke of Austrian rule, ironically, this opera opened in post-Napoleonic Paris, where it was received coolly. The composer duly retired at the grand age of thirty-seven, handing the baton of Italian opera's newly discovered militant liberalism to Giuseppe Verdi (1813–1901).

Every town in Italy has a street or square named after Verdi, not because he composed war cries for just the rebellious workers, but because he gave anthems to the resurgent voice of the whole Italian nation in its most heroic hour.

During the early years of the Risorgimento, Verdi turned grand opera into nationalist propaganda, with works like *Nabucco* (1842), *I Lombardi* (1843), *Attila* (1846), *La Battaglia di Legnano* (1849), *Simon Boccanegra* (1857) and *Don Carlos* (1867), whose plots were thinly disguised allegories of the contemporary political situation. His name was scrawled as graffiti on walls throughout the peninsula – VIVA VERDI! – conveniently an acronym for Vittorio Emanuele Re d'Italia! (Long Live Victor Emmanuel King of Italy). In fact Victor Emmanuel was crowned King of Italy in 1860, the same year that Verdi, the national hero, was elected to the Italian Parliament. After a few years, though the King was still king, Verdi gave up parliamentary politics and returned to composing full time, which is probably just as well.

The Italians (who up to this point couldn't accurately be described as a distinct *nation*) discovered that opera could invent for them a sense of national identity – it could create a mythical and heroic history, and set it to passionately stirring tunes that made one want to rush off and drive the foreigner off one's native soil.

Unhappily, they weren't the only Europeans to see this potential in what had become, in the nineteenth century, the most populist of musical experiences. Verdi's German contemporary, Richard Wagner, used his operas to reinvent Teu-

Giuseppe Verdi

tonic culture, myth and legend, culminating in the baldly anti-Semitic paean to Aryan Christianity, *Parsifal* (1882). He even tried to force the Jewish conductor of *Parsifal* to renounce his faith and accept Christian baptism before 'touching' the precious score (I'm delighted to report maestro Hermann Levi told him where he could stick his baptism and conducted it anyway). Fifty years later Wagner's operas (and his many feverishly offensive articles and books) were to be hideously exploited by the Nazis, and he can't escape blame entirely, since he knew more than anyone how potent a cultural weapon opera could be. His agitprop pamphlets and subversive behaviour suggest that he was no political innocent, even if he was somewhat mad. His contribution to the musical and dramatic development of opera is unquestionably immense, but he was every bit as much the propagandist as his rival Verdi.

These days it is operatically p.c. to let Wagner off the hook vis-à-vis his political stance and the undertone of Medieval

Germanic menace that runs through his operas, on the grounds that the music is superb and the story-telling, as music drama, second to none. This is fine, so long as we always remember his underlying attitudes. Successive post-war productions, especially and significantly by modern Germans like Wieland Wagner (the composer's grandson) in the 1950s, have in any case sought to debunk his Aryan pomposity and re-examine the work in a different light. Their imagination and intelligence in this respect has probably rescued this great composer's mammoth output.

At the same time as thousands of the Nazi faithful were queuing up to be seen alongside Hitler at Bayreuth (Wagner's own opera house-shrine in Bavaria), Mussolini was trawling Verdi's operas, using them shamelessly in his nationalist crusade. A production of *Aïda* under his dismal Fascist regime in the 1930s had 'his' blackshirted troops masquerading as Ancient Egyptians marching off to conquer the supposedly 'racially inferior' Ethiopians.

Not *all* composers' political leanings, of course, incline them to fascism and xenophobic nationalism. Another German, Kurt Weill, who collaborated brilliantly with the Marxist playwright Bertolt Brecht, was engaged in a struggle *against* Hitler's obscene rise to power. Brecht's and Weill's cabaret-style operas, *The Threepenny Opera* (1928) and *Happy End* (1929), were followed in 1930 with a full-scale opera *Aufstieg und Fall der Stadt Mahagonny* (*The Rise and Fall of the City of Mahagonny*). Almost all the productions of these aggressively satirical pieces were accompanied by scenes of violent demonstration and disruption by Nazi thugs outside the theatre. After they came to power the Nazi regime treated Weill (as left-wing and Jewish) with particular venom and he was blacklisted as a writer of *Entartete Musik* ('degenerate music'). Had he not fled Germany for Paris and then the USA, he would certainly have died at the hands of the Gestapo. It is a rich irony that having been partly responsible, in *Mahagonny*, for a savage and uncompromising attack on America – as home to an ugly, uncaring, mercenary capitalism – Weill the refugee found there a welcoming sanctuary from

The fire at the Fenice in 1836: the opera house was rebuilt but
burnt to the ground again in 1996

persecution. He spent the rest of his life writing genial Broadway shows and died in 1950.

The contemporary world is not immune from the political implications of opera, either. The Fenice ('Phoenix') opera house in Venice was first erected in the era of Monteverdi. It hosted the premières of many of the world's greatest operas, including Verdi's *Rigoletto* and *La Traviata*, at a time when Venice was still a restless part of the Austrian Empire. Although Verdi himself had soon tired of the realities and disappointments of power politics, he had nevertheless set a ball rolling that was extremely difficult to stop. His motives and intentions were noble, but in Italy no one now thinks opera houses are merely there to provide light entertainment for toffs and tourists. The Fenice has been burnt down, twice, most recently in 1996 in an arson attack suspected to have been in some way connected with 'organised crime'. Whoever did it knew how significant and potent a symbol the Fenice was. But then, so do the people who will rebuild it and help the Phoenix once again to rise from its ashes.

While Verdi the crowd-pleasing nationalist was sweeping through Italy with his tragic and moral-laden music dramas, in Paris Jacques Offenbach was cocking a snook at the world of grand opera, and enjoying enormous commercial success. His satirical operettas, especially *Orphée aux Enfers* (1858), were characterised by much hilarity, topical political gags, popular tunes and saucy dancing: the 'Infernal Can-Can' still presented nightly at the Moulin Rouge is from that show. The successes of Offenbach's operettas were mirrored in England by the witty and tuneful diversions of Messrs Gilbert & Sullivan, though, of course – it being Victorian England – without the sex. Both Offenbach and Arthur Sullivan were composers of cracking hummable tunes, but one ingredient in their success was also the contemporary political satire running through all these works. William Gilbert's barbed comic assaults on the judiciary in *Trial By Jury* (1875), the Navy in *H.M.S. Pinafore* (1878), the army and the police in *The Pirates of Penzance* (1879), the House of Lords in *Iolanthe* (1882) and Civil Service superciliousness in *The Mikado* (1885) sit alongside his merciless lampooning of Oscar Wilde and the Aesthetic Movement in *Patience* (1881), and his smug mockery of the establishment of a *women's* college at Cambridge (Girton College), in *Princess Ida* (1884).

These hugely popular 'Savoy' operettas would eventually give rise to the musical, a form which has spread and thrived so rapaciously that there is barely a corner of the globe where one can't purchase the *Cats* mug and T-shirt, the *Whistle Down the Wind* whistle, the *Phantom of the Opera* face pack, or the *Chicago* thong. However, with one or two notable exceptions (Stephen Sondheim's *Assassins* or Kander & Ebb's *Cabaret* for example), in comparison to Gilbert & Sullivan this form has been almost entirely devoid of political edge, comment, satire or relevance. Nevertheless, one of the distinguishing features of the modern stage musical is how seriously it takes itself, with rarely a glimpse of the self-deprecating and ironic humour that enlivens its predecessors from Offenbach to Oscar Hammerstein, or, for that matter, Mozart's work with librettist Da Ponte.

Opera, the parent of the modern musical, exists and thrives side by side but *separately* from its wildly successful offspring. New operas are still being commissioned and produced around the world, and many have an energy and relevance that refutes the notion of opera as a form in terminal decline. Indeed perhaps the greatest living 'classical' composer is the American John Adams, whose 1987 opera, *Nixon in China*, is one of the masterpieces of our time.

Unlike most contemporary composers, Adams turned to recent political events for his subject (Nixon's historic 1972 visit to meet Chairman Mao in Beijing). Not unlike the audience at Monteverdi's *Orfeo*, *Nixon in China* was performed to many of the 'movers and shakers' in American political life. But as he told me when we met, Adams saw the commission as an opportunity to widen the appeal of the medium:

Opera doesn't necessarily have to deal with contemporary events, but it's really very seductive to draw from our present day experience – I look around me and I see all the great American authors, whether they be Russell Banks, John Updike or Toni Morrison – they're all drawing from contemporary experience and the same goes for film makers, so why not opera?

There was a witticism going around that first week of *Nixon in China* in Houston that this was court entertainment for the Reagan era. I myself like to think of it as an opera for 'Communists and Republicans', but I wasn't thinking about it as an opera to be tasted and appreciated by the elite. I was thinking about it as a statement of American art types and I really wanted to reach the kind of audience that an American like Mark Twain or Walt Whitman or Hemingway or Gershwin would, to use a work with genuine and deep American themes to express the 'zeitgeist' (to use a German word!).

Trudy Ellen Craney as Madame Mao in Act 2 of John Adams'
Nixon in China, Houston 1987

I think that opera can handle big, big subjects, like sexual identity, national myths, collective experience (in the Jungian sense) and so on. I think it can handle these issues because fundamentally it's a very unreal art form. The movies, despite montage and surrealism and also techniques you can have with experimental film makers, is fundamentally a very realistic art form in the way that photography is. But opera, from the moment we walk into it, is a ridiculous state of affairs – with the orchestra in the pit, people singing, poetry, dance – this union of art forms, it's a very unreal experience. It's always occurred to me that opera functions on the archetypal level, that it seems to go beneath the level of consciousness to make its effect. When the lights go down in the theatre and the music starts, we really do enter a world of suspended belief.

Largely because of this unreal experience it has a certain kind of magical, totemic power and I think that's why you can have Wagner talking about human interaction and dynamic whilst using this ridiculous vehicle of Teutonic mythology, or you can have Mussorgsky talking about the major themes of Russian culture. So these were the models that gave me the courage to go ahead and write my operas. What opera wants is a theme that has the power to go deep, deep down and stir up those dark, muddy waters and I think in a way I did that with *Nixon in China*, by taking themes which were so much part of the American experience.

For Adams and his librettist, Alice Goodman, the American experience of the twentieth century was epitomised by the Cold War collision of capitalism and communism, hence the subject of the opera. His second opera, *The Death of Klinghoffer* (1991), took the story of the Palestinian hijacking of the cruise ship *Achille Lauro* (and subsequent murder of disabled Jewish passenger Leon Klinghoffer) and tackled the 'Sophoclean' dilemma of the Middle East conflict. *The Death of Klinghoffer* was picketed by demonstrators during its opening run and Adams and Goodman both received hate mail and death threats. He is adamant that they did not choose their story to court controversy, but to examine their own ambiguous feelings as modern Americans about the Jewish–Palestinian question.

I was attracted to this story because it was so much like the *Passions* of Bach, that it was a story almost of a crucifixion: this murder of this retired Jewish man, who unknown wandered into a political maelstrom. This whole event took place within a stone's throw of the birthplace of the three great Western religions. On the one hand it was as lurid, as brutal, as gruesome as something coming at us over CNN, some hideous event that's produced for television and on the other hand it had a kind of archaeological gravitas, like something you'd read in the Old Testament or the Koran. So it was an opera that dealt, I think very honestly and sincerely, with contemporary issues but created a kind of timeless resonance at the same moment.

Monteverdi's first opera was performed in February 1607 to about thirty people in a private apartment in Mantua. The form he so expertly coaxed into life is now a huge, worldwide phenomenon as the building of ever more spectacular new opera houses all over the world continues apace. Western opera is even finding an audience and a purpose in the People's Republic of China, which has had its own idiosyncratic form of music drama (sometimes called 'Beijing Opera') since the sixteenth century. In it, myths and legends are told with singing accompanied by folk instruments, elaborate hand and body gestures, sometimes acrobatics as well, beautifully colourful ancient costumes, plenty of pantomimic comedy, and archetypal characters. The 'singing' style is highly stylised and archaic (this and other elements of the form are unchanged in centuries), and there is no harmony as such.

There are, though, many resonances with European opera, like its growth among the cultured elite followed by its expansion and popularity amongst ordinary people. Until the twentieth century, boys usually played women's roles, and successive political rulers discovered opera's excellent potential for propaganda purposes, in particular Madame Mao, the great leader's wife. She sought to commission and tour hundreds of 'new' operas with allegorical, political and moral tales during the Cultural Revolution. Perhaps the fact that Western opera is so alien and apparently indulgent compared to these dour social commentaries is what has lured a Chinese audience to it in recent years. Or perhaps it is because China is now actively looking outwards to the rest of the world for the first time in many decades, and sees Western opera as an enjoyable way of empathising with Western culture.

Whatever the reason, the new appetite in China for Western opera is likely to have an impact on opera itself within a gen-

Chinese Opera

eration or two. Each culture that has embraced it has played its part in its development and mutation.

Opera does have universal appeal. Harvey Goldsmith, the British concert promoter, broke new ground in 1991 by presenting a spectacular version of Puccini's *Tosca* at Earl's Court Arena in London, with rock-style lighting effects and PA system, to 6,000 people a night for a week. The same opera was seen in larger-than-life scale at the Albert Hall in 1999 by 60,000 people. Verdi's *Aïda* and Puccini's *La Bohème* have sold out the vast National Exhibition Centre in Birmingham, the 'Three Tenors' have sung opera arias by satellite to two billion people on the eve of Football's World Cup, and so on.

Some would argue that the real reason opera has found a wider audience through 'arena' productions is that people are merely enjoying the spectacle. Both opera and the musical have been bedevilled by the charge that they are primarily concerned with spectacle, not humanity. Even Monteverdi felt moved to comment on the matter in a letter, expressing the fear that opera would be swallowed up by the need to create ever more exciting effects. In *Miss Saigon* (a musical that owes a huge debt to Puccini's opera *Madama Butterfly*) a helicopter lands on stage. In the very earliest days of opera, musical spectacles were devised which depicted real sea battles – in fact, even the Greeks and Romans mounted such extravaganzas (the amphitheatre at Taormina still has its under-stage water tanks for such entertainments). A recent production of *Aïda* used a herd of real camels, and elephants have been known to be used in operatic stagings, never mind a visiting spaceship, in Michael Tippett's *New Year* (1989).

The idea, though, that opera's new broad audience is only there for the special effects is extremely patronising. The audience for the *Tosca* I saw at the Earl's Court Arena in London a few years ago was full of people who seemed to be having their first experience of opera. Sure, they were amazed and delighted by the pageant and scenic magic of the first act. But the second act of *Tosca* is about two people alone in a room for the best part of an hour. No set changes, no dry ice, no projections or pyrotechnics, just a woman begging (in Italian) for the life of her lover with a cruel police chief who wants to sleep with her. I swear you could hear a pin drop. Whatever reason people had had for entering that arena that night, once inside they were gripped by Puccini's musical drama, by the tragedy, the narrative and the sweeping music.

It is quite clear that opera has in the past played an important part in people's real lives, and there is no doubt in my mind that it still can play a role in modern society.

Opera *is* an expensive art, yes, but then so are symphony orchestras, art galleries, science museums and playhouses. Culture didn't come cheap to Pharaoh Rameses II or the Doges of Venice either. But great art is the footprint of our civilisation, the measure of our learning and our understanding. Is the debate going to be reduced simply to cost? I hope not. I like to think of Monteverdi and his tragic hero in the Underworld. Monteverdi sincerely believed that the intelligent and humanistic values of his opera would have a civilising, enriching role to play in his society.

Io la musica son, ch'ai dolci accenti
So far tranquillo ogni turbato core,
Et or' di nobil ira et or' d'amore
Poss' infiammar le più gelate menti.

I am Music, who in sweet accents
Can calm each troubled heart,
And now with noble anger, now with love,
Can kindle the most frigid of minds.

FOUR

'JE SUIS COMPOSITEUR'

I have often been asked what it is like to be able to compose. The truthful answer is I don't know what it's like *not* to be able to compose. Sometimes I reply by saying that composing is a bit like dreaming. Composers are people who hear the echoes and fragments of completed music in their heads all the time, and what they're doing is attempting to capture it before it escapes, to write down the sounds they hear. But like a dream as soon as you start to write it down it becomes less and less like the music you heard in your head and more and more like the new music that is forming in front of you. The creative journey from subconscious to conscious seems both fruitful and forgetful, productive and wasteful.

Every summer I migrate to France to spend nearly two months working on commissions that don't need my London studio's technical back-up. A pencil and a pile of blank manuscript paper or a musical laptop are all I need. I have been doing this since 1991, taking my car and roaming the wide, inspirational plains of Burgundy, the Drôme, Languedoc-Roussillon and Provence.

In July 1992 I was driving south-east towards the Route Napoléon, which winds its craggy way through mountains from Grenoble to the Côte d'Azur. The commission I was to embark upon that summer was a daunting one – a Latin Mass for double choir – and on the previous ten days of touring I had busied myself with lesser tasks to put off the inevitable confrontation with this piece. Unusually for me, not a note of it was lurking around in my head, I couldn't 'hear' any of it.

You see, by the time I actually write the notes down on paper the composition part of it is virtually over, since I come up with the raw material itself, editing and modifying it along the way, purely in my head. For a work like this I wouldn't use nor need a keyboard for reference at all, in fact it can be a hindrance if writing something for voices or instruments very alien to the piano's sound and layout. It does mean, though, that I rely heavily on my imagination tapping into the musical 'source' in my head. Improvisation at the piano would have been an admission of failure at this point in composing my Mass, though I might have resorted to it as a last desperate measure if all else had failed. I had even banned myself from listening to tapes of other people's music in the car, in an effort to kick-start my own musical 'imagination'.

There were reasons for this mini-block. For a start, I was feeling intimidated by the existing repertoire of Masses available to your average cathedral choir. I mean, when the world already has fabulous Masses by Byrd, Lassus, Palestrina, Vittoria, Haydn, Mozart, Schubert, Poulenc and Stravinsky, who needs another one? All I could imagine at this point was something that sounded like everybody else, but not as good, frankly. Secondly, I had been a chorister myself and knew only too well what impossibly high standards we expected as a matter of course from newly commissioned works. I remember with shuddering embarrassment the cruelly frank judgements we 8- to 13-year-olds delivered on new pieces (always hideously difficult to sing in the 1960s, by the way, when new music was only taken seriously if it was unfeasibly complex or unpleasant), with the poor wreck of a composer quivering nervously nearby. On the other hand, the speed with which new commissions returned to the library shelf after their triumphant première was (and still is) a pretty reliable litmus test of the grown-ups' more diplomatic judgements.

The Mass is a tricky article anyway. When translated into English, even the Common Prayer version, it sounds disappointingly unpoetic and rather, if I may say so, repetitious. However, in Latin it is magnificent, resonating across the ages with its broad open vowels and powerfully evocative refrains. There was a time when you could hear this same Latin Mass in any Catholic church anywhere in the world, it was a truly universal sacred language, but now it has been driven out to the margins by a hundred or more vernaculars. I am a Protestant Humanist and even I love the sound of sung Latin in church or chapel. It is a link with our extraordinary Christian past, and it is patronising to assume congregations are too stupid to read the translation in front of them. The repertoire of wonderful settings listed above is now heard only in isolated pockets, English cathedrals – Protestant and Catholic – being some of them. Once I had a robust exchange over lunch with the Archbishop of Canterbury about Latin. He offered the opinion that people needed to understand what was going on in church if they were to be fulfilled by and committed to it (I hope he won't mind my paraphrasing of his views). I replied by saying that I thought there were one or two more pressing matters of incomprehensibility for congregations than the translating of Latin to attend to first, namely the Virgin Birth, the Resurrection and almost all the Miracles.

The Archbishop is a supremely sympathetic, intelligent and genial man but I don't remember being in any way moved by his reply. Indeed, I cannot for the life of me remember it at all. I then launched into my musings on the dearth of poetry, lyricism or imagination in the texts of modern hymns in comparison with the exotic and eccentric grandeur of hymns of yore. I must have sounded like some curmudgeonly old-timer and no doubt at this juncture lost both my audience and case entirely. Before I move on, though, I ask you to decide which of the following you'd rather sing:

> Lead, kindly light, amid the encircling gloom,
> Lead thou me on:
> The night is dark, and I am far from home;
> Lead thou me on.
> Keep thou my feet; I do not ask to see
> The distant scene; one step enough for me.

I was not ever thus, nor prayed that thou
Shouldst lead me on:
I loved to choose and see my path; but now
Lead thou me on.
I loved the garish day; and, spite of fears,
Pride ruled my will: remember not past years.

So long thy power hath blessed me, sure it still
Will lead me on,
O'er moor and fen, o'er crag and torrent, till
The night is gone;
And with the morn those angel faces smile,
Which I have loved long since, and lost awhile.

J. H. Newman (1801–90) 'Lead, kindly light' in
Hymns Ancient and Modern

Or:

Life is great! So sing about it,
As we can and as we should –
Shops and buses, towns and people,
Village, farmland, field and wood.
Life is great and life is given;
Life is lovely, free and good.

Brian A. Wren (1936–) 'Life is great', no.149 in
Hymns for Today

I'm not on my own with this one, am I?

Back to my Mass. The long and the short of it was that I couldn't 'find' this music anywhere inside my head and was beginning to worry about it.

I was winding my way through the spectacularly beautiful mountains south of Grenoble when my car began to develop a strange and worrying rattle. As I was in hostile, mountainous terrain, switchbacks and sheer drops all round, I was not inclined to ignore this grating, metallic obbligato, especially as it became increasingly noisy as kilometre followed sun-scorched kilometre. I decided to have it checked out as soon as I could, consulted the *Guide Michelin* and found there was a garage in the nearby town of Gap, but as it was Sunday I had to tread water till Monday morning and my car's appointment with destiny. I looked at the map to find somewhere sweet and small near Gap to spend the night.

I chose a hilltop village called Embrun for the reason that the *Blue Guide* said its thirteenth-century cathedral contained within it the oldest working organ in France. For someone like me, this is too good an opportunity to pass by, and gingerly I drove my rattling car back up into the hills. In Embrun's charming and minute square I found a fountain, a small *bar-tabac* and the kind of *pension* I remembered from my child-hood summers in France: dark, tiled and moodily monastic. Madame had one remaining single room, one basin, one loo (down the pitch-black corridor) and no discernible bathroom or shower. There was a single crucifix above the huge old-fashioned bed, a rolled-up sausage pillow, and breakfast (a bowl of *chocolat chaud* with fresh hunks of baguette) would be at 8.30 sharp. Blissfully installed, I went off to examine France's oldest working cathedral organ. If I was really lucky, I might find a postcard of it too, which I would send off there and then to my friend Charles Hart in London with the rib-crackingly amusing words 'unlike mine' scrawled on the back. I did, and I did.

Embrun's old organ is rather unprepossessing as a tourist attraction, one has to admit. The cathedral is beautiful, but so dark it may as well be closed to the public permanently. I stumbled into a few chairs before I realised I was in the main aisle of the nave and crashed into a few more until I found myself standing amid a circle of children enduring a Sunday School talk from a nun. How their tiny eyes had adjusted suf-ficiently to the cave-like gloom to be able to discern she was a nun and not a dismembered ghostly head with bifocals I do not know. I was amazed to note later that they had been look-ing at drawings in books at the time, surely 100 per cent invis-ible to the naked eye. I edged my way carefully forward like a somnambulist and searched absurdly for a sixteenth-century organ. I can't believe God approves of this level of darkness in His House, after all that effort on paintings and towering altarpieces, all to no avail. I did manage to identify the organ loft at least, and behind it sulked a few pipes. The idea that anyone might still play it for services is pure fantasy, as the Roman church from Palermo to Boulogne has given up on its heritage of ancient music in favour of electric organs and droning priests, but I have heard since that the federal or regional government has helped pay for the restoration of the historic instrument and they probably have one or two concerts and recitals on it by now. Good for them.

When I came out of the cathedral into the late afternoon sun I thought my eyes would pop out of their sockets with the shock. I had hoped, naturally, that the holy visit would have helped me get in the mood for composing a Mass but I must confess I went off in search of a Pastis and a bag of crisps. It's a gorgeous place, Embrun, and wandering around it on a sweltering August evening is a delightful pastime. I returned to my room to write the postcards and lay on the bed with the shuttered sun streaking across the starched white sheets.

All at once a bell for evening service in the cathedral started to chime – a persistent but unhurried F#. Soon it was joined by another, a G#, as if ricocheting against it in rhythmic sympathy. What I thought I'd do was get my manuscript paper and just for fun write out (in real time, as it were) the bell concert I was hearing – all the notes, harmonics and rhythms. This is the musical equivalent of doing a crossword or a brainteaser. Then a second church seemed to join in from somewhere else in the town, and the competing bells fought for attention on the page. To this layered chiming were added the bells of further-off churches across the valley – it being a mountainous region with lakes between the perched villages, the sound could carry greater than normal distances and soon I was enveloped in a grand chorus of bells far and near, intermingled with their echoes bouncing off the valley walls. Bells have very heavy harmonic overtones (extra notes you hear alongside the main one, creating an effect not dissimilar to a chord each

'The Bells'

time the bell is struck) and keeping up with them, analysing and transcribing them was a frantic job. Eventually, after about 10 or 15 minutes, the bell orchestra subsided, leaving only my original F# bell from the nearby cathedral chiming slowly and fitfully. Then it too died and left behind a strange, calm silence.

I sensed something in me had changed. I could 'hear' the bell concert as a sort of choral wash, as if it hadn't really ended but was now being sung instead. Within a few minutes I realised the sound had a top, middle and bottom, it wasn't simply a generalised wash, it had crystallised into a form. Now I could hear the bells as individual voices singing *Sanctus*. Imagine you are wearing a Walkman and you are hearing a piece of music you've never encountered before. This is what it felt like. I could 'see' (probably a combination of hearing, feeling and seeing the music laid out on a mental manuscript score in front of me is a more accurate description than 'see') this piece of music. I could sense that it had a shape but not how long it was nor where exactly it began. Was it just a *Sanctus* movement from a Mass, or did it stretch on into other movements, like the other tracks of a CD? I 'selected' the

Gloria movement to see if any music now existed in my head for that section. It started like the track on a CD, it came out like completed music – all the tunes, all the melodies all the rhythms. I could easily identify who was singing what and what key the music was playing in. It carried on, seeming to know exactly where it was going without any assistance or prompting from me. I tried the *Benedictus*, the *Agnus Dei*, the *Kyrie Eleison* and the *Credo*. It all seemed to be there. I had had this experience before, many times, but before I had heard fragments of the total piece – 'cells' some composers have called them – which I had eventually knotted together into a whole. I had heard tunes too, in isolation, running from start to finish, but without their accompaniment or without their overall context. This Embrun experience, on the other hand, seemed to be offering me the music ready-made.

Before I describe what happened next I should freeze this moment in time and analyse the material entering my head. When I say it appears to be complete, it is. If the piece is destined to be scored for orchestra, an orchestra is playing it, if it's going to be sung by a choir, then a choir in my head is singing it as if it were the first performance, and so on. However, it isn't set in concrete; I can alter and modify it at will. I can change the sounds, put in new instruments, give the tune to different voices, speed it up or slow it down, make it softer or louder, turn a chorus into a solo – anything, in fact. The 'revised' version will then play back to me like the original, and rather like a computer's method of 'saving' work, the new version replaces the old as the working model. It may seem strange or ungrateful, but I do discard some of the material I receive in this raw form. I play around with it and add new bits.

Why don't I, or any other composer in the same situation, leave it as it is? We mess about with it because we apply to the raw material a second layer of taste, a conscious level. It's as if we are embellishing the story of a dream to make the punch-line funnier or give the tale more meaning or substance. We are all familiar with the concept of taking an event in our lives, tarting it up and turning it into a full-blown anecdote. We

Composing

retell old favourites as if they happened yesterday. To suit our audience we might tailor the names of the characters to make it more personal or we might alter a detail of a story to make it more suitable for children, and so on. We all do it all the time. Composing is no different. I embellish and simplify, I add on and subtract, I colour and shape the raw material of music I hear in my head because I can, because it's fun, because I am turning it into something that can be reproduced at will by other people in the real world. I am a conduit for the music, so it can make the journey from my head onto the page and then into other people's heads. But the process of transcription to the empty manuscript page is one that modifies it, willy-nilly. If I transcribe it on a hot day in France it will end up on the page in one way, if I do it on a cold day in New York it will end up in another. The cultural environment is one major influence, as are my state of mind, my mood, and the mish-mash of music I have been listening to or playing over the previous few days or hours. Transferring the notes onto the page is extremely slow and time-consuming. Sometimes I will alter the original simply to alleviate the tedium of the task, just for the hell of it.

Sitting on the bed in my room in Embrun I couldn't quite believe my good fortune. Normally, if a tune is any good when I first encounter it, it will stay lodged in my head for as long as I need it to, but on this occasion I was uncharacteristically frightened that I'd wake up in the morning and find it gone as quickly as it had appeared. So I grabbed my manuscript paper and headed for the little restaurant in the square. At some point in the next few hours I must have ordered wine and food and consumed it, but what I remember most is poring over the page intently from about 7.30 p.m. till 1.00 a.m. without moving, scribbling away at an exhilarated, breakneck speed. Writing down the piece properly, all parts vocal and instrumental, and all 35 minutes of it, would have taken several weeks, but what I had to do was jot down in shorthand the salient information – the outline of the tunes, the basic harmony, the 'feel' of the sections, the overall skeleton plan. By one o'clock the sympathetic restaurateur was hinting that she might like to get home to bed and maybe I should continue my mighty task elsewhere. When I went to bed that night I was feeling a mixture of excitement and apprehension as to whether the music would still sound OK in the morning. Perhaps it would be enough for it to be there at all in the morning, as full and rich as it had been that evening. Well, it was all there the next day and I went on to finish the fair copy of the *Missa Aedis Christi* later that summer. The car turned out to have one tiny screw loose and the Gap mechanic thought me most amusing and English with all my anxiety and pessimism.

A year or two later, when I recounted the Embrun episode to a roomful of people, a man punctured the silence with the assertion that it was the most convincing proof he had ever heard for the existence of God. I have wondered about his comment often since then. It does indeed appear as if the music is emanating from some other source, but is this just an illusion, a trick of the brain? What I sometimes feel like is a skilled interpreter, able to pilot the music from the 'dream

The Sanctus, from Missa Aedis Christi

world' to the page, but I don't know if the place the music is coming from is God's place, as the man's remark implies. It has been suggested that music comes from some kind of central bank of consciousness that is the common inheritance of humanity. It may be that I am so lost for a description of the process that I fall back on tired references to a 'dream world' or a 'collective subconscious' or a heaven of some kind. Perhaps it is simply a chemical or biological reaction going on in my head and I have fallen back on other people's imagery to explain it away. Does it mean there is a God, as the man suggested?

I know that Christianity has had a considerable, if not decisive effect on the music of Western Europe – in some respects it is our music's midwife. Yet Christianity, like all the world's faiths, is an amalgam of many different things. For some, it is a philosophy for living, a template for well-integrated, compassionate human societies. For others, it is a story to explain and illustrate the mystery that undoubtedly surrounds us. But every time someone tries to explain or pin down the mystery of God it seems, to me, to drift further away. Even those who have had profound spiritual experiences find it difficult to relate these to the vocabulary of the average church service. The Bible contains amazing poetry and much truth about humanity, but the stories of Moses, of the loaves and fishes, Jonah and the Whale or St Paul briefing the Corinthians don't in all honesty tell you much about the spiritual, non-conscious world. Music, because it is by and large mysterious and inexplicable itself, seems to edge back to the heart of it, to step cautiously towards the feeling of a spiritual dimension. It may be our last remaining link, in our most concrete of concrete worlds, with a way of being that we once enjoyed and have long since left behind. We cannot *prove* music has a power, we simply surrender to it, because we want or need to. We *let* it move us. People with unshakeable faiths, I suspect, would describe God in such a way. When deeply religious people replace a sense of mystery, though, with a sense of *certainty* they are marching back down a man-made road of proof and empiricism.

Music is not certain or solid or real. It operates solely through our heads and our bodies. It contains doubt and uncertainty, it exudes sadness and longing. It radiates into us, or floats past us. It is not really under our control, it has a chemistry all of its own that composers tinker and dabble with. Composers are merely carriers, hauling water from a gigantic well to some parched and needy tribe, stranded far away from their natural homeland. When they first taste the water, the tribespeople think they can see their old country, hear their lost children playing, feel the old breeze on their faces. After that first heavenly sip they feel sure they will be able to find their way back home. But soon the cup is empty and they are standing once again in their new, empty surroundings, thirsting for more.

When I compose I am afforded the privilege of dipping into that deep, magnificent well.

FIVE

ACCIDENTALS WILL HAPPEN

The Invention of Temperament

I have already pointed out that there is Western European music, and All Other Music. There are many reasons for this, one of which is a concept of 'tuning' that no other system has attempted. Even non-musical people in the West say something sounds 'out of tune', a phrase that might strike an Indian, Japanese, Chinese or Indonesian musician as hopelessly misleading.

The reason for this is that during the seventeenth century, European musicians and their technical colleagues tampered with nature and came up with a fixed method of tuning instruments which not only altered the way all music was composed and performed, but also changed fundamentally the way we hear music. Because of this tuning system, to our ears music sounds weird or dissonant if it doesn't conform to our artificial standard – and most of the world's ethnic music falls into this category.

Equal Temperament is probably the single most important development in Western European music in the last 400 years and yet most people haven't even heard of it. Even musicians don't really understand it, but an enormous amount of the world's most beautiful music wouldn't exist without it. Equal Temperament is the tuning system by which practically all the notes in our Western music are organised and structured. It is to music what the calendar is to the days and nights or what the 24-hour clock is to the minutes and seconds. As with the calendar and the clock, Western man has taken what nature gave us and manipulated it artificially – every single note of our musical repertoire is a monstrous compromise. The road from the raw sounds of nature to the artificial smoothness of Equal Temperament is long and tortuous – a Big Bang with a long fuse – and it stretches back to ancient Greece.

It was in Greece in about 580 BC that Western musical theory more or less began, with the establishment of a specific palette of notes, arranged into a neat functional ladder – that is, the first scale. And the man credited with this original musical theory is Pythagoras, the very same man who brought us the mathematics of triangles.

That's not to say that there was no music before Pythagoras. On the contrary, music was extremely popular in ancient Greece, as it had been in the Egypt of the Pharaohs. But it must have had a certain anarchy to it, since Pythagoras decided that music needed a vocabulary and structure like any other language. In essence, what he discovered was that certain notes in nature created harmonious sounds and that these notes had a mathematical relationship. His discovery, according to legend, happened by accident – he was passing a blacksmith's when he heard a harmonious chord of chimes coming from the sound of the hammers on the anvils.

On investigation he discovered that the weights and lengths of metal that produced these harmonious notes were simple ratios: 1, ½, ⅔, etc. What Pythagoras was actually hearing was a demonstration of simple harmonics. This is how harmonics work.

Take an object. Any object – an empty bottle or a piece of metal, for example. If you hit it, it makes a *ping*. There is a ping, or note, to every hard item that you might care to mention. Its material, length, breadth, weight, height and volume will all affect what note the ping is. If you put water in the empty bottle its ping, or pitch, changes. This is the natural order of things.

If you take a length of catgut or wire, stretch it and pluck it, it makes a *boing*. The 'note' of that boing is also affected by the material, length, tautness, and so on, as with the bottle. If you halve the length of the wire and pluck it again you get a replica version of the first note, but higher. Little boing, as it

Woodcut from Gaffori's *Theoria Musica*, Milan 1496, showing Jubal,
Pythagoras and Phyloaus as the first musical theorists

were. Halve it again, and it goes up even higher (this time, it's
a *new* note, known as the 'dominant', an influential and sympathetic colleague of the first note). If you go on dividing the

103

string or wire it would produce other little notes. This is called the Harmonic Series.

Just as halving, then halving again, the length of wire produces a new 'dominant' note, this same 'dominant' can be produced by dividing the original wire not by half but by two-thirds. Similarly, striking a piece of metal two-thirds the size of the original gives you a 'dominant'. This is because $\frac{2}{3}$, as it happens, is a natural, harmonious ratio in maths.

It was this creation of new notes using the harmonious ratio of 2:3 that caught Pythagoras' imagination. By experimenting further he found that if you carried on dividing your metal bars by $\frac{2}{3}$ you could create an endless cycle of harmonious new notes (a dominant of a dominant of a dominant and so on). As a mathematician Pythagoras believed that everything in the universe could be reduced to numbers. The planets were numbers and their relationships were ratios. It therefore followed that music had a mathematical basis too. Hence his quest for a way to define music using maths. Certain numbers had special significance; the first three numbers were considered particularly powerful, so the ratio 2:3 was especially attractive to him as a basis for musical theory.

Let us go back to our original note. If you had an oscilloscope (something that analyses sound waves and shows them on a graph for you), it would tell you that the ping contained *several* notes all at once, that there are overtones connected to the ping that you didn't think you could hear, but you are nevertheless being affected by, and which help make the ping into the ping it is. Sounds behave in this respect like light – contained within sunlight there is a whole spectrum of different colours that are only visible when seen as a rainbow or through a prism.

Those overtones are the same as the notes you get if you keep halving the length of the wire or piece of metal. Once again, these phenomena are known as the Harmonic Series. This is nature's aural spectrum.

Pythagoras discovered the Harmonic Series two and a half thousand years ago. In his time he was as famous for being a mystic as for being a mathematician. He believed that the

universe had its own music, a harmony created by the movement of the planets in relation to one another. He was revered
by his disciples as a demi-god – an incarnation of Apollo, the
God of music, who had the ability to perceive tunes outside
human hearing. He claimed to be able to hear the 'music of
the spheres' and used to sing the hidden tunes to his disciples.
The idea of a 'music of the spheres' has persisted throughout
history, including in our own time. Broadly speaking it pro-
poses that music on earth is a reflection or echo of the music
created when planets fly in orbit around us in the solar
system. According to Pythagoras, we mortals have lost the
ability to hear 'cosmic music' because it is ever present and
we have therefore 'tuned it out' in our brain. (In fact, the idea
of music being all around us in the air isn't all that far-
fetched. Whenever we turn a radio on we pick up invisible
waves with music in them that are around us at all times.)
Pythagoras' teaching on the natural science of notes had a
profound influence on early European musical theory. He
saw the cosmos as one vast harmonic ratio made up of lots of
smaller ratios. Just as the sea's tides were affected by the
moon's relationship to earth, so everything on earth, he
believed, was affected by the movement of the spheres. Music
was the link between man and the universe. Later medieval
theorists took Pythagoras' assumptions largely as read,
though they did modify it by placing God at the top of the
heavenly hierarchy.

Perhaps you are wondering why Pythagoras didn't generate
his new notes from another division of the string or metal bar
($\frac{1}{3}$ or $\frac{2}{5}$, for example), since other notes are present (like the
colours of a rainbow) in the original sound too. Well, the
'dominant' derived from a $\frac{2}{3}$ fraction is so called precisely
because it is so powerful an influence on the overall tone – the
human ear can actually hear it quite clearly alongside the fundamental note in some cases (bells sound very 'dominant'-
heavy). Since this dominant is ever-present in natural sounds
you may as well use its ubiquity to your advantage. Pythagoras was using nature's inherent musicality to create new notes
from one original.

In theory, you can create an infinity of new notes with this method, like a spiral staircase that never ends. A medieval philosopher or theologian might have seen it as a musical Jacob's Ladder stretching from the earth to the heavens. Once you have created your notes you can then arrange them however you choose, but there are all sorts of reasons why you would need to limit the infinity of notes available. In fact, all of the world's musical systems have drawn the line somewhere for practical reasons (all of the world's musical systems, apart from the Balinese and Javanese ones, created their notes from the same natural formula). One reason is the need to make instruments that can actually be played with human hands. For a keyboard instrument that's going to be played by a ten-fingered person of average dexterity and intelligence it is certainly necessary to limit the number of notes on offer. A modern piano, for example, has 88 notes, comprising 7 'octaves' which are themselves made up of 12 subdivisions (making 84), plus four bonus notes. We shall see what an octave is and why Westerners chose to divide it by 12 shortly.

At various times in the period 1000–1700 manufacturers and musicologists came up with keyboard designs which had more than 12 notes in an octave, but none caught on because of the hideous difficulty of playing them and the equally hideous task of tuning all their strings. There are one or two of these freakish instruments still in existence. In the Teylers Museum in Haarlem there is an organ built to the specification of the Dutch physicist Fokker (1887–1972) dividing each octave into 31 parts. This would mean that for Fokker's organ to have a 7-octave range it would require, instead of 84 notes, a total of 217. There were antique keyboard instruments called *arcicembali* and *arciorgani* made in the 1550s with 31 keys in an octave. The physics and astronomy giant Christiaan Huygens, inventor of the pendulum clock, had also proposed a 31-tone scale at this time. In modern times some composers have reverted to an idea of more than 12 notes per octave, like the American Harry Partch who made up a scale of 43 pitches and designed an instrument to play it (this would need 301 notes to make 7 octaves). Others experimented with a 19-note division – the Russian-Swiss composer Jacques Handschin in 1927 and the Polish-American Joseph Yasser in 1932. It's fair to say, though, that these experiments were very much outside the mainstream thrust of European music.

Keyboard instruments are not the only ones limited for practical reasons to less than infinity notes in a scale. An oboe, clarinet or bassoon has to have its holes bored at predetermined points, so a decision as to what the notes are is a vital precondition. Violinists and cellists, on the other hand, are free of these strictures since the strings on their instruments are themselves infinitely divisible – they have no 'frets' that lay down the law about the positioning of the tuning, and their strings are easily and accurately tuned by the player. A fret, incidentally, is a horizontal line along the neck of the instrument that determines where one's finger might be placed on the string to obtain a certain note; they are essential on the guitar, which inherited them from its predecessors, the lute, the chitarrone and the theorbo.

So, on the one hand, a piano has to give each note its own separate finger-sized strip of wood and hammer with a pre-ordained and calibrated pitch, an oboe gives each note its own pre-drilled hole and a guitarist is given neatly divided-up frets for the placing of the fingers. On the other hand, a violinist, a cellist or a singer is as free as a bird. However, if a violin is to play a piece with the same agreed selection of notes as a piano, or a clarinet, it follows that someone, somewhere is going to have to compromise. Total freedom and total predetermination are uneasy bedfellows at the best of times. In practice what has happened is that the totally free instruments like violins have had to live according to the rules laid down by the strictly controlled group of instruments. This has meant, in effect, the (some would say) brutal restriction of the infinite choice of notes.

But there's another, more scientific reason why you have to limit your infinity of notes and it's called – mysteriously – the Pythagorean 'comma'.

We have already established that if you halve a tightly stretched length of wire or catgut you create a mini-version of

your original. The distance between the original note and its
offspring is called 'an octave'. Those of you who sense the
number 8 might have something to do with all this are right,
but you'll have to wait, I'm afraid, for the explanation of 8's
involvement in all this. The distance between your original
note and its 'dominant' (created by dividing the wire by ⅔) is
called a 'fifth', but the reason for that will also have to wait for
the time being.

Let us once again make new notes by using Pythagoras'
cycle of dominants. Starting from our original note, 'ping', the
first 12 'new' notes we can generate from it get higher and
higher, as you'd expect. We can, though, take the higher notes
we've created and find lower versions of themselves (their
lower 'octaves') so that all our first 12 new notes are close-ish

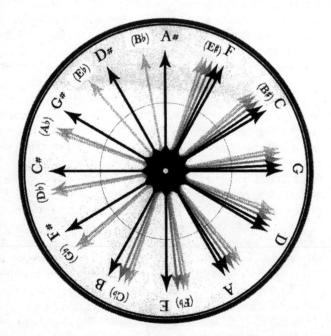

'The Pythagorean comma' – there are twelve notes within an octave span,
but in the next octave the thirteenth note is just out, 'teeth-gratingly close'
to the first, causing a horrible dissonance if you play them together.

together. In fact, we can arrange it so that all 12 make a ladder within a single octave span. This ladder is called a scale. Now these notes within the octave end up spacing themselves through the scale at *roughly* equal intervals. It's like a clock-face in which the hours find themselves *nearly* evenly spaced around the circle. So far so good. The *13th* note, however, causes the first of a series of horrible dissonances. This is because note 13 is dangerously, uncannily, teeth-gratingly close to the very first note. It is as if we are looking at a 24-hour clock in which 13.00 hours isn't precisely where 01.00 hours is placed but fractionally close to it. The 14th note is grimly close to the 2nd (or 14.00 hours and 02.00) the 15th to the 3rd, and so on. Now, two notes very, very close together is an extremely unpleasant sound, believe me. You never want to make that mistake twice once you've tripped into it. So you wouldn't want these pairs of notes, the 13th and the 1st, the 2nd and the 14th etc. to coexist within the same scale. It would be like two incompatible neighbours being forced to live in the same house. This is part of the dilemma known as the Pythagorean comma.

These next three paragraphs are for the musically advanced. If you're not in this category, it doesn't matter, just skip on. I simply don't want the musically advanced to think I am short-changing them.

You can see a Pythagorean comma at work if you create your own cycle of dominants. Starting with any note you like, go upwards in 5ths, thus:

F C G D A E B F# C# G# D# A# are the first 12 notes, as you can see. But the next note, the 13th, is E#, isn't it? E#, the unhappy bedfellow with F, that is. And the 14th note is B#, unhappy bedfellow with C. Going downwards in the spiral from F does the same thing with flats, by the way. Whichever way you go, wherever you start from, the 'comma' kicks in on the 13th note. If you allow all the keys of all the notes to have their full complement of accidentals (i.e. letting G# be a separate note from Ab and so on), you end up with extra – dissonant – notes from 13 to 21.

There is, unfortunately, yet another difficulty thrown up by the science of this all. Pythagoras made his notes, you'll remember, from perfect mathematical ratios and fractions. The tonic–dominant relationship C to G should be a 'perfect' interval. But what they all soon found, to their dismay, was that if you started making new notes from C to G to D to A to E, etc., then the *other* spin-off relationships between notes when re-shuffled into a scale didn't tally with each other. For example, in the above cycle C to G to D to A to E, the relationship between G and E is either a '6th' apart or a '3rd' (if you position your E lower than your G). Unfortunately, these other intervals, the 3rds and 6ths, don't produce the perfect 3rd and 6th ratios that would occur if you were generating notes in the first place from *nature*'s 3rds or 6ths. Nature only gives perfect ratios to its first-generation offspring – all the intervals you create indirectly from them are treated like second-class citizens. Perfect natural dominants, or 5ths, means imperfect 3rds. Perfect natural 3rds means imperfect ratios for 5ths. The reason for this is that a new-note generating sequence starting on C obeyed the laws of *that* particular piece of string at that length, thickness and tautness but there was no way it was going to abide by the laws laid down by other notes and their own foibles and desires.

Pythagoras knew all about this 'comma', but music in his day was so simple compared to ours that the average instrument could only cope with a 'scale' of 6 pitches, A B C D E and F. He must have chuckled at the thought of the difficulties in store if ever musicians wanted to push the boat out and have more than 6 notes in their scale.

However, we also know that Pythagoras *wasn't* the first person to figure this out. The Chinese had got there first. Quite spectacularly so, as it happens. Some evidence has come to light (in the form of dug-up ancient flutes) that suggests the Chinese had mastered the cycle of dominants *four* thousand years ago. At any rate, by the fourth century BC the Chinese were producing the same written theory on dominants and the Harmonic Series as Pythagoras had, which leads me to wonder whether merchants and travellers were passing information across the two worlds of East and West rather more than we used to think.

The Chinese case deserves a little examination, as it's fascinating. Their musical theory is highly imbued with Confucian thought. They too believed that music was from, and of, nature, and that it was organically integrated with the universe.

They took the first 12 notes of the cycle and made a scale out of them. These notes, the Lü, they thought of as 'the cries of the phoenix' and divided them into two equal groups, male and female. Though they had twelve notes to choose from (as a modern piano does), they were principally concerned with the first 7 of the series as it suited their instruments better, in particular the *qin* – a delicate wooden zither with 7 silk strings. Even within these 7 they narrowed their choice still further by making a 'pentatonic' scale of just 5 notes.

These five notes had great significance and represented: Earth, metal, wood, fire, water.

Or: Centre, west, east, south, north.

Or: Saturn, Venus, Jupiter, Mars, Mercury.

Or: Cow, sheep, fowl, pig, horse.

But the Chinese and Pythagoras both came across the same fundamental flaw in the cycle of dominants, the inconvenient mathematical blip, the Pythagorean comma. This flaw so upsets the way these notes operate together, so disrupts the harmony and stability of the scale, that theorists and musicians spent the next two thousand-odd years trying to resolve it. The story of that struggle to square the circle, to tame nature's perversity to make it work for man's hearing equipment, is the story of the search for an 'Equal Temperament'.

The Chinese worked out how to solve the mathematical puzzle, but never implemented it. The Europeans desperately wanted to find out the solution, and eventually did, and indeed put it into practice (uniquely so), but never thought to ask the Chinese, which would have saved them a lot of hassle and heartache, not to mention bad-tempered academic dispute.

As it happened, the Chinese never implemented the solution because they were happy to circumvent the problem altogether by sticking to the first few notes of the series. So why did Europeans become so interested in finding a fix for the comma? What was it that was driving them on feverishly? Why didn't they just leave things be, like the Chinese or the Balinese, and accept that nature's music is full of irregularity and dissonance?

The reason they bothered seeking out a solution to this conundrum was a uniquely European one. They wanted to be able to combine instruments together, creatively, and they wanted to do what no other musical culture seemed to want to do: they wanted to make *harmony*. If you only want to sing melodies with a bit of percussion, fine, nature's series will do the business for you. No questions asked. For the bulk of the first millennium after Christ, European music mainly used only 8 of the 12 notes – A B C D E F G A – living obediently within the restrictions this imposed. It is because of the medieval scale of only 8 notes that we call an octave (an '8') an octave, and why a dominant is a 5th (e.g. A to E), a subdominant a 4th (e.g. A to D), and so on. Later on, when the scale had more notes in it, the old names (5th, 4th, octave, etc.) were retained even though they didn't make as much sense as before. In crude terms, the medieval musician used only the 'white notes' of a modern keyboard, and their arrangement became the model for all the other scales. The 'black' notes weren't really *invented* later, they had always been there, it's just that they weren't used. If you only use the white notes your 'home' key has to be C major (C-D-E-F-G-A-B-C), or, at a pinch, A minor (A-B-C-D-E-F-G-A in its medieval version). All the other keys need one or more of the 'black' notes to replicate C's model scale and therefore came along much later. Now you know why 'C' is regarded with such fundamental reverence in the music world. Everything is fine with the 8 simple 'white' notes as long as you don't start making complex music with them.

But if you want to have chords, if you want to play notes simultaneously, if you want to have twenty different instru-

The Muses, from *Champion des Dames*, 1441. The women in the front
are playing a flute and a tamborine, cornet and dulcimer, while behind
them others play on a portative organ, a different dulcimer, a bass flute,
a mandola and a second flute.

ments playing happily together, you have to turn your back on
nature and create an artificial musical language. You have to
dismantle the gentle simplicity of those 8 notes and go off in
search of pastures new. Which is exactly what Europeans did,
starting in about AD 1000.

The development of harmony was a seismic change in the
history of music, a change moreover that separated the European tradition irreversibly from all its counterparts elsewhere
in the world. If you can hear harmony – chords of one kind or
another – in Indian music these days, it's because it has been
borrowed from Western music some time in the last fifty years

or so. Chordal harmony, until the current age of cultural crossbreeding, was a European phenomenon. For harmony to work, a pretty drastic solution to Pythagoras' comma had to be established.

Around the year 1000 musicians working for the Church began the combining of notes for rich and novel effect. Initially these note combinations were pretty simple. For a start, only two notes were ever sung together at the same time. Even this was considered radical – it took a good two hundred years to try singing three notes together at the same time. At first they only felt comfortable combining the most obvious of nature's notes – so a note might be combined with its own octave, with its dominant and with the note below it ('subdominant'). The reason for the inclusion in this exclusive list of the sub-dominant (known nowadays as a 'fourth') was its 'clean' natural ratio ($\frac{3}{4}$). The other curiously popular note combination was what we would now call a 'second', i.e. a note and its neighbour one degree up or down. This is because the note in question is found very early on in the Pythagorean cycle of new notes (it's the one after the dominant, in fact – the dominant of the dominant). This is crucial. The pioneer notecombiners knew they were doing something dodgy and that these experiments were fraught with risk. Better then to stick gingerly to the most reliable notes, the ones closest to your original source, with the simplest, most natural ratios. Combinations of notes that derived from 'impure' ratios were frowned upon by the Church. More unusual intervals between notes that 'didn't work' because of the mathematical errors they would trigger were simply not used. Given that *every single piece of music* written after 1600 up to the present day uses these 'forbidden' and 'unworkable' intervals, they were missing big opportunities, and some people knew it. The ground beneath musicians' feet began to rumble at the beginning of the fifteenth century, when composers started to experiment with previously unfashionable intervals. In particular, they were seduced by the 'unstable' intervals of medieval music: 3rds and 6ths. The wind of change was detectable by about 1420 when Continental composers like the flamboyant Guillaume Dufay (1397–74), from Flanders, began imitating the top English composer of the time.

The English have traditionally been musically rather conservative, to say the least. This Englishman, though, was a composer with a particular fascination for all things numerological and astrological and though we know very little about him it is fair to say that he was the most influential English composer in Europe before the Beatles. His name was John Dunstaple.

Dunstaple must have known that his use of 3rds and 6ths was going to cause trouble, but he indulged himself nonetheless. As long as you kept well away from organs, whose tuning was already fixed and inflexible, you could get away with these new combinations. You just make sure your singers take extra care during the singing to produce a clear, natural, sweet sound on the 3rds whenever they occur. What the singers have to do is 'retune' their voices carefully against one another every time they come across one of these intervals. This would be like a guitarist twiddling the pegs at the neck of their instrument hundreds of times during the performance of a single piece of music.

But if you constantly re-tweak the 3rds and 6ths, if you favour their sweet and strange new sound, the other intervals have to shunt around as a consequence, trying to fit neatly within an octave, like the hours on a clockface jostling for position around the circle. Once Continental composers took up the challenge of these possibilities, it was only a matter of time before the order and structure of the medieval scale started to fracture and disintegrate. This would probably have happened eventually, but it accelerated dangerously during the fifteenth century, thanks to the vogue Dunstaple unleashed. How did his music come to be heard in Europe anyway?

Dunstaple wrote a motet, *Veni Sancte Spiritus*, for a special service of thanksgiving held in Canterbury Cathedral in 1416 following the English military victory at Agincourt. Henry V himself was present, as was the Holy Emperor Sigismund. The composer then travelled with the victorious English court to France after the Treaty of Troyes, which ceded much of

Northern France and Burgundy to the English crown. Henry V set up a Regency under his brother the Duke of Bedford, who was evidently a great admirer of Dunstaple's many gifts, and accordingly, Dunstaple's music, with its risqué, avant-garde sounds, became well-known and imitated throughout the Continent. Once they had tried their own 3rds and 6ths, Continental composers soon became obsessed with them too and the course of musical history veered off into uncharted waters. Dunstaple's music must have sounded startlingly modern. He was taking brazen liberties with the rhythm as well as the harmony of the period. He didn't think of himself as a revolutionary but with the benefit of hindsight we can see what an effect he had. His music is the first sign of a great shift in composers' attitude to harmony. Nature was being left behind and replaced with something much more man-made and seductive. Dunstaple and Dufay stand on the cusp of the Middle Ages and the Renaissance: the reason why medieval music sounds to us rather barren is because it lacks the warm harmonies that 3rds and 6ths gave to later music.

The Pythagorean tuning system, which had coped pretty well with 5ths, 4ths, 2nds and octaves, was now in crisis. Amusingly, neither Dunstaple nor Dufay had any suggestions as to *how* to solve the problem they'd created, they just went on writing their ripe harmonies and assumed the keyboard makers, who were the main victims of the tuning nightmare that 3rd and 6th combinations produced, would come up with some solutions.

The process of tuning keyboard or fretted instruments so that the notes 'fit' neatly together inside an octave is called 'tempering'. What musicians, craftsmen and theorists of the Renaissance and Baroque periods were trying to do was make an ideal 'temperament', one that would make all this harmonic activity work successfully together. For these people it became the equivalent of scientists and philosophers looking for the Alchemist's Gold, or navigators looking for a measurement of longitude.

So it was that during the early Renaissance, with the increased use of 'new' intervals and combinations, musicians were striving energetically to develop a form of 'tempering' the notes that increasingly allowed 3rds and 6ths to prevail harmoniously. This they did with variable success, but they had to make endless compromises vis-à-vis the 5ths, 4ths and 2nds. If you pull the distance between the numbers of the hours on your clockface this way or that, the other hour-numbers become distorted accordingly. Renaissance temperaments that favour 3rds and 6ths to the detriment of some 5ths and 4ths are called 'meantone'.

A whole *new* set of chords and intervals became forbidden or unusable. There were certain keys you couldn't use at all. The complexity of the 'meantone' temperaments meant that they were difficult to understand for the ordinary musician and varied absurdly from town to town, country to country. Everyone had their version of it, and what worked for one piece of music on one instrument in one place almost certainly wouldn't in another. Proponents of this system say it provoked enormous diversity and character in the music because it was practically never the same twice.

By trying to make the ratios work for 3rds, and altering the fundamental ratios for the 5ths in the process, Renaissance musicians were perverting the 'natural' resonance that was inherent in the 5ths from the Harmonic Series. Some sounds created by these temperaments were considered so appalling that they were called 'Wolf tones'. To our ears, adjusted to the relatively calm and bland modern tuning system, meantone temperaments sound at best, piquant and exquisite, at worst, 'out of tune'.

Whilst Renaissance artists were experimenting with the new concept of perspective, which gave greater depth to the image, composers were also trying to give music greater depth by making richer and richer combinations of notes – chords.

The arrival of 3rds and 6ths made popular a chordal harmony based on the 'triad' (you take a note, add a 3rd to it, then a 5th, e.g. C-E-G, and you get a triad). The chord of three notes we call a triad produces harmony that is the antithesis of medieval sparseness and austerity. From the early Renaissance on, composers are writing music that sounds to our modern ears warm, 'filled-in' and familiar: this is the all-pervasive effect of the triad. But chords weren't the only things experiencing growing pains during the Renaissance; the other aspect of music that was beginning to cause problems was the whole business of keys.

THE MYSTERY OF KEYS

Let's go back and make ourselves a scale of notes the Pythagorean way. We start with a sound – let's call it the note C – and create a simple ascending ladder of C, D, E, F, G, A, B, then C again. This family of notes belonging to a root note of C is the key of C. If we had started with the note D instead we would have created an ascending ladder called the key of D. It really is as straightforward as that.

These families or keys are like individual planets in a solar system. They have their own peculiarities, sounds and colours. Once you start to create keys from outlandish notes like G# (the note between G and A), very complex and unusual timbres can be made. If you think of Earth as C, then G#'s key is a bit like Mercury or Pluto. Different, to say the least. But they are both nonetheless swinging round in orbit in the same planetary system. They have a faint but significant pull on each other; they have elements in common.

The difficulty arises when you try to move from one to another within the same piece of music or when you try to combine notes from one key with those of another. Nature likes its differences and is obstinately unhelpful when it comes to this. Moving from one key to another in the old way was unheard of in the Middle Ages and fraught with trauma and danger in the Renaissance. Composers, though, began to spit in the face of these obstacles and wanted to use more and more unusual keys. Then they wanted to move from one to another. Finally they wanted to be able to combine notes from one with those of another. But how on earth were instruments supposed to play all these many different notes from different families?

'The mystery of keys'

For many instruments, the solution was simple. They didn't. Even as late as Bach's time a trumpet could only play in one key and only played a few notes of the complete palette of 12, to boot. Horns and sackbuts (early trombones) were more or less the same. If you wanted a trumpet to play in a key other than its basic 'default' key you had to make a new trumpet of different length, shape and weight. Even today you have trumpets in B♭, C, D, E♭; clarinets and saxophones in B♭, E♭, A, E, and so on. Nowadays, thanks to modern engineering, these instruments can at least play the whole palette of 12 notes in a key, but before the baroque period all this was a pipedream. If you wanted your trumpet to play your piece in, say, the key of B it was just hard cheese: you couldn't. Putting together a trumpet in D and a recorder in F was also not really a possibility. Now perhaps you can appreciate how nature's laws of harmonics and sound were getting in the way of the desires and ambitions of European composers as time wore on. Nature's key system was becoming a liability.

Worse still, keyboard instruments were expected to be able to play all the notes in all 12 keys, and for all the hundreds of notes available to be in tune, i.e. compatible with each other.

Keyboard instruments – harpsichords, organs, clavichords – weren't allowed the cop-out of being in just one key all the time. They were supposed to be all things to all people. 'Tempering', or creating temperaments, was the method by which keyboard makers went about this seemingly impossible mission.

If you are trying to make compatible all the 12 key families you come across the dreaded Pythagorean comma on a grand, Tyrannosaurus Rex scale. I will give you one example of this, although it is, I'm afraid, devilishly tricky.

The key of C has as its '6th' the note of A. A also acts as the 3rd note of the key of F, the fifth note of the key of D, the second note of the key of G, and so on and so forth. I hate to be the one to break the grim news about this, but all those As are slightly different. The solution to this nightmare scenario is pretty obvious. You *make* them all the same. This, though, is much, much, much easier said than done. This was the tempering task *par excellence* for keyboard makers and tuners of the period 1400–1700.

By trying manfully to cope with all the extra notes composers wanted, to tune their strings to fit with all those other instruments in the orchestra, keyboard tuners ended up with some deformed and mutated note relationships, the Wolf tones we encountered earlier. A whole science grew up dedicated to adjusting a keyboard's tuning system so that it could make its myriad notes interlock. Controversy raged throughout Europe as to how one made the key families work harmoniously together on a keyboard.

Lurking behind all this tempering, tuning and wolfing about was a simple, terrifying truth waiting to be unearthed. This was the concept of an 'equal temperament' – in other words, a tuning system that artificially divided up the octave of 12 notes into 12 mathematically equal parts. Though it would in effect banish the remote 13th to 21st notes altogether, it would make all As, all Gs, all Cs the *same*, and it would make all notes disobey nature's harmonic laws; it might solve the keyboard's mounting tuning difficulties in one go.

During the Renaissance everything was being explored with reference to numbers – mathematical perspective in art,

Wind instruments with string bass, a detail of *A King kneeling before an altar*, engraved by Master L.D., 1540s

the pendulum clock, the fibonacci sequence, and so on. In music too, a quest began to find a mathematical solution to the Pythagorean comma. Most great mathematicians and physicists of the period 1550–1700 were intrigued by the science of music, from Galileo Galilei's study of sound and vibrating strings of 1600 to Robert Boyle's experiments on sound in 1660. Johannes Kepler used musical analogies to explain the movement of the planets and Christiaan Huygens experimented with the layout of the keyboard, but a crucial contribution to the practical implementation of an equal-tempered tuning system was made by the great Dutch mathematician and engineer, Simon Stevin. Stevin, a contemporary of Galilei, was the founder of the modern decimal system, among other things, but between the 1580s and 1600 he also put his mind to working out the precise calculations required to tune a keyboard to an Equal Temperament, based on

Pythagoras' original scheme. But knowing the precise distance that notes in your scale should be from each other (1.059463094 times the frequency value of the note below, as it happens) is one thing. Being able to implement it is quite another; no one in Stevin's time had the technology to act on his figures. Indeed, he had no idea that in the musical world the various 'trial and error' forms of temperament (tuning the 12 notes by ear) were getting closer and closer to his calculated measurements by sheer human graft.

Amid all this, many composers were still uncomfortable with the idea of a standardised, mathematically even scale, believing that the purity of the 'old' note discrepancies gave music a certain richness of tone which would be lost in an all-purpose system.

But then, out of the blue, a genius burst abruptly onto the scene and changed musical history with a single composition. The Big Bang actually occurred within the walls of Cöthen Castle in East Germany, and the man behind it was none other than Cöthen's head of music, Johann Sebastian Bach.

In the early years of the eighteenth century, keyboard tuners had been getting closer to their aim of providing the all-singing all-dancing all-keys-available keyboard. Suddenly, though, they were faced with the possibility that someone had got there first. Geniuses force the pace of change and progress, and Bach was no exception. He published a collection of preludes and fugues for the harpsichord (or clavichord) that included in it pieces for every single known key. Bach had managed to tune an instrument capable of playing all the keys at one sitting. He knew what a breakthrough his book was and called it *The Well-Tempered Clavier*, announcing proudly on the cover of his manuscript that the preludes and fugues (24 in the first book) were to be played at the keyboard (clavier) in all the major and minor keys. We don't know if it was Bach himself who tuned the instrument to achieve this amazing feat, or one of his pupils, but the challenge to the world's keyboard makers was now clear: it *could* be done.

The publication of Bach's *Well-Tempered Clavier* in 1722 is one of the landmarks of European music history. If you had to

Johann Sebastian Bach

find the ten most important pieces of music ever written, it would be in the top 5. In Bach's own lifetime its influence was rapid and dramatic. Later, both Mozart and Beethoven paid homage to the collection's brilliance and importance. Composers and players throughout the Continent treated 'the 48' (as it later became known after he released a follow-up second volume) in reverential awe.

Bach himself moved to a more prestigious job as music director of the St Thomas Church in Leipzig not long afterwards. Leipzig then, as now, was a major trading and cultural centre, and by the time, a half-century later, the Leipzig music publishers Breitkopf and Härtel published an edition of Bach's keyboard works Europe-wide, the well-tempered keyboard was a universal fact of life.

While it was undoubtedly a gigantic landmark in the story of the keyboard, it wasn't, strictly speaking, the very first use of all the keys. This had been possible on the (fretted) lute for some time. A composer called Giacomo Gorzanis wrote a collection of twenty-four dance suites in the 1560s using all 12 keys in quasi major and minor arrangements for the lute, but you were expected to be able to retune the instrument between pieces to suit the new key you were going to use. Bach's achievement was greater because a keyboard instru-

The title page of
*The Well-tempered
Clavier*, 1722, and the
Fugue in C Minor

ment's tuning is fixed at the outset and you couldn't possibly retune all the strings every time you turned the page. Even before Gorzanis's lute collection, the fourteenth-century Robertsbridge Codex, a manuscript anthology of keyboard pieces, contains music using all the sharps and flats, but these pieces were never meant to be played in one go. The Codex itself was compiled from many different sources at different times. Moreover, the distinct identity of many of the keys used would have been fairly murky in the fourteenth century, since no one knew what tuning system the writers of this music would have expected, nor precisely what the different keys were supposed to sound like.

Bach's work, whether he intended it to or not, opened up spectacular new possibilities and began a new chapter in Western music. But 'well-temperament' was in fact the *penultimate* step in a process that led to the introduction of 'Equal Temperament', a system as important to music as penicillin was to medicine or the internal combustion engine was to the motor car. Equal Temperament was a Big Idea, one that had been around for ages, but it took a surprisingly long time to take centre stage. What's more, its propagation and its adoption as a universal language for music owes a huge debt to inventors quite outside the world of music.

You won't be surprised to learn that the Chinese had looked at the notion of a mathematically equal division of notes in the scale too. Indeed, anyone who has observed the annoying discrepancy of the 'Pythagorean comma' comes up with the same question. The concept of Equal Temperament, in which all 12 notes within the octave are equidistant, is easier to talk and write about than do. Which is why it took so long for it to prevail. For a start, it requires some extremely detailed mathematical data, which is all very well, but fiendishly difficult to apply to a musical instrument when all you've got is a tuning spanner and a pair of ears.

It seems that Chinese musical theorists were coming to the same conclusions as their Western counterparts at roughly the same time. In 1584, a certain Chu Tsai-yü (Zhu Zaiyu) mapped out an equal-tempered scale of 12 notes by dividing the fundamental number by the twelfth root of 2. No one in China, as far as we are aware, took up his suggestion, as they were quite happy with their pentatonic scale of 5 notes and couldn't see any point in making their music-making more complicated.

Meanwhile, in Europe, theorists were looking at exactly the same proposition. Vincenzo Galilei, for example, wrote about it in 1581. Did the Easterners and Westerners know about each other's findings? Later documents survive, notably a 1735 treatise by a Jesuit missionary working at the court of the Manchurian Emperor Kangxi (1662–1722), detailing Chinese musical practice and theory. But this man, Jean Baptiste du Halde, claimed that the Chinese had, by the time of his sojourn there, lost virtually all of their ancient learning in the art of music.

Craftsmen were making lutes and viols (precursors to the modern violin family) whose frets were laid out as a series of equally distanced notes, although this method was thought to be unworkable for all other musicians. Early advocates of an Equal Temperament system were the abbot of San Martino in Sicily, Girolamo Roselli, and Gioseffe Zarlino, the head of music at St Mark's, Venice (easily the most influential musical appointment in Europe), who published the seminal treatises *Le Istitutioni harmoniche* in 1558 and *Sopplimenti musicali* in 1588. Zarlino's pupil was Vincenzo Galilei.

In the seventeenth century, some composers, such as Girolamo Frescobaldi and his pupil Johann Jacob Froberger began suggesting the idea of Equal Temperament for keyboard instruments, but a workable method of implementation was still deemed impossible. By the time of Bach's *Well-Tempered Clavier* an actual attempt to tune an instrument into 12 equal notes was still out of reach. But the publication of his collection set musicians thinking. Why, you may be wondering, didn't Bach's Well-Tempered system prevail as a new standard?

The reason is that it was one man's tuning, at one particular time, on a few instruments, in one region of Germany. Bach never wrote down precisely how it had been achieved, so

'An instrument maker's workshop', from the *Grand Encyclopédie*, 1755

students and scholars can't with any certainty recreate his methods. His pupil Johann Philipp Kirnberger later developed a temperament (now known excitingly as Kirnberger III) thought to be fairly close to his ideal, but the art of tuning is so delicate and personal that it is unlikely that many other people outside his immediate region knew of it for some time. His temperament was so particular and subjective it couldn't become a standard. The ideal of an all-key-families keyboard instrument was the same for all, but the ways of achieving it varied enormously from region to region.

For a while the older 'meantone' temperaments, Bach's 'well' temperament and the notion of a new Equal Temperament coexisted. Partisan schools developed for and against the new ideas. J. S. Bach's son Carl Philipp Emmanuel Bach seems to have been converted to the goal of an Equal Temperament, and the French composer Jean-Philippe Rameau became a powerful voice in its favour. But coexistence probably couldn't last. One French contemporary of Rameau summed up the tussle:

After these motley combats, one system will become victorious. If fortune favours the best system, music will gain thereby a real advantage; and in any case it will at least profit from the convenience of having the same ideas and the same language accepted everywhere.

By the end of the eighteenth century, the eventual triumph of Equal Temperament was increasingly seen as inevitable. Its adoption in the 1840s by the London piano firm John Broadwood, then the undisputed leader in the market, was decisive. The older meantone systems never recovered.

Broadwood's adoption of Equal Temperament, though, was only made possible by the intervention of another inventor from outside music, Henry Maudslay. Maudslay's perfection of the precision metal lathe in 1800 was one of the momentous events of the industrial age. The Maudslay lathe made it possible to build other lathes of unprecedented precision, which in turn could calibrate the tuning of assembly-line pianos with great accuracy. The strings could be strung, three to a note at extremely high tension on iron frames and mathematically tuned to Equal Temperament. The magic number that Stevin calculated in 1584 could at last be applied with accuracy and ease. With all the 12 keys now easily available, composers exploited the new facility with reckless abandon, changing key all over the place in a desperate pursuit for more dramatic, disturbing or sensuous effects.

The problem with Equal Temperament to this point had been that it was notoriously difficult to tune, as in effect tuners tuning by ear had been required to nudge the notes slightly *off-centre* to make the maths work. In Equal Temperament, you see, *all* the notes in a scale are a little 'out of tune'. They all shift over from their proper natural positions to accommodate the 'comma' – the leftover amount at the end of a scale. To make the 13th note the same as the 1st note all notes must be shunted away from their rightful home. The old Pythagorean 'just' ratios have to be abandoned: the most basic note-creating ratio of all – the $^2/_3$ ratio that gives you a dominant or 5th (C to G, for example) – is no longer a true,

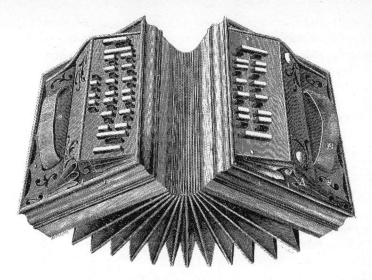

Victorian accordian

natural dominant but an artificial, not-quite-right dominant. This is why Equal Temperament is such a compromise. Even the instruments that don't have to have a temperament, like the violin family, are obliged to play by the same rules and regulations obeyed by those that do. There's no point playing a true, perfect dominant (5th) on your violin if the pianist accompanying you can't. He's louder and more powerful than you, and he's got hundreds and hundreds of dominants (5ths) tuned his way to your puny few. Consequently, you conform to his standard.

With Victorian precision engineering, Equal Temperament could be applied to many other instruments. With the use of the industrial lathe, it was now possible to bore woodwind instruments with pinpoint accuracy and create beautifully even brass valves and moulded horns. All manufactured instruments became standardised to Equal Temperament, mass-produced and exported. The Victorian Empire of Equal Temperament set out to conquer the world, suffocating the gentler but less reliable old systems. Indeed, one of the most devastatingly effective weapons in the triumph of Equal Temperament was the seemingly innocuous piano accordion. The accordion, a Viennese invention of the late nineteenth century, was the world's first portable keyboard – it reached parts other keyboards couldn't reach and it had two important characteristics.

First, it made its sound by pressurised air passing across wafer-thin metal reeds (when you blow across a piece of grass and make a horrid squeaking noise you are using the same technique). These metal reeds were fixed mechanically to a board and almost never lost their factory-set perfect pitch. They therefore stubbornly adhered to the Equal Temperament system given them by the manufacturer (the accordion's name actually means 'tuned'). Secondly, an accordion was loud – louder than any other of the folk instruments around at the turn of the century.

Over the course of the twentieth century the accordion gradually became integrated into remote folk cultures with its promise of a fuller sound. Wedding and dance music in particular benefited hugely from the accordion's greater firepower. In the process it drowned out the old temperaments, forcing voices and stringed instruments that had hitherto used antique or exotic tuning styles to conform to its Westernised standard.

In classical or concert music Equal Temperament was a universal norm from about halfway through the nineteenth century. It took another hundred or so years before its victory over ethnic music in Europe was to be almost as complete. As you can now appreciate, Equal Temperament has been a mixed blessing. Only in remote areas where the accordion never penetrated, like cut-off parts of the Arctic Circle, do the old 'just' intonations survive. The Chinese, having worked out the mathematics of Equal Temperament, made a conscious decision not to use it. They wanted to keep the harmonious relationship between music and nature – they feared the artificial grip of a man-made tuning. For them, the soothing, healing, physical power of music is too valuable to lose in the search for music of greater ambition and scale, and it's true that in the long struggle for Equal Temperament we have lost a connection with the natural world. From Pythagoras to Dunstaple, Stevin and Bach, we in the West have deliberately turned our back on nature and forged a man-made compromise. Western music has a vibrancy to it, which feeds directly off the tension (between natural and artificial) in the tuning. Even in China, though, the old system is in retreat. Young Chinese people are becoming more and more exposed to Western tuning and gradually their indigenous ancient style is starting, to them, to sound out of tune. In future this last stronghold of the non-Western approach will inevitably begin retuning itself to the louder, more insistent voice of equally tempered music.

The advent of recorded sound and portable electronic keyboards has played a critical role in this musical 'Westernisation'. Every time contemporary Indian composers switch on their electronic keyboards to write, even if they are using sampled sounds of antique ethnic Asian instruments, they are slamming another nail into the coffin of their own ancient musical tuning system. As the sampler samples its sitar or tabla it converts the sound onto a chip and thereafter onto a Western keyboard laid out with our 12 equal notes. Its calibration and sampling frequency are designed, of course, for Western music.

Standardised tuning was always going to benefit from technological advances. Equal Temperament was such a tuning. Many believe that the total dominance of Equal Temperament's 12-note system is as much driven by commercial and business pressures as musical. With the advent of electronic instruments and an electronic standard of fixing pitch (A=440 Hz) in the 1920s, Equal Temperament was made irreversible.

We now hear all music through the filter of Equal Temperament. The deliberate imperfections of Equal Temperament now sound 'right' to us. We have lived with its distortions for so long we have lost the ability to hear the many other colours and shades available in nature's music. It has made much of the rest of the world's music sound discordant and whiny to our ears, because the nuances and subtleties of their pitching do not fit its mathematical logicalities. It has, in short, made us intolerant of other less-familiar music systems. Even as early as 1751 the French writer Charles Fonton, writing of Oriental music, compares the tranquil sound of Chinese music unfavourably with the energetic, restless music of Europe:

> Adapted to the Asiatic genius, it [Oriental music] is like the nation, soft and languorous, without energy and strength, and has neither the vivacity nor the spirit of ours. Indeed, if a music is monotonous, admirable as it may be otherwise, it will inevitably cause drowsiness and sleep. Reiteration of the same impressions on the fibres of the organ of hearing slow down the movement of the animal spirits by suspending activity and action, not allowing any other change, and by natural consequence, promoting sleep.*

A common complaint directed at Equal Temperament is that the differences between its keys are equalised and therefore bland and colourless. Paradoxically, it has also been described as 'aural caffeine, overly busy and nervous-making' and that it makes the intervals between notes 'buzz' too quickly. Because, in effect, *all* the notes in Western music are a bit out of tune, it has been suggested that this is the reason why it can't be used, like Chinese music, for meditation (or sleep, apparently). The American composer Terry Riley, who has written pieces deliberately contrary to Equal Temperament using specially constructed instruments, has said, 'Western music is fast because it's not in tune.' What he means by this is that Western music is not in tune with nature, it is incapable of finding a calm, neutral state, so to avoid the discomfort of this situation it keeps moving relentlessly on – it is generating movement because it cannot be at peace with itself. The sound waves emanating from Western instruments are

---

*Translated by Margaret Murata and quoted in Strunk's *Source Readings in Music History*, W. W. Norton & Co., New York & London, 1998.

vibrating too quickly, they are 'sharpened' (raised) to higher than their natural position. This gives the impression to the listener that the music is undoubtedly effervescent, but also that it is 'speeding'.

In recent years, as part of the so-called 'authentic' performance movement, some musicians have begun reproducing music from before 1800 in its older, meantone temperaments. Indeed, there are people who can recognise a Werckmeister temperament from a Vallotti, a Neidhardt from a Kirnberger III, who talk of tuning to 415, 420 or 440 hertz. Sufficient reliable research now exists to enable tuners and instrument manufacturers to prepare for such performances and recordings. To the tutored ear these experiments sound fresh and unusual. To the untutored ear, I'm afraid, they sound a little rough and ready or, dare one say it, 'out of tune'. The old tunings are so unstable that performing a 30-minute-long piece for a CD will require countless stops and pauses to allow for retuning the instruments along the way. Such recordings will have hundreds of edits and invisible joins so that the modern listener is cheated into thinking the old temperaments are no less workable than the modern. The fact is, though, however piquant and quaint the old temperaments may sound, none work as well in practical terms as Equal Temperament. I do prefer to listen to Bach or Mozart on original-style instruments because their sound is so delicate and sweet, but I know I am only able to do so thanks to modern trickery and sleight of hand.

Hearing Bach or Mozart on original instruments is one thing, but music after their time (from Beethoven onwards, more or less) is not feasible at all without the structure and stability of Equal Temperament. Composers are using keys that would be totally unusable without at least a Well-Tempered basis, and making changes from key to key, that most certainly do need Equal Temperament to work.

Much Western music is so exquisitely beautiful it's impossible to imagine a world without it. Most music written since Bach's time actually needs Equal Temperament for it to function properly, and that includes nearly all popular music. I for one believe its rewards have far outweighed its flaws. I can even think of individual pieces that justify its invention on their own. Every time I hear Richard Strauss's 'Four Last Songs', Gustav Mahler's Ninth Symphony, or the magnificent grandeur and power of the music of Dmitri Shostakovich I am reminded of the unique scope of Western music. All these composers play merry havoc with keys, shifting promiscuously across the broad palette of notes within all the scales. Their music is highly 'chromatic' – meaning that its sound glides through all the different notches in the musical scale, treating them all with equal interest and fascination. As the name 'chromatic' suggests, this is music of dazzling, rich colour and variety. It has exploited Equal Temperament's possibilities to the full. Despite its weaknesses, Equal Temperament has been a great enabler. Without it, Western music would have been deprived of many of its most precious jewels.

SIX

BARTOLEMEO CRISTOFORI

and his Amazing
Loud and Soft Machine

European music has given the world many things, but its most popular, durable gift is an instrument invented in Italy 300 years ago which can now be found in every nook and cranny of planet Earth. It has no equivalent in any other culture, has an astonishingly broad repertoire and enjoys pride of place in virtually all forms of music. It is of course the piano.

The piano can be all things to all people – an intimate accompaniment to a solo song, a whole orchestra of sound commanding the concert stage, a bridge between the worlds of classical, jazz and popular music, the musical equivalent of the artists' palette and the ultimate composers' companion. It is equally at home in Oasis's 'Don't Look Back in Anger' and in Schubert's 'Trout' Quintet. For earlier generations than ours the piano was the home entertainment medium *par excellence*, and the creaking, clattering bandleader in the corner of a bar. Its invention, around 1700, was one of Western music's most impressive achievements.

The emergence of the piano as an instrument so ubiquitous, versatile and prevalent – a state of affairs we nowadays take for granted – did not follow the gradual curve that characterised the emergence of other modern orchestral instruments. It was more like the steam locomotive; it had to be devised. It had to be constructed and exhibited by one person to lift it away from the many also-rans, to catapult it forward. The designer in question we shall meet later, but we should first of all look at its family tree.

Practically all musical instruments are derived from four basic family roots: things you hit (drums), things you blow (wind and brass); things you pluck (guitars), and things you bow (violins). All orchestral instruments started this way, in the bush, in the cave, in the tribal village or in the sacred and ritual gathering place. However, Western European music is different from all others in a number of ways. One of these is its tendency to continue inventing new instruments as time goes on. In fact, the development and exploitation of new instruments could be described as something of an obsession.

The transformation of the hollowed-out animal horn into the orchestral French horn we know today, with its valves and coiled brass tubing, is a good example of the amalgamation of techniques from many different sources. Take the original animal horn, such as the ancient Hebrew *shofar*, borrow the resonances of the subtler Polynesian conch-shell, then fashion your own artificial horn from metal as seen on horns brought from Central America or as found amongst Nordic mining peoples. The National Museum of Denmark in Copenhagen have some amazing 3,000-year-old metal ritual horns, called *Lurs* – that one wrapped around one's torso – beautifully preserved all that time in a frozen bog. Bore a few holes in the bell so that when you cover and uncover them you produce more notes, attach 'crooks' (removable sections of extra tubing to give you even more notes), then allow to simmer for a few hundred years. Finally (in about 1815) invent and add valves to your brass tubing to facilitate play and add yet further notes and range. *Voilà!* the modern orchestral horn. Meanwhile, in the Pacific, the conch-shell potters on amongst the sun-kissed palms.

Instruments from around the world were brought to Europe by traders and explorers, all of them undergoing radical modification as they were absorbed and exploited. The rustic panpipe became the multi-keyed, sideways-on, fully chromatic orchestral flute; the ancient aulos, reedy and crude, became the oboe and the cor anglais. The gentle and courtly Moorish lute and guitar ended up as the amplified, electric sex machines strapped rampantly to the bodies of James Brown,

Jimi Hendrix or Eddie Van Halen. Desert nomads are by and large still content with their reedy mizmārs as the tribes of the upper Andes are with their bamboo panpipes. But Europeans just wouldn't let it lie. No one has yet made headway redesigning the Aboriginal Didgeridoo, but I have heard whisperings of an 'Electric Didgeridoo' being touted around, so perhaps it's just a matter of time.

The most spectacular example of tampering and fiddling came with a family of instruments that was not around in the time of early hunter-gatherers. The keyboard family owes its existence simply to mankind's ingenuity and imagination. Keyboards are *machines,* in contrast to the natural simplicity, say, of the clay pipe and whistle.

Organs were the first to appear, being well established by Roman times, and thriving by AD 1000. The concept of adding a line of keys to a series of pipes was presumably dreamt up to overcome the impossibility of one poor player trying to blow his way down a long row of pipes himself. Once musicians hit upon the idea of a scale of keys that you press with your fingers, this was transferred to other types of sound. Foremost amongst these was the sound of high-tension strings across a soundboard – the underlying principle of all guitars, harps or violins.

A popular ancient instrument that exists in almost all civilisations is a coffee-table-sized wood box with strings fixed at either end. It's a bit like a guitar with 30 strings, lying on its side, or a mini harp, in a case. These instruments are called by a multitude of different names all over the world, from the Chinese *Yang q'in (chyn)* to the Finnish *kantele.* The popular alpine version is the *zither* and in India it is the *vicitra vīnā.* To play a zither you pluck the strings either with your fingernails or (rather more comfortably) using a plectrum of some kind. Having established that plucking the strings is easier with a plectrum, the next evolutionary step might be to get a mechanism to do the plucking for you. If you fix a keyboard to the mechanism you can access a wider range of notes and appear to leap and bound dextrously over the strings like a gazelle. Which is exactly what someone did in the Middle Ages,

Hydraulic organ and cornu, detail of a Roman mosaic, AD 230-40, Trier

creating the first plucked-string keyboard instrument. References to such instruments are found from the fourteenth century, though they are not generally described as if they had *just* been invented. The oldest *surviving* string-plucking keyboard instrument in the world is now in the museum of London's Royal College of Music. It is called a clavicytherium and is thought to have originated in southern Germany in about 1480. Despite its obvious link to the zither family, the clavicytherium most resembles a harp in a (beautiful) case, as it stands upright in front of the player. In fact, the upright structure and shape of it indicate that it owes much to the design of the small organs of the period, and indeed small organs were the only other keyboard instru-

A medieval zither

ments around at the time to furnish any kind of template. The reconstructed copy of the 1480 clavicytherium sounds like a harpsichord whose strings are allowed to ring on as long as they like – it is a ghostly, jangling sound. Although upright clavicytheriums continued to be made well into the eighteenth century, the harpsichord proper that developed from the clavicytherium usually favoured a horizontal, tabletop design.

Harpsichords started small and delicate, not much larger than a zither itself. Baby harpsichords are often called spinets or virginals. Though these terms are more or less interchangeable, nowadays we would differentiate between harpsichords, spinets and virginals by looking at their shape. Like the zither family, a spinet's strings usually run across the case from left to right with the keyboard set in the middle of the line of the strings, rather in the position you might have your computer keyboard, in the central front position on your desk. A spinet's case may be slightly rounded or even oval. A virginal is roughly the same, though it may be completely rectangular in shape and the keyboard may be shifted more to the left or right side of where it would be on a spinet. Spinets and virginals only have one string per note. The harpsichord, on the other hand, orientates itself round to the *end* of the set of strings – the player is now sitting in a position at one side of the rectangle only. The strings – often if not always two per note – are longer too, stretching away from the player like railway tracks, not across from left to right.

The etymology of the virginal's name has perplexed and tickled scholars for centuries. Some suggest that it derives from the fact that in courtly Renaissance life the virginal was the young maiden's favoured instrument. Others think it might be because the sound of it is sweet, pure and gentle, like a virgin, as it were (only plausible if teenage girls have changed beyond recognition in the intervening centuries). Hitherto it was thought that the instrument may have been named after the English Queen Elizabeth I, the 'Virgin Queen', but references to virginals predate her reign. Another explanation is that the name comes from the Latin word *virga*, meaning rod or stick, and refers to the small protruding wooden prong ('jack') that plucks the strings. Delightful though the earlier versions are, I can't help thinking that this is the most likely possibility. One other piece of information you may enjoy about the virginal is that in proper old-fashioned usage, the expression (as in trousers and scissors), is 'a pair of virginals', as in 'I am going downstairs, Mother, to play on my pair of virginals'. Need I say more?

English Tudor composers were particularly distinguished by their enthusiasm and output for the virginal, and the titles of the pieces they wrote would provide for an entire evening's stand-up comedy if you are ever invited to be after-dinner speaker at a convention of Elizabethan keyboard instrument manufacturers. I list, without further comment: *My Lady Wynkfyld's Rounde, Put Up thy Dagger Jemy, The Duchesse of Brunwick's Toye, Quodlings Delight, The K(ing's) Hunt, Up Tails All*, and *My Lady Carey's Dompe*.

Notwithstanding England's nimble-fingered virgins, there was in fact another branch of the keyboard family altogether. These didn't pluck the strings, they hit them.

An Open-air Concert, with a spinet, lute, flute and bass-viol,
Italian school 16th century

These derived from another version of the zither, the cimbalom. It too has many different names and variants around the world – the tympanon, hackbrett, santur, tsimbal, koto, oud, tjelempung and psaltery (salterio) are all members of this group. In English it is called the hammer dulcimer. Instead of plucking the strings you strike them with two sticks known as mallets. One crucial aspect of the dulcimer's sound is that it has a much wider range of dynamics – loudness and softness – than its plucking competitors. When you *pluck* a string with a mechanical device it's always the same loudness or softness no matter how hard you press, but when you *hit* a string you can vary the volume considerably depending on how forcefully or gently you strike it. The dulcimer these days, however, has retreated to the fringes of mainstream music, though it is alive and well in ethnic and folk circles – a staple of eastern European gypsy bands. It did, though, strangely, have one brief, glorious moment, when it looked as if it might turn into the piano all by itself.

An inventor and musician called Pantaleon Hebenstreit, from Leipzig, came up with a mutant dulcimer, 9 foot long, with 186 catgut and wire strings, one each per note, struck with two 'baguettes' (mallets), and double soundboard, which he proudly toured around Europe to great acclaim between 1697 and 1730. He caused such excitement at the court of Versailles that Louis XIV, Le Roi Soleil, imaginatively dubbed his novel instrument 'the Pantaleon'. Intriguingly, it is now believed that Pantaleon demonstrated in Florence with his contraption in the 1690s, at the precise time when Bartolomeo Cristofori was there, putting the finishing touches to his new instrument soon to be known as the pianoforte.

Hebenstreit, by all accounts a fine violinist, composer and dancing master, as well as Pantaleonist Extraordinaire, became Kapellmeister for Augustus the Strong in Dresden, and died in 1750. His few surviving compositions were lost in the 1944 Allied bombardment. But it seems the operational complexities in playing the Pantaleon consigned it to a footnote in music history, like the Claviorganum, the Tangentenflügel, the Lyraflügel, the Enphonicon Harp-piano, the Orchestrion, Thym's Grand Piano with Bassoon and Janissary, Pichelbele's Orchestra-Harpsichord, and the Clavecin-Oculair, which attempted to replace sound with colour, all of which are to be found in museums around the globe.

After the enterprising Hebenstreit himself passed away the pantaleon lived on only in name and memory. In Germany people had grown fond of the sound, particularly the way the strings carried on reverberating after you struck them (there were no dampers), so later piano builders sought to emulate this effect with the sustain pedal. They even occasionally used the name *pantalon* [*sic*] to describe various types of pianoforte.

The ordinary, non-Pantaleon hammer dulcimer, meanwhile, continued to be played. Since it was considered rather rustic and vulgar by musical snobs of the Middle Ages and Renaissance, they developed a smarter version of it with a keyboard attached: the clavichord.

The clavichord is basically a hammer dulcimer with a whole regiment of mallets fixed under the strings, operated by a keyboard, and this mechanism, of course, made it the closest antecedent of the pianoforte. Like the dulcimer, it is extremely sensitive to touch. If you press harder on a key you can make the string wobble and bend before releasing it. It became immensely popular in the Baroque period and every self-respecting composer or conductor in Europe had one in his or her front room. But despite its popularity and the delicacy and expressiveness of its tone, the clavichord had one serious drawback which left it stranded by history, so much so that today the only ones you can buy are more or less faithful reproductions of those favoured by Bach and his ilk (in fact you can order copies of exact instruments known to have been owned by famous old master musicians). The drawback is that it's incredibly quiet. It has a dynamic range from soft to unbelievably soft, and that's it. You could play as hard as you like on a clavichord standing next to a light sleeper prone to insomnia and they wouldn't wake up. Which meant that it was popular as a practice instrument at home, and to accompany vocalists who sang extremely quietly in very small rooms, but it could never integrate with other instruments or be a reliable back-up to a choir.

There were other problems with the clavichord, such as its inability to stay in tune for any length of time (the strings were constantly being stretched and bent by the mallets for expressive bendy tone effect, so lost their tension), but it was undoubtedly an exquisite sound.

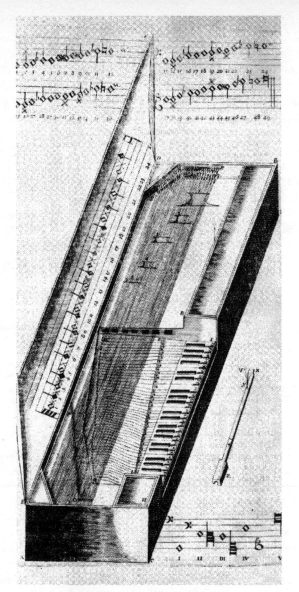

The clavichord, from Martin Mersenne's
Third Book of Universal Harmony, 1636

While the clavichord was quietly pitter-pattering about in people's back rooms and attics, the plucky spinet and virginal had started developing. Little table instruments were getting bigger and bigger, turning into fully grown harpsichords. Consequently, they were getting a lot louder.

In 1700, on the eve of the invention of the piano, the harpsichord was the principal keyboard instrument of choice in Europe. Four or five octaves of high-tension strings were laid across a rigid wooden frame and plucked with mechanical plectra operated by keys. Some had two manuals (keyboards) like an organ, with additional rows of higher (or lower) strings to allow layering of sounds and echo effects – and many came with decorative cases designed to grace your palace or stately home. But the harpsichord, too, has one fatal flaw: its lack of expressiveness. The mechanics of it were such that the string was plucked with same force all the time. Like the organ, your note was either on or off, and so, like the organ, the harpsichord lacked 'soul'. Harpsichord builders tried everything in their power to solve this – they devised strips of cloth to be placed on the strings to muffle the sound, they used less brittle materials to pluck with, and different textures of string, they even offered a lid that opened and shut with a foot lever to vary the loudness of the sound, but there was no getting away from it – this instrument could not respond to the touch of one's fingers when playing, and they knew it.

At the very end of the seventeenth century, with composers writing ever more ambitious keyboard music, there seemed to be a gap in the market for an instrument that could combine the expressive nuances of the hammer-action clavichord with the range and power of the plectrum-action harpsichord. For a big step forward like that, you need a big patron to fund the research and development: cue the Medicis.

The Medicis' Florentine palace, now the Uffizi gallery and Pitti Palace, had by this time become a musical powerhouse. Though Duke Cosimo footed the bill for this burst of artistic munificence, it was his intelligent, pretty son Ferdinando de' Medici who masterminded the projects. Ferdinando, a fine

and knowledgeable musician, began to amass not just a world-class art collection but also a huge array of musical instruments. The collection's curator was Bartolomeo Cristofori, a leading harpsichord maker and restorer who had been headhunted, it seems, from Padua. Flamboyant bon viveur Ferdinando, by all accounts, had a soft spot for his keyboard technician. Indeed, some say he preferred the company of Cristofori and others (like the composer Alessandro Scarlatti, for example, with whom he enjoyed a long and warm 'correspondence') to that of his neglected Bavarian wife Violante. One cannot but feel tremendous sympathy for Violante who was young, bright and artistic, but had to languish at her in-laws' home in Florence (where she knew no one) while her husband pursued his indulgences elsewhere. Ferdinando's penchant for dressing up at the Venice carnival and gallivanting with assorted eurotrash apparently prevented him from consummating his marriage. He staggered back to Violante towards the end of his short life, riddled with syphilis, and received total care and compassion from her until his death. But then, that's women for you.

Ferdinando's plan was to accumulate not just artefacts – paintings, sculptures, harpsichords – but artisans, and he established an impressive workshop. Painters, sculptors, clockmakers, printers, restorers, craftsmen of all kinds, rubbed shoulders in a hum of creative activity. Cristofori, however, complained of the noise and distraction at the palace's open-plan studio and spent much of his time beavering away at his own premises nearby. Little is known of his pre-Florence training, but it seems his methods were idiosyncratic. All the instruments he designed, of various kinds, that survive today betray an individualistic streak that took many liberties with accepted practices and techniques. His biggest experiment was to tackle the harpsichord's lack of subtlety and expression head on. He took the basic skeleton of the harpsichord and the hammer-action of the clavichord, and

Opposite: A harpsichord with two keyboards.
Adelaide de Guiedan and her sister, by Nicolas de Largilliere

invented a completely new instrument, described in the Medici inventory of 1700 as an *'arpicimbalo di Bartolomeo Cristofori, di nuova inventione, che fa il piano e il forte'* ('Bartolomeo Cristofori's harpsichord, newly invented, that is capable of playing soft and loud'). History had been made.

Only three of Cristofori's historic piano prototypes still survive: one is being restored in the splendid Leipzig museum of musical instruments, another in the Museo degli Strumenti Musicali in Rome, is unplayable, and the third, playable since a slightly dubious restoration in the 1930s, is in the Metropolitan Museum of Art in New York. Though it has been much modified and enlarged over the years, the pianoforte that Cristofori invented is clearly the ancestor of the instrument we know today.

The first thing that hits one immediately on seeing this 300-year-old instrument is that while the shape and size of the case are obviously that of the harpsichord, the look of it is radically different. Gone are the florid case paintings and decorations. Cristofori's pianos look like serious musicians' tools, simple prototypes even, not just aristocrats' playthings. In fact, for something that gave birth to an entirely new branch of the keyboard family, it looks remarkably like a coffin. This may have something to do with Cristofori's seeing himself as more of a scientist–inventor than as a restorer–carpenter, but the plain, workmanlike design is prophetic of the piano's later spread right across the class spectrum. What Cristofori did understand was acoustics; his piano, despite its delicacy and subtlety compared to modern models, really 'sings' thanks to its cleverly placed soundboard, strings and action.

He started with the idea employed by the clavichord – small hammers, levered upwards on a pivot, striking the high-tension strings from below. But the similarity ends there. For a start, when Cristofori said soft and loud he wasn't making a wild boast – the dynamic range and the power of this piano far outstripped the tiny sound of the humble clavichord. Secondly, instead of the hammer staying in direct contact with the finger once it has found and struck the string, the hammer falls away immediately, letting the finger continue downwards

Pianoforte, made by Bartolomeo Cristofori in Florence in 1726

on the key a little further. This 'escapement' mechanism was one of Cristofori's most brilliant innovations, and proved crucial to the success of his new instrument. He had to make sure that the hammer fell away from the string *far enough* to prevent it rebounding accidentally, but also to be available for a rapid response if the player wanted to repeat the same note again, immediately afterwards. His solution was to include a padded landing strip, or check, and a 'halfway house' holding area for the hammer to facilitate the rapid repeat. The mechanism had to be flexible enough, and the string tense enough, to cope as well with a terrific thwack as with a gentle prod. Cristofori therefore increased his dynamic options by doubling the number of strings. Harpsichords had for a while

149

been able to play more than one string per note, but in their action two separate jacks plucked two separate strings (sometimes of different octave pitches). Here one hammer hit two strings of the same pitch.

Despite the popularity in Germany of the pantaleon's ringing tones, and the clavichord's tiny sustaining sounds, Cristofori decided that the pianoforte would be better served if you could dampen the sound of the string once it had been struck, rather in the manner of the harpsichord. With a louder instrument than either the dulcimer or the clavichord, the effect of letting the strings continue ringing would be cacophonous. He reasoned, correctly, that if you have strong, long strings that can be hit with force and passion, you can't just let them linger on after they've been played. They create too much reverberation and hangover, making the piano sound too wishy-washy. So Cristofori added small padded strips attached to a pin that automatically lifts off the string when you hit it, but falls back again – using gravity – immediately the hammer's out of the way. Very ingenious, very Cristofori. Indeed, when one examines the playing action that he developed during the piano's Year Zero, it's hard not to come to the conclusion that subsequent efforts to improve and enlarge the instrument have only really been the icing on the cake. All the fundamental things you need to build a good piano are found on Cristofori's original. As far as we can tell (since only three out of his twenty or so still exist), no two Cristofori pianos are exactly alike. He was clearly still working on it himself when he died in 1731.

Coincidentally, 1731 is also the year of the publication of the first surviving example of music especially written for the new instrument, Lodovico Giustini's sonata for 'soft and loud' harpsichord, commonly called the 'mallet harpsichord'. In his twelve sonatas for 'piano e forte' in the following year, we can see the first ever expression and dynamic markings for keyboard music. Imagine what a liberating experience it must have been for a writer to be able to put 'get louder' or 'get softer' on a passage of music.

With the benefit of hindsight, it is strange that Cristofori's own compatriots showed hardly any enthusiasm for his amazing new instrument. After his demise, this particular Big Bang might never have taken off at all had it not been for the fact that some of his pianos found their way out of Italy to Spain, Portugal, Germany and England. The few that existed were occasionally imitated, and everywhere in Europe they caused considerable interest and curiosity. The most famous of the new pianoforte owners was the legendary castrato Carlo Broschi ('Farinelli' to his many adoring fans), J. S. Bach, no less, tried one out and even allegedly included piano in one of his pieces (*Das Musikalische Opfer* – 'Musical Offering' – of 1747), but he wasn't too impressed. There is a certain amount of speculation and debate as to whether Georg Friedrich Handel also had one at some point. Soon the piano was given an important lifeline by the Saxon organ builder Gottfried Silbermann who in the 1720s, started making instruments closely resembling Cristofori's. The stir that the pianoforte created outside Italy gave it a powerful new lease of life and its subsequent development was a perfect example of successful pan-European cooperation.

In the second half of the eighteenth century power, wealth and influence were shifting to Britain, and in 1761 the new King George III married a cultured and intelligent princess from Germany, Charlotte of Mecklenburg-Strelitz. George was also from a German family, from Hanover. There was tremendous excitement bordering on hysteria surrounding the arrival of the seventeen-year-old new Queen, with enormous crowds gathering to catch a glimpse of her wherever she went. Horace Walpole wrote in his diary, on 8 September 1761, of her arrival:

> The Queen . . . is this instant arrived; the noise of the coaches, chaises, horsemen, mob, that have been to see her pass through the parks, is so prodigious, that I cannot distinguish the guns. I am going to be dressed, and before seven shall launch into the crowd.

As luck would have it, Charlotte was intensely musical. In the wake of her arrival, many German musicians and instrument builders came to London, whether to capitalise on the English fashion for all things German or all things musical, or to escape the economic depression caused at home by the Seven Years War. Handel, who had died two years before, had been Britain's favourite composer in the previous generation. Present-day London bears many street names and references to this heady period – Charlotte Street, Charlotte Mews, Charlotte Place, Mecklenburgh Square, Brunswick Square, Hanover Square and Handel Street are a few. This was the time when the fashionable 'West End' really was the western perimeter of the city. After the Peace of Paris in 1763 a building boom began, with stylish, grand architecture from Robert Adam, and William Chambers (the designer of Somerset House). Theatres were opening everywhere, larger and rowdier than ever – the two biggest were Drury Lane, which had seating for 2,000 in 1780, where one might see the great David Garrick perform, and Covent Garden, with a seating capacity of 2,100 in 1780, reaching 3,000 after a refit in 1792. The Theatre Royal, Haymarket, was probably the most popular, managed astutely by the one-legged comic and playwright by the name, I kid you not, of Samuel Foote. Johann Christian Bach's operas were as popular here as they had been in Italy, where he had lived before moving to England in 1762 to become music master of the royal household. As well as Germans, London was home to different populations from many countries, like the Huguenot refugees who had fled from the religious wars in France, bringing with them their multifarious skills and trades, turning eighteenth-century Clerkenwell, Spitalfields and Soho into something more like the cosmopolitan melting pot of 1920s New York than the grandiose Imperial capital it became after the defeat of Napoleon. Thanks to trade within the growing Empire and the wealth pouring in from the slave trade, industrialisation and colonial plunder, London was booming. Into this whirl came the teenage Princess Charlotte with her coterie of Saxon musicians and took the place by storm.

The talk in London musical society was of an amazing new keyboard instrument that Johann Christian Bach had recently played for the Queen and her court. Concerts in Soho had demonstrated that this instrument could indeed play loud and soft, was most beautiful and delicate and that quite honestly my dear the harpsichord has become so *passé*. The pianoforte had arrived, and thanks to a resourceful German émigré, Johannes Zumpe, working out of premises at no. 7 Princes Street, off Hanover Square itself, it soon acquired a popularity it would never again lose.

Johannes Zumpe, who came from the town of Fürth near Nuremberg, was by trade a cabinet maker. The square piano that he designed and sold with such spectacular and immediate success is, like Cristofori's, a plain, no-nonsense box cleverly conceived to exploit fashionable London's interest in the new instrument. His piano was portable, reliable and relatively affordable, a third of the price of the rival harpsichords on offer. The unusually high quality of the materials used reflected his furniture-making training but also the availability in London of finest mahogany from British colonies in the West Indies. The square piano's success probably had as much to do with its suitability for sensitive accompaniment of the singing voice as its pleasant solo qualities. Particularly for young ladies, playing and singing light songs was a common way of spending an evening; before long, the square piano was on every young madam's Christmas list.

Zumpe clearly had some knowledge, possibly first hand, of Cristofori's revolutionary instruments, as can be seen from his neat economical action. The case shape, however, owes more to the rectangular German clavichord of the moment, whilst other aspects betray ideas from the keyboard pantalons, also being produced in Germany (for example, hand-operated levers to switch on or off the treble or bass dampers). Zumpe never patented his design, with its standard 58 keys, two strings per note, of iron, brass and copper, soft leather hammers and well-proportioned, portable case. Between 1766 and 1779 he made about fifty pianos a year. His reputation and his courtly clients ensured that he never needed to advertise. A veritable army of composers churned out repertoire specifically for the English square piano, and its fame led entrepreneurial craftsmen across Europe to drop everything and start building instruments after Zumpe in the 'English' style. The music teacher and friend of Samuel Johnson, Charles Burney, summed up Zumpe's achievement:

> After the arrival of John Christian Bach in this country . . . all the harpsichord makers tried their mechanical powers at piano-fortes, but their attempts were always on the large side, till Zumpé . . . constructed small piano-fortes of the shape and size of the virginal, of which the tone was very sweet, and the touch, with a little use, equal to any degree of rapidity. These, from their low price and the convenience of their form, as well as their power of expression, suddenly grew into such favour, that there was scarcely a house in the kingdom where a keyed instrument had ever had admission, but was supplied with one of Zumpé's piano-fortes for which there was nearly as much call in France as in England. In short he could not make them fast enough to gratify the craving of the public.

Zumpe died in 1790, retired and wealthy, and his success spawned an epidemic of imitators in Britain and across Europe. Among them was John Broadwood, a self-aggrandising Scot living in London, who became the foremost piano manufacturer of the period following Zumpe's death. His company expanded impressively to emerge after the Napoleonic Wars as the world's leading piano makers. Broadwood owed a huge unacknowledged debt to the brilliance of Zumpe, as he did to another north European living in London, Americus Backers, the man who can be credited (though again, not by Broadwood or his descendants) with the launching of the grand piano proper.

While Zumpe was busy producing his delightful square pianos in London's West End, across Europe in the shadow of the Alps, Austrian and South German keyboard makers were also waking up to the possibilities of the instrument. In October 1777, a young man was making his way by stagecoach in the dead of night to the magnificent Bavarian town of Augsburg. His final destination was Paris, but he had an urgent appointment the next morning with a piano maker called Stein. The 21-year-old traveller was to unlock the musical secrets of the piano and give it some of its most astonishingly beautiful music. This young man in a hurry had been christened Johannes Christoffus Wolfgang Theophilus, and was known to his friends as Amadeus Mozart.

Mozart and his sister Nannerl had come to Augsburg, birthplace of his formidable father Leopold, to visit Johann Stein and play one of his celebrated instruments. The experience was to change Mozart's life, nudging his interest away from the keyboard of his youth, the harpsichord, and towards the newer, more expressive pianoforte. From this moment on Mozart's piano writing gradually deepens, with the undoubted dexterity and showmanship of his earlier style giving way to a beauty that is less about performance and more about sensitivity. His later piano concertos have never been surpassed. This is how Mozart himself described the visit to the workshop in a letter to his father on 17 October 1777:

This time I shall begin at once with Stein's pianofortes . . .

Now I much prefer Stein's, for they damp ever so much better than the Regensburg instruments. When I strike hard, I can keep my finger on the note or raise it, but the sound ceases the moment I have produced it. In whatever way I touch the keys, the tone is always even. It never jars, it is never stronger or weaker or entirely absent; in a word, it is always even. It is true he does not sell a pianoforte of this kind for less than 300 gulden, but the trouble and labour that Stein puts into the making of it cannot be paid for. His instruments have this special advantage over others that they are made with escape action. Only one maker in a hundred bothers about this. But without an escapement it is impossible to avoid jangling and vibration after the note is struck. When you touch the keys, the hammers fall back again the moment after they have struck the strings, whether you hold down the keys or release them. He himself told me that when he has finished making one of these claviers, he sits down to it and tries all kinds of passages, runs and jumps, and he shaves and works away until it can do anything . . . his claviers certainly do last. He guarantees that the sounding-board will neither break nor split. When he has finished making one for a clavier he places it in the open air, exposing it to rain, snow, the heat of the sun and all the devils in order that it may crack. Then he inserts wedges and glues them in to make the instruments very strong and firm . . . Here and at Munich I have played all my six sonatas by heart several times . . . the last one in D sounds exquisite on Stein's pianoforte . . .

During his brief but momentous visit to Augsburg, Mozart's enthusiasm for Stein's piano led him to agree to give a concert of one of his works, a concerto for three keyboards, to be performed in one of the town's glittering Renaissance halls. His famous virtuosity and youth must have dazzled the audience, but his own attention was firmly on the versatile new instrument he was playing. When Mozart first moved to Vienna in 1781, before he had his own (Anton Walter) piano, he used a Stein piano belonging to his friend Countess Thun for composition and concert performances. Whereas Zumpe's English square piano popularised the instrument among the aristocracy and merchant classes across Europe, Stein's more powerful German piano set in motion a tidal wave of composition by the greatest of composers, in a lineage that stretched from Mozart and Beethoven to Debussy and Shostakovich.

The piano's overwhelming dominance amongst instruments during the nineteenth and early twentieth centuries was due to several factors. One was its central role as the ideal accompaniment for the human voice. From Schubert to Lennon–McCartney, from Tchaikovsky to Elton John, from Ella Fitzgerald to Robbie Williams, the tone and expressiveness of the piano has given it a unique place in the history of song. From Mozart onwards, the piano became *the* accompanying instrument, swiftly supplanting the harpsichord, and

Beethoven's Broadwood Fortepiano, an engraving of 1828

as such came to have a disproportionate influence on chamber music of all kinds. It was the instrument to which others tuned and referred. It was able – uniquely until relatively recently – to stand in for practically every other combination of instruments.

Mozart discovered the rich subtlety of the piano and Schubert was to be the first of many to exploit its relationship with the singing voice, but Beethoven took an instrument that was still relatively delicate and refined, and stretched it to the limit, turning it into the concert powerhouse that thrilled packed audiences throughout the nineteenth century. Beethoven gave the piano the test drive of its life. By the time he had finished with it, the nineteenth-century piano was both the instrument of the extravagant and celebrated soloists, of whom Franz

Liszt and Frédéric Chopin were the greatest, *and* the favourite instrument of the amateur musician. These two functions were fuelled by each other. Pianists at home, thrashing through their Chopin mazurkas before tea, dreamed of emulating the great stars they saw on the stage of their local town halls. In nineteenth-century Europe and America, music-making was an active, participatory matter. The piano itself duly expanded with the repertoire. It gained an iron frame, tougher wire strings, a bigger range to fill big concert halls with sound, like a one-man or -woman orchestra. The iron frame was first applied to square pianos in America in the 1820s, but was not generally available in Europe until well into the second half of the century. (Those of you who saw Jane Campion's haunting feature film *The Piano*, starring Holly Hunter and Harvey Keitel, with its disturbing drowning scene near the end, may be amused to learn that Holly's pre-1830 English piano would have had a frame made entirely of wood and would therefore have floated, not sunk.)

Music's answer to the industrial age was a titanic instrument that people did not so much play as grapple with. The piano could represent man's epic and violent struggle with rugged nature, and composers supplied the stormy sound-track for the age. The piano's impact went far beyond its own repertoire. Composers treated the instrument as a *sine qua non* for the construction of their huge symphonic works. The structure of a vast amount of *orchestral* music owes its shape to the mindset of the piano. The harmony and rhythmic energy of an enormous amount of music is in fact that of the piano, transcribed and arranged for other ensembles. Even very famous orchestral pieces often began life as piano compositions (Elgar's evergreen 'Nimrod' from the *Enigma Variations* falls under the hands at the keyboard with amazing ease – it plays like a Victorian harmonisation from *Hymns Ancient and Modern*). Glancing through the pages of a glossy coffee-table book entitled *Composers at Home* or some such title, in a bookshop in Milan, I noticed that almost all of the composer sanctuaries and studies had a piano as the main focus of the room. In portraits and photographs composers

The mad pianist'

are inevitably sitting at the piano contemplating their latest masterpiece or scribbling feverishly at the score with their heavily nibbled pencils. The hut in which Gustav Mahler composed his Second and Third Symphonies, on the banks of the Attersee Lake near Salzburg in Austria, is typical. As well as a desk for the manuscript paper there is the obligatory piano, the perfect natural vista, the tranquillity, the solitude and harmony away from the bustle of the world. At least this was true in Mahler's day. The much-visited hut-shrine in the village of Steinbach is in fact a replica: the original is now a toilet block for the caravan site and scuba diving centre that surrounds it. In the visitors' book, one wit from London opines that Mahler would probably have rather appreciated the joke, and might have had jarring, bombastic caravan music come marching past in one of his pastoral movements (as he was wont to do with the military bands recalled from his childhood, living next to a barracks). Neither the piano nor the semi-historic hut's other contents are original, but it doesn't seem to matter when you're standing there. (Ken Russell made his own replica and stuck it on the banks of Lake Windermere in Cumberland for his film *Mahler* in the 1970s.) Nonetheless, at Steinbach the lake is still calmly beautiful, the mountains still loom above, the hills still roll romantically down to the water's edge.

Mahler did not write music specifically for the piano, but its influence is everywhere in his orchestral works. His method was to compose first a 'short score' sketch – a piano template for the whole piece, then, using the short score as a guide, realise the work into a full orchestral canvas. When he died, leaving his tenth symphony unfinished, a reconstruction of it (by Mahler scholar Deryck Cooke in the 1960s) was considered feasible, since he had written the music for the entire work from start to finish in short (piano) score, but had yet to orchestrate large sections of it. Cooke, knowing Mahler's other orchestrations, was able to bring the notebook symphony back to life. Several of Mahler's symphonies contain material that started life as songs for piano and voice. Here again, he would take the piano part and rearrange it for full orchestra, sometimes absorbing the vocal line into the band, sometimes leaving it sung. For me, the most obvious reminder of the pianistic genesis of much of Mahler's orchestral writing is one of his hallmarks: the gently rippling, arpeggiated chords of the harp beneath a slow-moving carpet of strings. This can be heard clearly in his most famous movement, the Adagietto from his fifth Symphony. You may know this ravishing, sad piece from the film *Death in Venice* (and countless commercials that have exploited its desperate beauty). When you next listen to it look out for the harp, oscillating away as if 'inside' the strings. Its fractured chords are so like the undulating notes one uses in a piano accompaniment to keep the rhythmic pulse ticking quietly away that I can't believe this music was not conceived at the piano. The movement is entirely orchestral, but it feels like a song – indeed, its closest relative amongst the rest of Mahler's output is his song for contralto and orchestra, 'Ich bin der Welt abhanden gekommen', from the *Five Rückert Songs*, which uses the harp in exactly the same manner.

Mahler's influence on the young Viennese composers that followed him was seminal, but the epicentre of the musical tremors that ran through the first fifty years of the twentieth century was not Vienna but Paris. Here, inventive French composers such as Maurice Ravel and Francis Poulenc rubbed shoulders with key exiled Russians, like Igor Stravinsky, and touring musicians from America with their startling jazz. Even after the Second World War much contemporary music found a home in the French capital, in the conflicting camps of modernist Pierre Boulez and mystic Olivier Messiaen. The godfather figure behind all these movements was Mahler's contemporary, Claude Debussy. Debussy was first and foremost a pianist and a brilliant writer for the piano. His greatest gift to music was a radical approach to harmony which he explored in a magnificent collection of piano music. However, the inspiration for these experiments came not from the repertoire of European piano music, but from another source altogether. It all started at the great Paris Expo of 1889 for which the Eiffel Tower was built.

At the 1889 Universal Exhibition, musicians and performers from all over the world gave Europeans their first exposure to the music of exotic cultures. Artistes from Africa, the Middle East, Russia, Central Asia and the Orient were to be seen. Hungarian and Romanian gypsy and folk bands, and choirs from Finland and Norway also gave concerts, but it was the Javanese gamelan orchestra from the city of Joyga and their *bedaya* dancers, in the Dutch pavilion, that caught Debussy's eyes and ears.

The gamelan orchestra (*sapangkon*) is so called because it comprises a large collection of different instruments – gongs (*gong, bonang, kempul, klentong*), bells, metallophones (*saron demung, saron barung, saron panerus*), xylophones (*gambang*), bronze slabs (*gender*), cymbals (*kemanak, tjengt-jeng*), drums (*kendang, ketipung, batangan, tjiblon, bedug*), inverted kettles (*kenong, ketuk, engkok, kemong, kempyang*), bowls (*réjong, kadjar*), flutes (*gambuh, suling*) and spike fiddles (*rebab*) – played by a small ensemble of coordinated players. Each gamelan (meaning 'to hammer') is unique, but the predominance of certain scales and tunings give it a special, shimmering, colouristic effect. Debussy was hooked, returning day after day to the exhibition to soak up this extraordinary sound. His friend Robert Godet commented:

Many fruitful hours for Debussy were spent in the Javanese kampong of the Dutch sections listening to the percussive rhythmic complexities of the gamelan, with its inexhaustible combinations of ethereal, flashing timbres, while with the amazing Bedayas the music came visually alive.

Debussy himself wrote of them many years later,

Javanese music is based on a type of counterpoint by comparison with which that of Palestrina is child's play. And if we listened without European prejudice to the charm of their percussion, we must confess that our percussion is like primitive noises at a country fair.

Debussy set about trying to translate the weird and wonderful far-eastern sounds onto the European piano with its rigid western scales, and in a series of pieces written at the beginning

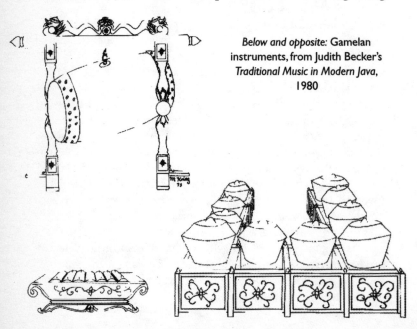

Below and opposite: Gamelan instruments, from Judith Becker's *Traditional Music in Modern Java,* 1980

of the twentieth century his experiments began to bear fruit. In his cloud-picture, *Nuages*, he used the sonorities of the piano in a startlingly new way. One technique he favoured was to let the natural harmonics of the strings rebound and ricochet on each other – created by letting chords 'hang on' over each other much longer than normal, lifting the dampers off the strings in an almost pantaleon-type way. Chords with apparently superfluous notes in them were able to effect the overall resonance of the harmony – the superfluous notes, of course, turning out to be critical in changing the colour of the sound. Though he hated the term with respect to music, his use of sound colours in these pieces has some similarities with impressionism (or pointillism at any rate) in painting. On close inspection, a pointillist painting is made up of tiny specks of colour that seem to be incongruous. When taken as a whole, from a little distance, the 'incongruous' colour specks act on those around them to create a shimmering view. Debussy's use of 'unwanted' extra notes within a chord, or indeed a chord

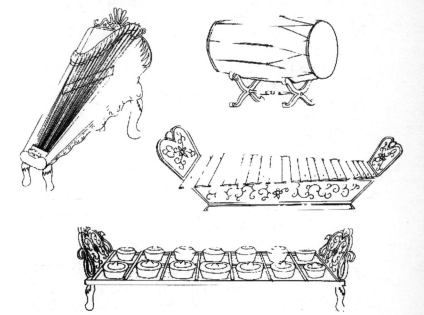

itself hanging mischievously over into another 'main' chord's airspace, does much the same. The bells and gongs of the gamelan nearly all ring on carelessly once they've been struck: it was their overlapping waves of sound, echoing and fading away, that Debussy was trying to imagine.

Debussy made full use of the piano's rich palette of sounds and effects in his attempt to unlock the old harmonic rules and clichés. His skill in so doing was taken up by France's foremost composer of the later twentieth century, Olivier Messiaen. In his *Vingt Regards sur l'enfant Jésus*, written after his release from Nazi internment camp in 1944, the colouristic hand of Debussy is everywhere in the piano writing. His masterpiece, the monumental *Turangalîla-symphonie* (1948) for orchestra, is – amongst other things – an unabashed homage to the sound of the Javanese gamelan.

Debussy's interest in the exotic and foreign did not stop at Java. At the same Universal Exhibition he also became acquainted with the music of several unknown Russian composers – Rimsky-Korsakov, Mussorgsky and Balakirev – and also with African tribal dance music. There was, however, another musical trick up Debussy's sleeve, one that he might have picked up on his numerous long evenings at Le Chat Noir café in Paris's red light district, near Montmartre. Suddenly, as if from nowhere, something popped up in his piano music that was derived from far away across the Atlantic: syncopation.

Syncopation means the deliberate delaying or anticipating of the beat. You push or pull the notes away from the place you're expecting them to be when your foot is tapping along to the beat. Syncopation is so commonplace in all popular music now that it hardly seems worthy of mention, but it was once quite a novelty. Syncopated piano playing was the foundation stone of early jazz and popular song. Whether Debussy had heard some of this newfangled syncopated music played by visiting African-American musicians in Paris or on an early recording no one is quite sure, but he was definitely influenced by the style known in America as Ragtime, in pieces with, I'm sorry to say, titles like 'Golliwog's Cakewalk' and 'The Little Nigar' (*sic*).

Ragtime originated in the USA at the end of the nineteenth century, its most celebrated and brilliant exponent being Scott Joplin. Joplin, who was born and raised in the American Deep South, came to prominence with the publication of his 'Maple Leaf Rag' in 1899, when he was living in Sedalia, Missouri, and working as a pianist in bar-brothels, one of which was called the Maple Leaf Club. Two (or more) theories circulate concerning the name 'ragtime' to describe the lightly syncopated piano style he excelled in. The official musical-dictionary version is that the rhythm was considered 'ragged'; the other, unofficial, explanation is that ragtime music first emerged in brothels, so when the prostitutes were having their periods (at the same time, since they were all living under one roof) the piano players took over entertaining the clients. When it was – literally – 'rag' time, this was the music that took centre stage.

At the root of ragtime is a kind of marching music (as played by popular bands of the time), the left hand supplying the tuba bass notes and – by leaping energetically up a couple of octaves – the chords in the middle as well. The right hand looked after the tune and its embellishments. Once again, the piano was being all things to all people, in this case acting as one-man band. Making the journey from band to solo player naturally caused certain compromises and adjustments, such as a leaping left hand and a right hand trying two-to-the-dozen to fill in the melody and all the mini-melodies normally added by piccolos and other high wind instruments around it. This busy approximating of several melody instruments by the right hand fractures the rhythm, syncopating it. The fracturing of 'normal' rhythm was a crucial step in the breaking away of jazz from 'classical' music. The two streams became more and more separate as the century progressed. The common link between the two remained the piano – energetically involved in all stages of jazz and, as we saw with Messiaen, equally so in the European branch.

Joplin died in Manhattan in 1917 still vainly hoping, ironically, to be accepted as a serious, classical composer. Despite the commercial success of the 'Maple Leaf Rag', which sold

A bar piano in the American West in the 1870s

half a million copies in his lifetime, Joplin's life was desperately sad, not least because he suspected his music would one day, long after his death, make much more of an impact than it did while he was alive. This turned out to be prophetic. His music inspired a generation of players of syncopated piano, like Jelly Roll Morton, Willie 'The Lion' Smith, Eubie Blake and Jimmy Johnson. Even as late as the 1940s, in the swing era, ragtime was making its presence felt, while modern audiences know his music from the 1974 hit film *The Sting*, starring Robert Redford and Paul Newman. What Joplin demonstrated, as did Fats Waller and Oscar Peterson, was that the piano made an easy leap from classical to popular. It was the catalyst in a process that took classically trained musicians, like Joplin, into jazz. Whereas the guitar was the instrument of early blues, the piano was the harbinger of early jazz.

The fact that the piano was the natural instrument of a poor brothel pianist in the Deep South just one generation from slavery shows how profound its penetration into every level of society it had become. The piano democratised music. It found its way into living rooms, parlours, schools, church halls, missionary stations, pubs, clubs and cafés. It was the 'entry point' into music for millions of people. It was the way ordinary folk got to hear the latest popular songs (before broadcasting and records), the latest symphonies (reduced and transcribed, of course) and even film music before the talkies. With a piano you could mount your own village production of a pantomime or operetta; with a piano you could put on a proper concert. The piano age was one in which amateur music lovers played for themselves the music they adored.

Pubs and bars have now replaced their pianos with computer games and Muzak and a family's evening entertainment no longer consists of songs round the joanna, but the piano is still a formidable force in our musical life. From the opening bars of 'Let it Be' to the long queues of fans that follow the young Russian virtuoso Evgeny Kissin around the globe, we readily submit to its power and beauty. People still buy pianos in large numbers, but the sales of traditional instruments are puny in comparison to those of its most successful spin-off, the digital keyboard. I wonder what Bartolomeo Cristofori would make of these electronic hybrids? Well, he would recognise the weighted hammer action and probably smile at their huge range and heaviness. He would definitely find the range of extra sounds available at the flick of a switch miraculous, as the keyboard suddenly transforms itself into a harpsichord or an organ or a choir going 'Ah'. He would wonder where the strings and the wooden case had gone, but the thing he would find most baffling would be the volume controller. After all that effort I put in, he'd say, to make a keyboard that gets louder and softer through the contact of your fingers on the keys – and now you've replaced the infinite variation of human touch with a plastic knob? You call that progress?

SEVEN

CHOSEN PEOPLE

Zog nisht keinmal az du
gehst dem letzten veg
(Never say that you are on your final journey)

Western music was born in the Roman Catholic Church and
weaned from its maternal clutches during the Renaissance. It
gave a voice to the Enlightenment (with help from the reforming spirit of Protestantism) and spread across the industri-
alised West. In the twentieth century two great influences
came to bear on it, both emanating from races whose origins
were outside Europe altogether. The impact of African music
was one, particularly on all forms of popular music. The
equivalent in classical music was the influence of the Jewish
community, whose gradual emancipation and assimilation
into European life, beginning in the last half of the nineteenth
century, transformed musical culture as profoundly as it did
science, law, philosophy, medicine, literature, art and politics.
Any list of seminal figures in twentieth-century civilisation
would be unthinkable without the towering figures of Karl
Marx, Leon Trotsky, Sigmund Freud, Albert Einstein,
Gertrude Stein, Primo Levi, Franz Kafka, Ludwig Wittgen-
stein, Marc Chagall and Charles Chaplin – and a host of influential composers and musicians.

The musical foundations of European music, Gregorian
chant in the West and Byzantine chant in the East, can actually
both trace their roots back to Jewish religious music, but the
Jews in Europe had little influence on classical music before
Napoleon took control of France. After that period, however,
the situation started to change in an extraordinary fashion.

The French government's enactment of a law in 1791 granting full equal rights to Jews did not suddenly relieve Jewish communities of the anti-Semitism and prejudice that had always plagued them, but it did begin a process of emancipation that was taken up in most other countries – especially those conquered by Napoleon's armies – with the exception of Imperial Russia. The Enlightenment had also stirred into life a movement separating Church from State, thus reducing the ability of the Vatican to promote doctrine harmful to Jews. The nineteenth century saw a gradual loosening of restrictions on the Jewish way of life but at the same time a tension developing from within European Jewry itself as to whether it was possible to be assimilated into the (still largely hostile) majority culture and retain the special character and laws of Judaism. Integrationist tendencies, especially amongst educated Jews in Western European countries who thought of themselves as quite different from the poor rural communities in Central and Eastern Europe, found expression in a growing 'reform' movement. Influential leaders like the Rabbi Samson Raphael Hirsch (1808–88) taught that Jews could indeed live within a secular society without contradiction or turning their backs on fundamental religious laws. Abraham Geiger (1810–74) went further by propounding a universal enlightenment in which Jews might take their place in society alongside Gentiles in a future that would gradually dispense with everyone's religious observance.

Migrations played their part. Mass movement to the United States in the period 1882 to 1914, and from isolated rural settlements to urban centres within Europe, dramatically accelerated the assimilation of 'reforming' Jews into mainstream European culture. Many intellectuals found the strain of reconciling their roots in closed, traditional communities with their new lives in cosmopolitan cities so great that they converted to Christianity. Some abandoned religion altogether, turning to alternative philosophies – many of the early proponents of socialism and communism were of Jewish origin. The influx into previously Catholic cities of Jews from more remote parts of the Austro-Hungarian Empire, which bore such remarkable cultural fruit, can be seen most emphatically at its centre, Vienna. Between 1848 and 1914 the Jewish community in Vienna increased 35 times from a mere 5,000 people to an impressive 175,000, 9 per cent of the total population. Most of the arrivals came from poverty-stricken areas of Galicia, Bohemia and Moravia. Once they had resettled in the city, their impact on the professional classes was markedly disproportionate to the size of their community. By 1936, 62 per cent of Vienna's lawyers and 47 per cent of its doctors were of Jewish origin. It is a sad fact that the enthusiasm with which Vienna's new Jewish community embraced the majority culture of the Imperial capital was not reciprocated. The election of an openly anti-Semitic mayor in 1897 was a foretaste of things to come. Vienna's most notorious anti-Semite, Adolf Hitler, articulated the envy and hatred that many Austrians felt towards their brilliant and successful neighbours. Even after the Holocaust, modern Vienna, unrepentant and unreconstructed, finds it necessary to post a 24-hour police guard outside the city's synagogue.

Many reasons have been given for the explosion of Jewish talent throughout Western culture in the twentieth century. When Jews began their absorption into European society they brought commercial acumen, but their impact on the professional classes, on further education, scientific investigation, on the law and spectacularly on the arts across such a vast swathe of the Continent was exceptional. They had had this effect once before, in Islamic Spain between 700 and 1490. Here they had been granted rights and privileges by successive Moorish administrations, becoming the backbone of the Imperial civil service and leading research in science and technology. Yet what followed the emancipation of Jews in the sophisticated emirates and caliphates of Córdova was the crushing intolerance and genocide of the Reconquista, in which Jews were once again victimised and persecuted. How horribly prophetic this tale of events in Southern Spain is of those in Central Europe between 1850 and 1945.

Doubt and insecurity haunted both Jews who had renounced their religious roots (like Marx and Freud) and those who chose to hang on to them in the teeth of suspicion or disapproval amongst Gentiles. Jews turned their doubt and insecurity into feverish activity and struggle. In creative terms, their status as exiles within their own home towns made them perceptive and accurate observers; their longing for acceptance, their sense of disorientation and homelessness gave their artistic work a poignant, distressing voice. This melancholic, displaced quality in Jewish art and music may have seemed out of place amidst the confident Imperial pomposity of the nineteenth century: in the twentieth, it became a lamentation with which all humanity could identify. The terror and agony of the First World War darkened and deepened European culture, and two of the Great War's most troubled and percipient writers were Jews, Siegfried Sassoon and Isaac Rosenberg.

As for music, Felix Mendelssohn (1809–47), Jacques Offenbach (1819–80) and Giacomo Meyerbeer (1791–1864) were successful Jewish composers of the nineteenth century. While their music is often charming, rich and eloquent it is of a quite different order to what followed. At the end of the century two composers emerge whose work is profoundly, disturbingly moving. The first of these is Alexander Zemlinsky (1871–1942), a half-Slovakian, half-Bosnian Jew. The other is his Viennese colleague Gustav Mahler (1860–1911), a native of Bohemia (now the Czech Republic) who later converted somewhat half-heartedly to Catholicism when it transpired he would not be appointed musical director of the Vienna Staatsoper if he did not renounce his Jewishness. Both were opera conductors of some fame and distinction in Vienna, but neither received recognition for their brilliant compositions during their lifetimes. Both were celebrated teachers, Zemlinsky nurturing the precocious talent of Erich Korngold, a Moravian Jew who wrote swirling, romantic orchestral music in Vienna, and swirling, romantic film scores after he had fled Europe for Hollywood. For many years, Mahler was seen chiefly as the mentor of the flawed geniuses Arnold Schönberg, Alban Berg and Anton Webern, known collectively as 'The Second Viennese School'. These Jewish composers, all working in Vienna at the turn of the century (alongside the *Sezession* painters Oskar Kokoshka and Gustav Klimt) sought to dismember and reorder the whole lexicon of Western music, culminating in the devising of the so-called '12-tone' or 'serialist' system. The 'serial' approach to the musical scale was to have enormous repercussions inside the classical music world, especially amongst young and iconoclastic composers. The modernist movement in music was triggered by the methods and theories of these three radical figures. The fact that music, seventy years later, shrugged off the effects of serialism and reverted with a sigh of relief to old-fashioned 'tonality' does not diminish the importance of Schönberg, Berg and Webern.

A sense of foreboding runs through much music written by Jewish composers in the twentieth century. As Germany was disintegrating into the gang warfare and instability which underpinned the rise of the Nazis, the angular, political songs of Hanns Eisler and Kurt Weill etched their own version of events into musical history. Eisler and Weill both collaborated with Bertolt Brecht, both escaped to the States before the Second World War and both tried their hand at film scoring. Hollywood had by the 1930s become the principal sanctuary for artistically minded Jews fleeing Europe, though the finest film scores came from the pens of dedicated film composers rather than classical writers trying to get by. The best film music ever written is that of Bernard Herrmann (*Psycho, Vertigo, North by Northwest, Citizen Kane*) – whose scores are characterised by an uncompromising darkness and sombre urgency, the likes of which no modern film producer would ever allow.

It is misleading, though, to think of the Jewish contribution to twentieth-century music as one entirely ridden with angst and melancholia. When one considers the quintessentially American exuberance of Aaron Copland or Leonard Bernstein, the beauty of the works of George and Ira Gershwin and the joyful optimism of Rodgers and Hammerstein, Irving Berlin, Jerome Kern and Loesser and Loewe, another side of the Jewish character surfaces. The two sides coexist in an uneasy equilibrium in the outstanding songs of Stephen Sondheim, Cy Coleman, Jule Styne and Paul Simon. The many hundreds of world-class Jewish conductors and soloists that so dominated music-making in the twentieth century are both a living defiance of the attempt by Nazi policy to erase the cultural contribution of the Jewish people, and an indication of the scale of the loss that occurred in the death camps. Vladimir Ashkenazy, Daniel Barenboim, Jascha Heifetz, Myra Hess, Vladimir Horowitz, Otto Klemperer, James Levine, Yehudi Menuhin, David Oistrakh, Eugene Ormandy, Itzhak Perlman, André Previn, Anton Rubinstein, Arthur Rubinstein, Georg Solti, Isaac Stern, Georg Szell, Michael Tilson Thomas, Bruno Walter, Pinchas Zukerman, Larry Adler, Emanuel Ax and Murray Perahia are a tiny proportion of that number. Popular music lists Bob Dylan, Randy Newman, Billy Joel, Leonard Cohen, Marvin Hamlisch, Neil Sedaka, Bette Midler, Herb Alpert, Danny Kaye, Stan Getz, Carly Simon, Carole King, Neil Diamond, Barry Manilow, Barbra Streisand, Benny Goodman and Al Jolson. If these are the survivors, the children of the survivors and the ones whose families escaped the Holocaust by lucky accident of geography, how many others do they stand in for?

African music brought rhythm back (with a vengeance) to Western music, but what did Jewish composers bring to the development of the classical repertoire? Are there not composers from a non-Jewish background whose work is also dissenting and dark? The Russians, Igor Stravinsky and Dmitri Shostakovich come to mind. The music of these monumental composers is indeed nervous and dissonant, but in place of dismay and a fatalistic surrender, their suffering has an anger and aggression to it. Whereas Mahler, Zemlinsky or Weill yearned for acceptance, Stravinsky and Shostakovich were iconoclasts, welcoming or provoking confrontation. Shostakovich's answer to Stalin's disapproval, his fifth Symphony, is on the one hand apparently an apology for the dissonance and austerity of his previous symphony and on the other a piece of such force and power it amounts to a sardonic riposte. Only an idiot or a megalomaniac would not have read the triumphant courage of the fifth Symphony as defiance in disguise.

The use of Russian folk tunes in Stravinsky is confident and unabashed; there is a rawness and savagery to his writing that seems to have been made to withstand the Siberian permafrost. For all its sophistication and conceit, Stravinsky's music is peasant music – tough, unyielding and crudely colourful. For musically educated Jews, though, there was neither nostalgia for the peasant life of the *shtetl* nor any sign of wanting to promote it with Stravinsky's strutting confidence. Klezmer music, the street sound of Jewish bands from communities throughout Eastern Europe, does not bleed into the late romantic symphonic style or the serialist experiments of the Jewish–Viennese composers. The folk style suggested in Mahler is more refined and Austrian. He conjures up childhood sometimes with an idealised vision of heavenly innocence, sometimes with menace and fear, recalling family conflict and the interfering racket of military bands in the nearby barracks. Stravinsky and Shostakovich lean back upon their Russian past with ferocious pride. Mahler looks back with insecurity and pain. Mahler's music is often powerful, brash and vast, but it is almost never fearless in the way Stravinsky is. What has he to fall back on? He is a wandering Jew, seeking a new identity in someone else's homeland. Jewish artists spent the first half of the twentieth century running away from terror to wherever would give them temporary asylum. Shostakovich, on the other hand, was resident in the world's second largest superpower, acutely aware of his identity and place.

However, comparing Mahler with Stravinsky and Shostakovich is unsatisfactory since both Russians knew and admired his work. Shostakovich would listen to records of Mahler smuggled in from the West (Mahler's music was banned in Stalinist Russia) and Stravinsky admitted to the influence of Mahler and his Viennese protégés on many occasions. A more revealing comparison is with a devoutly Catholic Austrian, a composer Mahler himself looked up to: Anton Bruckner.

Bruckner came from Linz in Upper Austria but ended up in

Gustav Mahler

Vienna as Brahms had done before him and Mahler would do after him. He wrote ten symphonies on a colossal scale, three grand Masses, a *Te Deum* and some smaller-scale motets (his best pieces, these). Because he was Austrian, wrote ten huge symphonies and was in awe of Richard Wagner, Bruckner's name has always been paired with Mahler's. There are, undoubtedly, some stylistic similarities in their respective efforts, but that is as far as it goes. For all its lush melodiousness, Bruckner's music is long-winded and simplistic when compared to the neurotic energy of his younger contemporary. Bruckner symphonies never tire of repeating the same phrases over and over again until you are gasping for release, Mahler struggles quixotically with every nuance and detail, unleashing new ideas and layers with every page of the full score. Mahler never settles – this is restless, wandering music, filled with introspection and insecurity. He cannot even let the orchestral instruments alone, inventing new ones, making unexpected demands on familiar ones and endlessly experimenting with colour and combination. Bruckner, the settled and secure town organist, has none of this turmoil. His pieces build up inexorably to climaxes you can see coming half an hour off. At best, his work can be seen as a solid, broad-shouldered cry of praise to God, at worst it is bombastic, pompous and irritating. Mahler, confused and disorientated by his pseudo-conversion to Catholicism, cries out instead to God for answers, or replaces religious certainty with passionately wishful thinking about a collective spiritual vision for all mankind. Bruckner reminds me of Vienna. You can see what people like about it, it's grandiose in a touristic sort of way but it lacks the guilt and tension that would give it soul. Mahler is all soul and very little controlled decorum. Bruckner celebrates the calm, picture-book landscape of Upper Austria and its conservative gentility. Mahler, who composed in the very same neck of the woods, saw lurking behind those forests and fences something much more alarming. He was, tragically, right.

In the last four years of his life, after the death of his daughter, Mahler embarked on three last symphonies, written between 1907 and 1911. These works carry a desperate message, one that was to ricochet across the century. Scrawled across the margins of his scores are farewell messages and exclamations of despair: he was clearly disturbed by the possibility of death, but also preparing himself for it. The reason his beautiful, haunted music speaks to us with such unbearable power is that he seems to have intimated what was coming, not just for himself but for his world. These heartbreaking symphonies could not, I believe, have been written by someone who did not understand the predicament of the humiliated outcast – the stateless European Jew. In one of his earlier songs, Mahler set to music a poem by the Romantic poet Friedrich Rückert, 'Ich bin der Welt abhanden gekommen', which means 'I have become cut off from the world'. The sense of abandonment is everywhere in his music. A century later we approach another of his song cycles, the *Kindertotenlieder*, songs on the death of children, with a trepidation informed by the horrific events of the period following Mahler's life, in his country, amongst his people.

This is the music of the twentieth century.

Oft denk' ich, sie sind nur ausgegangen!
Bald werden sie wieder nach Hause gelangen!
Der Tag ist schön! O, sei nicht bang!
Sie machen nur einen weiten Gang.
Jawohl, sie sind nur ausgegangen
Und werden jetzt nach Hause gelangen!
O, sei nicht bang, der Tag ist schön!
Sie machen nur den Gang zu jenen Höh'n!
Sie sind uns nur vorausgegangen
Und werden nicht wider nach Haus gelangen!
Wir holen sie ein auf jenen Höh'n im Sonnenschein!
Der Tag ist schön auf jenen Höh'n!

Often I think they've merely gone out.
Soon they will return home.
The day's beautiful, O, don't be anxious,
They're only taking a long walk
Yes, surely they've only gone out
And will now come home.
O, don't fret, the day is lovely.
They're only taking their walk to that high point
    over there –
They've only gone on ahead of us
And won't be coming home again.
We'll catch up with them up at the high point,
    in the sunshine

EIGHT

MARY AND HER LITTLE LAMB

Thomas Alva Edison and the Invention of Recorded Sound

The easy availability of music is something that most of us take for granted. Before the age of recording, people heard a particular piece of orchestral music maybe once or twice a *decade*. Now anything can be listened to, instantly, at the flick of a switch, the drop of a needle or the aiming of a laser. But in the 120-odd years since we've been able to record sound, have we come to love the perfect copy a little too much? Are we more at ease with the reproduction than the genuine live experience, warts and all? Has recording spoilt us and numbed us to the excitement and drama of the Real Thing?

This is the story of the invention of recorded sound, the profound, irreversible effect it has had on music, and what we all, as listeners, expect from it. Recording unleashed on the twentieth century a massive amount of music in a multitude of forms, it gave music wings to cross the planet – but in the world of classical music it also caused a dramatic shift in emphasis, from an interest in the new and contemporary to the old and familiar.

Though the early gramophone came into being as a result of the desire to record speech not music, very soon its principal, almost monogamous marriage was with music. But although its impact on music was undeniably huge, this was a two-way process: the early imperative to improve sound quality, the search for an electrical recording solution, the development of stereophonic sound, and so on, would never have had the same urgency if the content had been only talk. We shall come back to the effect sound recording was to have on music later, but first we should examine the early history of the medium.

In a book in 1649, Cyrano de Bergerac (the real guy, that is, not the fictionalised swashbuckler) had a vision of a future visit to the moon, whose inhabitants (Lunarians) had ingenious 'talking books'. Little did Cyrano know that 350 years later every home on planet Earth – though not yet satellite Moon – would have such a speaking machine. Whilst such a fact might have amazed and delighted him, the knowledge that 'When 2 Become 1' by a 'girlband' called the Spice Girls would also be listened to by millions of young people across the globe thanks to the same invention might have had him wondering whether it had been worth all the effort. But there you go.

Just over two hundred years later, in 1860, an Austrian named Faber constructed a 'talking man' robot which had a bellows for lungs, a voice box (with ivory reed vocal cords), a larynx, diaphragm and mouth (with rubber lips and tongue), and a wheel placed in his artificial thorax to make R sounds. This talking miracle was operated by a series of levers and controlled by a piano-like keyboard. Mankind apparently loved the sound of his own voice so much that the idea of a machine that could reproduce his speech-patterns and talk gibberish was considered a vital area for scientific research.

Less absurd, and more germane to our story, were the Phonautograph, the brainchild of a Frenchman by the name of Léon Scott de Martinville in 1857, and the Paléophone, made by another Frenchman, Charles Cros, twenty years later. The idea of the former was that a wavy line would be traced onto a sheet of paper coated with lampblack (wrapped around a revolving cylinder) when stimulated so to do by the sound coming out of a horn. Across the end of the horn was attached a membrane which reacted to the sounds by vibrating and passing on these vibrations to a hog's bristle which in turn would scratch the coated paper. It may sound a bit daft, but it contained as an idea the elements of the device that was to become the first sound recorder. Cros's later effort, the Paléophone, was based on de Martinville's, but he refined it by suggesting that it have a more permanent and sinuous ridge (groove), that the hog's bristle might be replaced with an engraving implement of some kind, and that the material it etched could be more like zinc, say, than coated paper. It is unfortunate – some would say disastrous – for Cros that none of his 'Paléophones' have survived (if indeed they were ever constructed). His written specification for this sound-recording device was lodged with the Académie des Sciences in Paris on 30 April 1877. If this specification had been enough, Cros would now be the Father of Sound, instead of a meagre footnote in someone else's story, for just six months later, on the other side of the Atlantic, a great man of science blasted into posterity with his sound-recording novelty, stealing the limelight, the glory, the cash and the kudos. His name was Thomas Alva Edison.

Edison invented recorded sound by accident. He had really been working on improving the speed of telegraphy. Stung by Alexander Graham Bell's registering a patent for the telephone before him, he was feverishly investigating other possibilities connected with the telegraph network fast springing up across the States. Intriguingly, even at this early stage of its development, the telephone line was already being suggested as a possible carrier of fax-style messages. Edison was trying to see if the process of sending Morse messages 'down the line' could be speeded up. He was perfecting a machine that transcribed telegrams by indenting the message onto paper tape with the dots and dashes of Morse code, then later repeated the message back at high speed. To regulate the tape's progress through the indenting mechanism, he fitted a steel spring. When he ran the tape, with its engraved Morse code grooves and holes, back across the reading-head at high speed, the spring vibrated sympathetically: Edison noted that it gave off a 'light musical, rhythmic sound, resembling human talk heard indistinctly'. Surely, he thought, if these markings on the papery tape could create a responsive sound by accident, then they could be modified deliberately to that end? Perhaps in the manner of de Martinville's and Cros's scratched grooves on paper or zinc? The idea of a machine that could 'play back'

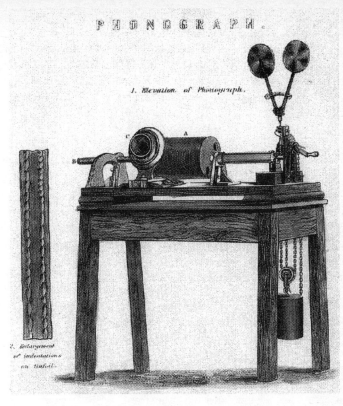

An Edison tin-foil phonograph of 1878

the sound of human speech was a hair's-breadth away from realisation.

His immediate aim was eminently practical. The new-fangled telephones, now only one year into their life, were still extremely scarce and expensive, so Edison reasoned that a small, portable talking machine could record a voice message by anyone, anywhere. This recording could then be taken to a central telephone exchange to be played back down the phone line in bulk sequences (rather in the manner of an Internet Server gathering and transmitting e-mail): in other words, an audio version of telegrams. Instead of 'telegraphs', these would be called 'phonographs' (*phonos* is the Greek word for sound).

He started with a lathe, onto which he fitted a slowly turning cylinder with a handle at one end. Then he wrapped a strip of paper soaked in paraffin around this barrel, smoothing it down neatly so that the slightest mark on it would be noticeable: he now had a roll of paraffin paper he could rotate from one end to another. Then he attached to the side of the lathe a funnel about 10 inches long, open at one end but with a diaphragm on the other. This was set at right angles to the rolling cylinder, with the wider, open end facing away from the barrel. Onto the diaphragm which covered the thinner end he fixed a small pin. If one shouted down the funnel, not surprisingly, the sensitive diaphragm wobbled and shook with the movement of air down the tube. The pin vibrated with it. The theory was, if you turned the handle so the paraffin paper turned, the pin engraved the paper as it rotated, with the vibrations and tremors produced as a result of shouting down the funnel. (I say theory, because I myself have tried this experiment on a replica of this crude recording lathe and it's pretty unreliable at the best of times.)

After engraving the paper you would then repeat the process in reverse. Turning the handle again, the needle or pin rests gently in the grooves you made the first time, retracing its steps, as it were, and what is supposed to happen is that the diaphragm shakes and trembles all over again, playing back to you your original shouting noise. Since running the needle along its grooves flattens them out, you only have one chance to 'hear' the recording back. After that, the paraffin paper is useless.

The first ever recorded phrase on such a device, indeed the first recorded utterance, was Edison himself reciting 'Mary Had a Little Lamb'. When the experiment actually worked, he said, 'I was never so taken aback in my life.' Very soon after his first historic attempt, Edison replaced the paraffin paper with tin-foil, but the foil was equally useless after one listening, and it was unusable once taken off its revolving cylinder. Still, it was a start.

Listening to the phonograph

This 'Phonograph' recording device (still on show at the fascinating and friendly Edison National Historic Site in West Orange, New Jersey) was registered for patent in late 1877, and immediately caught the imagination of an American public hungry for new inventions and novelties. The giddy speed and variety of scientific advance between 1860 and 1900, particularly in the United States, was highly infectious. Inventors of all kinds were spurred on by the thought of rags-to-riches tales and dreams of untold wealth and fame emanating from ingenious, life-enhancing gadgets. Bell and Edison were in the vanguard, but many others were active in their slipstream. This exciting era, galvanised by the relatively recent conquest of electricity, is comparable with that in Britain in the previous century, when the possibilities of steam power brought forth brilliant engineers and propelled the industrial revolution forward. Edison alone patented literally hundreds of new devices, from the Incredible Incandescent Electric Lighting Appliance (i.e. the light bulb) and the Amazing Mechanical Winnowing Contrivance, to the Revolving French Fried Potato Cooking Kettle and the Steam-Powered Ear-Trumpet, quite apart from the Astounding Paper-Sack and the Foldable Checkers-Playing Board.

Before we get carried away, though, it's worth pointing out that Edison's first recording contraption could not in any way be described as 'high fidelity'. It took an expert to get any sounds at all out of it, never mind musical ones, and the reason why no recordings survive from the phonograph's first few years is because the tin-foil impressions were irreparably damaged the minute they came off the cylinder. Well, you try recording 'White Christmas' with a drawing pin, a cardboard loo roll and a strip of bacofoil and you'll see what I mean.

Accordingly, Edison's legendary recitation no longer exists, though he did 're-enact' the experience in 1929 on his original phonograph, and this recording does survive. A man in Brooklyn called Mr Aaron Cramer has an 1878 recording, made on a tinfoil phonograph by engineer Frank Lambert with the words 'Four o'clock, Five o'clock, Six o'clock', etc. spoken by Lambert himself, which makes it the earliest recorded speech. The existence of this foil recording we owe to luck (that it fell to a knowledgeable collector) and inspired restoration. Mr Cramer bought the rusting, dilapidated lathe from a dealer twenty-odd years ago not knowing exactly what he was getting: certainly the vendor hadn't a clue as to its significance. After it was cleaned up and properly examined the cylinder was found to have a scratched recording still on its surface from which a new copy was made for posterity. I heard the recording and saw the famous lathe in the genial Mr Cramer's basement, sitting in amazed delight as I heard a voice speaking to me from the time of Richard Wagner, George Eliot and Charles Darwin.

Edison's invention was remarkable, but its birth was not intended to have any impact whatever on music. The first use to which music was put was in the service of the new phonograph, rather than as a partner in its development (a position it was soon to occupy and monopolise). Its ability to record and play back the human voice, or a dog barking – extremely crudely and virtually inaudibly by our standards – was demonstrated by travelling showmen who baffled huge fee-paying audiences all over the USA. The climactic trick of the evening would invariably be the 'instant' recording of a cornettist, with the machine wondrously copying every tiny nuance of the player's performance, ending with a speeded-up version from the phonograph (by turning the handle faster) that apparently brought the house down.

Meanwhile, the phonograph's formidable inventor, while understandably delighted at the wad flowing in from the new invention, had a more purposeful future for it in mind than novelty shows and attractions. In fact, he had *ten* projected purposes for it, as he made clear in an article of 1878. First amongst these (and the most commercially exploited in the early years) was office dictation and letter writing; next was talking books for the visually impaired, and third was the teaching of proper elocution.

In fourth place on his list was the reproduction of music (above 'archiving family sayings', toys, speaking clocks, preservation of endangered languages, distance-learning and an improved method of using the telephone). He did naturally foresee that bands and orchestras might be able to play down a funnel 'like those used in ventilating steamships', but he could not have anticipated how eagerly and rapidly the public would want to hear recorded music when it became viable and (more) audible after the turn of the century. When multiple phonographs were later adapted for use as coin-operated jukeboxes, public enthusiasm for them convinced Edison and many other rivals that there really were commercial possibilities in music.

The nickel-in-the-slot machine, using reliable and durable wax cylinders, a hearing device identical to a doctor's stethoscope, and pre-fitted with some popular march or song turned out to be a momentous breakthrough for the phonograph. Instead of being a sideshow, the phonograph could actually take centre stage and perform a function people actively enjoyed. The *Cincinnati Commercial Gazette* of 25 July 1890 summed up the public mood:

> The Musical Phonograph, which is now to be seen in every restaurant and bar downtown, is knocking the business of all other Drop-a-nickel-in-the-slot machines into a cocked hat. When a man can hear the 7th Regiment Band of New York play the Boulanger March, a Cornet solo by Levy or the famous song 'The Old Oaken Bucket', for 5 cents, he has little desire to pay 5 cents to ascertain his weight or test the strength of his grip. That is the reasons [*sic*] the musical machine has killed the business of the other automatic machines.

The craze for music from a box in the corner of a café, still popular today, evidently wiped out the public's interest in other slot machines at a stroke.

Edison's preliminary list of possible uses for his invention, however, was remarkably prophetic: how was he to know that 'archiving favourite family sayings' wouldn't take off until much later, when the age of the ubiquitous camcorder would allow grandchildren to capture their aged and wise relatives falling off boats, walking into transparent french windows, and having their knickers come down while ballroom dancing, to the cruel merriment and voyeuristic glee of an entire nation? Talking dolls arrived on toy-store shelves almost immediately, and never left them. Modern 'language labs' are merely an elaborate version of his projected phonograph teaching facilities, and he hinted at the idea of a telephone answering machine using recording.

But the first thing that followed Edison's invention of the phonograph was a bad-tempered and highly competitive scrap about patents, licences, trademarks, exploitation rights and modifications.

First Alexander Bell's cousin Chichester worked with an instrument-maker called Charles Tainter to develop an improved recording device they dubbed the Bell-Tainter Graphophone. This had the benefit of entirely wax cylinders and a floating stylus, as well as a foot treadle or electric motor to regulate the rotation of the cylinder (similar to those used in sewing machines). The point about the hard wax cylinders replacing tinfoil and paraffin paper was that you could now remove your recording from the machine and play it back again and again. It goes without saying that this vastly increased the prospect of selling the discs to the public – the nickel-in-the-slot machines wouldn't have been possible without this innovation. Then Émile Berliner, an émigré German, launched his new Gram-O-Phone, which very soon began to lead the field, as it had the advantage of using flat rubber discs instead of cylinders. The introduction of discs should not be underestimated, as it was now possible to make one 'negative' zinc master from which an unlimited number of rubber discs might be pressed, rather like the method of making prints from a photographic negative. Before that, musicians making recordings had had to perform pieces countless times onto each individual cylinder recorder (there would often be ten cylinder recorders in the studio recording simultaneously, but even then it might take a whole day to make 200 copies of the same three-minute song!). In the late 1890s the rubber discs were replaced with a brittle form of early plastic known as 'shellac' or 'Duranoid', which was made, believe it or not, from crushed Malaysian beetles. Berliner's company and its associates gave birth to virtually every major record company of the next half-century – he was truly the father of the modern music industry.

After his initial endeavours, Edison became distracted by other areas of experimentation, notably the invention of the carbon-filament electric light bulb, only to return to the improvement of his phonograph in 1888, when he realised that recording music was going to be such big business. It cannot be an overstatement to say that his contribution to life in the twentieth century is almost unparalleled. Most great scientists only manage one massive breakthrough in their careers; Edison's inventions, on the other hand, had an effect on almost all areas of modern domestic life.

The phonograph came into being as a result of the desire to record speech. From the outset, the phonograph pioneers felt it a worthwhile function of the medium to record famous voices for posterity. Typical recordings were those made of the voices of Sarah Bernhardt (performing dramatic excerpts) and Mark Twain (reading). Among other archival voice recordings made in the USA and Europe were those of Alfred Lord Tennyson, Robert Browning (at the Crystal Palace exhibition of 1888), William Gladstone (at the Paris Expo of 1890), Pope Leo XIII (at the Vatican in 1903) and Chancellor Bismarck (also at the Crystal Palace). Despite this, it was the appeal of music – not speech – that inspired the industry into action. It is therefore slightly surprising that at first classical musicians were so suspicious of the invention. Sir Arthur Sullivan (as in Gilbert and Sullivan) was typical of many when he declared (proudly, at the beginning of his first recording session): 'I am astonished and somewhat terrified. Astonished at the wonderful power you have developed and terrified at the thought that so much hideous and bad music may be put on record for ever.'

Sullivan's fears may have been aggravated by the fact that initially it was popular, light music that attracted the most interest and investment. For the next hundred years classical musicians were to echo his complaint about the huge popularity of what they considered to be inferior music. It is true that in the gramophone's infancy the best-selling releases were comic and sentimental vaudeville songs, marching bands and novelty whistling acts, but given his grim prophecies it's ironic that Sullivan's own compositions – the songs and choruses of his hugely popular light operettas – were also amongst the first 'hits' of the medium.

As for 'serious' classical music, it was slow to appear on the market. Commercial considerations and snobbery were undoubtedly factors, but the immense difficulty of capturing the sound was also a stumbling block. A recording of Handel's grand oratorio *Israel in Egypt*, made at the Crystal Palace in 1888, is thought to be the earliest surviving music recording. One intrepid engineer, a certain Colonel Gouraud, sat in the press box balcony miles away from the stage with a tiny cylinder phonograph, its recording horn poked over the edge. Goodness knows how much of the two-hour work he originally managed to record, what with cylinders only lasting two minutes at best, but a fraction of it can still be heard today. To be perfectly honest, if you didn't know beforehand that it was 4,000 voices singing Handel you'd never be able to guess.

It's clear that in the earliest years the main purpose of recording classical music was an historical, archival one. Someone thought to capture Brahms, for example, playing his Hungarian Rhapsody in Vienna in 1889 – less than a decade before he died, but the awfulness of the sound is less important than the fact that it exists at all. Much the same might be said of the celebrity 'piano rolls' that famous composers and pianists made for use on 'pianolas' (player pianos), except that the quality of the sound is better as reproduced by the mechanical piano rolls. Piano rolls became popular around 1900 and thrived until the 1930s, when gramophone recording techniques had improved sufficiently to be able to capture the sound of the piano more faithfully. Players performed their pieces onto a special piano machine that simultaneously made perforations onto rolls of stiff paper so that one could then 'play them back' on another player piano machine, using the technology of the barrel organ. Sophisticated versions, like those of the New York-based Aeolian Company, could vary the volume and sensitivity of the playing enormously and even operate the sustain and soft pedals. Piano rolls survive, for example, of Mahler, Debussy, Grainger, Granados, Prokofiev, Stravinsky and Gershwin playing their own works.

There are also early phonograph or gramophone recordings of Kreisler, Grieg and Debussy (in Paris in 1904). Perhaps most fascinating of all, though, the most peculiar and most valuable historically, are the two sessions recorded in Rome in April 1902 by Alessandro Moreschi, the last living castrato. Castrati, you may remember, are male sopranos whose testicles are removed before puberty to prevent the dropping of the range to baritone or bass. Not surprisingly, this once popular technique died out in the nineteenth century. The recordings of Moreschi, by then in his sixties, contain some of the most haunting and – let's be honest – frightening sung performances known to man. They have been reissued recently on CD. That the practice and tone of Italian solo singing can have changed so dramatically in under a century, so that what was then considered breathtakingly beautiful, subtle and stylish, should to our ears sound like an appalling caterwauling, as if the act of castration were actually being performed during the recording session, is a sobering warning for all musicians currently engaged in the re-creation and study of 'authentic' music performances.

Owing to the appalling quality of the sound reproduction in the first twenty or so years of the gramophone's existence, musicians were slow to come forward and make recordings. Undeterred, recording pioneers thrust boldly on. In 1893, an Italian New Yorker by the name of Bettini entered the fray. On a machine of his own design he began recording the leading opera singers and instrumentalists of the Metropolitan Opera, duplicating copies to be sold at very high prices for the connoisseur end of the market. His unabashed advertised aim was to provide 'High-grade Records, High-class music, and only by Leading Performers and World-Famed Artists'. The Met's finest singers would pop into the studio and sing an aria onto cylinder phonographs: tragically hardly any of these recordings survived the destruction of Bettini's collection, housed in a warehouse in France, during the Second World War.

The relative success of Bettini's venture, however, showed that it was indeed possible to record and market classical artists as long as you could identify and target your audience, and your audience had plenty of disposable income. The 'specialist niche' record dealer was born in Bettini, a tradition that sprang unexpectedly back to life again in the 1980s when (relatively) inexpensive digital recording became available. The effect of the Internet, bringing niche market providers to their disparate audiences all over the world through instant digital sound transfer, will in due course I believe prove to be an even bigger revolution in the growth of audiences for the classical repertoire.

It is significant that Bettini stressed the higher quality of his recordings over the competition, acknowledging one of the obstacles to the growth of the classical audience. All record manufacturers knew that there was much to be done in this area and there is no doubt that the inadequacies of early recording equipment with regard to music were the prime cause of the successive technical improvements to the gramophone which still continue today.

Before electrical recording in the 1920s, the only way to record musicians was to have them stand as close as possible to a horn or funnel of some shape or size, in whatever arrangement was deemed practical, discovered mainly through trial and error. Upright pianos were sometimes put on high rostra to bring their soundboards into alignment with the mouth of the singer they were accompanying (pianos were notoriously difficult to record at all). In 1899 an acoustician from Frankfurt, Augustus Stroh, patented a special violin that could play much louder than a normal one for recording purposes, even if it did look somewhat eccentric (a trumpet horn stuck to a violin skeleton). Pieces of music were savagely cut and re-ordered to allow them to fit onto the two- or three-minute discs. This might have been all right for popular songs of three minutes' duration, but for a concerto or symphony of 30 minutes' length, the effect was brutal. Orchestrations were also altered, for example by omitting double basses and replacing them with tubas (whose sound cut through a little better), or by dispensing with timpani and percussion altogether, since they annihilated everyone else in range. Orchestral music was performed by a fraction of the number of players used on the concert platform, as the recording rooms were tiny and only those instruments closest to the 'horn' would be heard anyway. The first complete recording of a Beethoven symphony (the Fifth, needless to say) in 1913, by the Berlin Philharmonic, was recorded without basses or timpani and with a severely reduced string section. A more drastic solution was

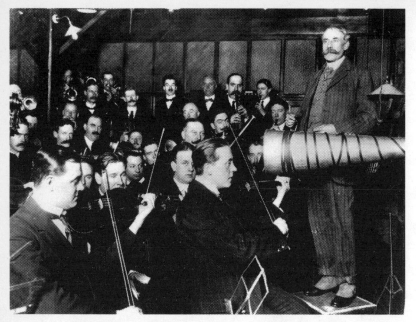

Elgar conducting his first recording – of *Carissima* – in 1914

simply to replace strings with brass and woodwind instruments altogether.

In the twenty years before 1900, the gramophone spread across Europe, with each country adding elements and modifications of their own. The French were quick to take up the new invention, and the brothers Pathé, having started with a coin-operated phonograph in the corner of their bistro near the Place Pigalle, soon moved into cylinder and player production themselves, their most popular model being 'Le Coq', the image of which became their trademark, as older viewers of the famous newsreels will recall. At their recording studios in the Rue de Richelieu they brought in both popular 'light' entertainers and the stars of the Opéra and Opéra-Comique. An enchanting innovation of their marketing was a sumptuous listening salon in the Boulevard des Italiens, where, by 1899, in palatial surroundings, one could, for 15 centimes, don compressed-air earphones and sample any one of 1,500 titles in the catalogue (in the cellar beneath them little men were actually putting the discs on for them to listen to!). In the end, though, the mass market only really came to classical music through the combination of an American engineer, whose family had come from Eastern Europe, working for a British company with an Italian artist. Recording, then as now, was an international pursuit.

In London, Émile Berliner's representatives had formed the Gramophone Company. It became world famous not only on account of its recording output but also because of a dog. Nipper, in a famous Francis Barraud painting called *His Master's Voice*, became one of the most recognised brands in the world. The Gramophone Company and Victor, its sister company in the States, were under no illusion that popular music was to be the real honeypot, but nevertheless they longed for respectability. This was something, they believed, that only classical music could bring. Like Bettini, the Gramophone Company tapped into a fashion amongst the bourgeoisie for grand opera, and sent scouts to find promising artistes in Italy.

Verdi had only recently died, in 1901, and his successors Mascagni, Leoncavallo and most of all Puccini, were alive and active. The Gramophone Company began a determined effort to ensnare the top operatic stars. They even started a special 'red' label for these records, to make them seem like champagne amidst the rest of the plonk on offer. But they were not only interested in the already-famous singers: their most successful breakthrough came with a young, virtually unknown artist from Naples – Enrico Caruso – who was to become the most famous singer in the world. With Caruso's rise to stardom, the gramophone was transformed from an interesting novelty for boffins into a populist worldwide phenomenon.

Enrico Caruso was one of seven children born to a working-class Neapolitan family living in the Via San Giovanello. He received his first singing instruction as a choirboy in a local

A Gramophone Company catalogue of 1905

church, and as a teenager he made a few lire every night singing favourite Neapolitan songs for the café customers on the harbour waterfront. He began work in a factory, but eventually he was able to turn professional with his outstanding voice. After a shaky debut in Naples – he vowed never to perform there again – he was invited to sing at the holiest of all opera's shrines, La Scala, Milan. It was here in March 1902 that Fred Gaisberg, the Gramophone Company's European representative, heard Caruso performing in Franchetti's popular opera *Germania*. Gaisberg offered the young unknown a deal to record ten arias for £100; Caruso duly accepted the offer, to the horror of Gaisberg's London office, which tried to forbid the spending of 'this exorbitant sum'. Gaisberg, however, backed his hunch, using his own money. That April, in Suite 301 in the Grand Hotel, Milan, the ten records were cut, beginning with 'Studenti, Udite' from *Germania*. Gaisberg went on to recoup his investment thousands of times over – and the records earned his company a fortune.

Most of the ten masters made on that occasion remain in perfect condition to this day. After their release, Caruso's fame spread dramatically throughout Europe and America. He made two recordings, in 1902 and 1907, of the aria 'Vesti la giubba', from Leoncavallo's opera *I Pagliacci*, which between them sold over a million copies. *I Pagliacci* was at this time a relatively new opera (it was given its first stage performance in 1892), based on a recent real-life criminal case. It's hard to find a modern equivalent for this – a modern opera being as commercially successful as *I Pagliacci*. Even the hit records released from the shows of Andrew Lloyd Webber are based on stories from the past (*Evita* is probably his most contemporary non-fiction subject). As for the work of contemporary 'classical' composers, the thought of Harrison Birtwistle writing an opera which included a million-selling song is, let's face it, laughable.

Caruso was to the early gramophone what Frank Sinatra or Maria Callas were to the LP, what Elvis Presley and the Beatles were to the 45-rpm 'single', and what Dire Straits and George Michael were to the compact disc: the 'software' of the music that drew listeners to the 'hardware' of the machines and materials. He was the first recording megastar, as much a household name in his day as Charlie Chaplin, prodigal son of another medium also in its infancy. Caruso's voice had a timbre and range that perfectly suited the limitations of the medium, it could soar and tremble with such strength and depth that the background hiss and the indistinct accompaniment were all but forgotten. To many people, hearing him scale the summits of high opera was both miraculous and moving and this was not just their first experience of the true potential of the gramophone but also a gateway to the whole classical repertoire. Edison's humble contraption was to become a universal gift with the popularity of Caruso, catapulting classical music out of the small, exclusive world it had hitherto known.

The Gramophone and Victor Companies were buoyed by Caruso's success. What's more, all the other top singers now wanted a piece of the action, hurriedly dropping their objections to the quality of the medium once they realised that it could make them rich. The female equivalent of Caruso was Nellie Melba, an Australian soprano with a peach of a voice and a good head for business, who held out until she got £1,000 – and her own unique label in passionate mauve.

The listening public grew relentlessly. By the beginning of the First World War something like a third of British homes had a phonograph or gramophone. The arrival of portable record players – first produced by Decca for use in First World War trenches – meant that music could not only be heard in the home, but just about anywhere.

Most of us have heard early 'shellac' recordings, and if we're honest, they usually sound as if someone is wailing incoherently to the accompaniment of a blizzard or at least a good fry-up. We are, though, generally hearing records that are extremely old and have been played and manhandled hundreds or even thousands of times. In fact, with the right equipment at the right speed, an unused copy of one of these early high-quality vocal recordings can sound astonishingly clear and enchanting. When early recordings are transferred on to

Enrico Caruso as the Duke of Mantua in Verdi's *Rigoletto*

CD for repackaging and marketing, the greatest care is taken to reduce the surface noise, which can be achieved in a number of ways. One method is to place the end of the horn

197

from which the music comes as far away from the actual needle and disc as possible. The specialist company Nimbus Records, for instance, have a playing horn about 12 foot long, so that the modern microphone picking up the sound is far enough away from the turntable not to hear the hiss and crackle of the stylus. The stylus itself might be made of soft-wood, so that its journey along the groove is as untraumatic for the disc as possible. In some cases the record itself may be 90 years old but is as new and fresh as the day it was released. In practice this means that huge collections are bought up in bulk to ensure that somewhere in the catalogue there will be some virgin discs. Varying the speed of the turntable until the voice sounds like a human being and not a chipmunk is a technique with an exact parallel in the restoration of early film; the manic and jerky movements of early twentieth-century film performers has nothing to do with their actual physical behaviour and everything to do with the speed of the film being incorrectly set.

The coming of the talkies radically transformed the movies, and the most important part of the technology that made synchronised sound possible came from radio – the electric microphone, first used in 1925. Not surprisingly, it was to have an equally dynamic effect on the recording industry.

Radio had emerged in the early 1920s. Apart from introducing the electric microphone to the recording world, it broadcast a wide range of music, so that many ordinary folk were exposed to classical music for the first time. What is more, certainly in Europe, it occasionally played more challenging contemporary music, or what was considered, believe it or not, unfamiliar 'early' music like Bach. Radio had a wider range of frequencies, better dynamics, and could play pieces in their entirety, so you didn't have to get up every four minutes and change the record.

Perhaps most notably of all, in Britain, the British Broadcasting Company, later Corporation, was founded in 1922, and the stated aim of its charter was to enhance the cultural life of the nation. Its commitment to the musical diet of its listeners was second to none, and the BBC even took over the

A native American Indian illustrates the volume problems
of early recorded sound

annual Promenade festival in London as a major showcase for
the world's finest music and musicians. Britain had been
described, rather cruelly, in the nineteenth century by the
super-musical Germans as the 'land without music' – a kind of
philistine's paradise. In fact the nationwide involvement of
amateur music-makers throughout the Victorian era would
probably have outstripped even Germany, but the comment
was no doubt directed at the professional arena. There were
certainly no British Beethovens, Wagners or Tchaikovskys.

Yet thirty years after the setting up of the BBC, Britain had turned itself into one of the world's chief musical centres with a capital city boasting more symphony orchestras than any other on earth. The contribution of the BBC in this change of attitude was pivotal.

As for the recording of classical music, the innovation of the electric microphone meant that at last the whole ensemble or orchestra could be heard – musicians didn't have to cluster around variously shaped horns and tubes, playing at full blast through pieces with as little subtlety and delicacy as they dared. Quieter instruments like the flute, mandolin and harp appeared as if by magic and the piano's wide range and tone came out of oblivion. The listener even had a fighting chance of hearing the bass line.

The electric microphone also revolutionised recording in the popular field. No longer needing to bellow into a tin funnel like a sports coach into a megaphone, singers like Bing Crosby could murmur intimately into the microphone, regardless of the strength of the accompanying band. 'Crooning' in a gentle and sentimental way with minimum effort made the singer seem more personal. From this moment on, popular singers developed their technique deliberately to exploit the microphone. Perhaps the most famous popular singer of the century, Frank Sinatra, was able to weave and linger around his accompaniment, stretch the rhythm mischievously and tease the song's melody precisely *because* of the rich, supportive power of the electric microphone. This was the aural equivalent of the cinema's close-up.

By contrast, opera singers continued to yell theatrically as if standing in front of 2,000 people, however close the microphone appeared to be. In recent years some have finally succumbed to the realities of the technology, but it has been a spectacularly slow learning curve. Why opera singers to this day are so resistant to the notion of subtle amplification of their voices in an opera house where they are competing with huge orchestral forces I do not know. The orchestral instruments have become louder and brighter (by design), the capacity of the halls larger, the ability of the audience to listen greatly reduced, yet the poor human voice is the same as it was in Mozart's day.

The advent of recorded sound vastly increased the audience for 'art' or 'serious' concert music, of course. If one adds to the equation the impact of broadcast sound and the sprouting of record clubs and subscription societies, the growth was incomparable with anything that had happened to music before. The great classical works from Mozart's operas to Brahms's symphonies had only ever been heard, and sporadically at that, by a tiny, educated, relatively well-off audience. But the huge new, egalitarian constituency for music naturally had different priorities from the courts and salons that had hitherto been the natural home of so much composition.

In the 1930s, relatively new music by composers like Prokofiev or even Ravel (who would nowadays be thought of as fairly 'easy' listening) would have seemed to many new gramophone owners like the sound from hell. A report of the première of Prokofiev's Second Piano Concerto is symptomatic of the general feeling, describing the audience as having been 'frozen with fright, hair standing on end'.*

Still, without Edison's invention most people would have gone a whole lifetime without hearing this music at all. At least they had the opportunity to be shocked by it.

The Second World War moved recording technology on with renewed vigour. The Japanese blockade of Malaysia had led to such an acute shortage of shellac (derived from those Malaysian beetles) that people in America could only be issued with new records if they brought old ones back. The American military were also using recycled shellac to coat the instrument panels of their bombers (it wasn't prone to condensation, apparently), putting further strain on the already short supply. Eager to find a replacement, the American record company Columbia developed a new plastic material – vinyl – no doubt to the huge relief of the beetles. Vinyl records were first issued commercially in 1948.

---

*Vyacheslav Gaurilovich Karatigin, quoted in Rita McAllister, 'Sergey Prokofiev', *New Grove Russian Masters*, 2, London, 1986, p. 118.

Not only was vinyl more resilient and flexible, it was also capable of supporting a 'microgroove' that meant that records could be played at a new speed of 33⅓ rpm and could thus contain more material. The Long Player had arrived. Finally, record listeners could hear something like 25 minutes of uninterrupted music. From day one, the LP seemed like a natural format for classical music in the way that the 45-rpm 'single' did for pop. The arrival of the LP encouraged everyone to update their record collections. The shellac '78' was consigned, albeit gradually, to the trashcan of history. With the LP came a great swathe of new repertoire and a host of new recording stars. This was the heyday, for example, of Maria Callas, the female successor to Caruso, who made a series of still-revered records, many of them at La Scala, Milan. Her performance of Puccini's Tosca, with the tenor Giuseppe Di Stefano and the baritone Tito Gobbi, is still considered by many buffs to be the finest operatic recording ever made. Like Caruso, Callas was made into a superstar by her recordings. The control and detail made possible by recording techniques meant that her vocal performances could be heard with absolute clarity, and the unusual passion of her interpretations was given an almost embarrassing intimacy.

Another key development also came from the Second World War. Captured German tape technology found its way to America, and sound, instead of being recorded onto a master disc – a tricky business at the best of times – could now be recorded onto magnetic tape. Different 'takes' of the same piece could now be sliced up and stuck together, and ever since the ability to cut tape was developed, classical music has become obsessed by the possibility of 'editing'. When you listen on record to the average Beethoven symphony, you're actually hearing hundreds of edited segments glued together; in an opera lasting two or more hours this might reach literally thousands of edits. Nowadays the process of 'cut and paste' is done by computers, but the principle is exactly the same. It is no exaggeration to say that a single note from one performance can replace a single note from another. With the recording of early or period instruments, the ability to stop and start hundreds of times has been a huge boon, since the instruments do not stay in tune with the stability and consistency we expect from modern instruments. You are in fact hearing 'period' music with 'period' instruments in 'authentic' editions thanks to state-of-the-art computer wizardry.

In some respects the editing revolution made things easier for musicians, who could redo their mistakes and wobbles as many times as they liked. On the other hand, an artificially high standard was being sought on record that couldn't possibly be matched in the concert hall. Either way, it led recorded music further than ever away from where it had started. The attempt to re-create as faithfully as possible the aural experience of the concert hall has been abandoned. What has emerged instead is the idea of a definitive performance of a particular piece, frozen in time – a false perfection, as it were. We have witnessed, since the advent of recording, a battle between the concept of music as a living, organic, breathing 'condition', ceaselessly reinventing and reprocessing itself, never static, never finished, and the concept of music as a *thing*, like a painting, sculpture, poem, or building. I believe no composers or performers before the twentieth century had to grapple with these conflicting views of music.

A further stage arrived with the development of stereophonic sound in the late 1950s and its marketing in the 1960s, when everyone began replacing their old mono LPs with stereo ones – indeed albums like the Beatles' *Sergeant Pepper's Lonely Hearts Club Band* made a special feature of the new technique. In the classical world, the stereo experience gave a greater sense of perspective and width to the sound, for example by laying a symphony orchestra across the two speakers from left to right, as if the listener were standing on the conductor's podium. Despite this, the private experience of listening to a recording was still very different from the communal one to be had in a concert hall.

To fuel the ever-growing demand for product, unlike the rock industry which favoured *new* artistes and composers, the classical sector began to trawl repertoire that reached further and further back in time. In the 60s and 70s, thanks to pioneers like David Munrow, Neville Marriner and Christopher Hogwood, early and baroque music found an enthusiastic new following. This rediscovery of lesser-known parts of the repertoire simply would not have happened without Edison's invention.

With every new improvement in the sound quality or format, a renewed project of recording and collecting began, and the central repertoire was re-recorded. This had two effects: it confirmed a sort of 'A' playlist of 'great' classical music of the past and it promoted a constant reassessment of the less central composers. The concept of composers being 'rediscovered' decades after their deaths (or even, in some cases, while they were still alive) and being repositioned on the ladder of fame is, with the possible exception of Mendelssohn's championing of Bach in the 1820s, a unique feature of the recorded age. The prominence of Mahler, Sibelius, Monteverdi and almost all music written pre-1600 in our classical mainstream is almost entirely due to this kind of reappraisal with ready reference to recordings of their music.

The twentieth century's preoccupation, through recordings, with a constantly updated living 'museum' of Western Music, resulted in a constant revision of our perception of the music of the past. This in turn led to a restless quest for the 'definitive' version, the 'perfect' interpretation, the search for 'authenticity'. It is as if modern artists were expected to paint their pictures actually inside the National Gallery and the Tate, alongside the masters of the past, whose reputations and achievements bear heavily down upon them, watching their every brush stroke. Prior to the arrival of recorded sound, the overwhelming majority of concerts would have included music of the present or recent past – it was the norm. The story of music-listening habits in the twentieth century, on the other hand, is more or less the triumph of the past over the present. Even a glance at current classical CD charts shows that our thirst for repackaged, recorded or edited antiquity far exceeds our interest in even the most popular of our contemporary 'classical' composers such as Glass, Nyman, Tavener or Górecki.

While mass audiences, though, were probably less likely to encourage the composition of new works (because they couldn't *own* them like a wealthy patron might – there was no vanity in the transaction), there is no reason to conclude that their taste, in the long run, was any less conservative than that of their aristocratic predecessors'. Intolerance to the unfamiliar and challenging is a pretty universal trait. But the public's tolerance was also severely tested in the first half of the twentieth century by trends in composition that tore up the rulebook of the previous 500 years. Modernism in music became a battleground whose combatants were prepared, it would seem, to fight to the death.

The avant-garde composers of the first sixty years of the twentieth century sought unapologetically to destroy the very language of European music as they found it. If that meant alienating audiences, driving them away from contemporary music in their millions, then so be it. Indeed, there was a school of thought throughout the musically grim decades that followed the Second World War which proposed that anything that *was* popular couldn't possibly be of value or interest. The smaller the audience, their logic ran, the more likely it was to be comprised of true believers who 'understood' the new music – almost as if the more offensive, austere or difficult a composition might be, the better chance it had of being 'real' music. Ironically, the very thing that such composers were escaping, namely widespread acceptance, was pursuing them through the medium of broadcasting, and ensuring that their alternative manifestos were as publicly proclaimed as possible. Without Cologne's ground-breaking public service radio station WDR, France's ORTF, or Britain's Third Programme' (Radio 3), composers like Pierre Boulez or Hans Werner Henze would have had a few hundred followers, if that, and disappeared into the mists of oblivion. By the 1990s contemporary classical music had reverted to its former role *within* the mainstream of the concert repertoire, with composers such as John Tavener, Arvo Pärt, John Adams, Philip Glass, Michael Nyman, Judith Weir, James MacMillan, Michael Torke, Toru Takemitsu and Henryk Górecki widely enjoyed.

One of the unique qualities of Western European music, as we have seen in an earlier chapter, is its system of notation. This enabled the separation of composers from performers (it wasn't compulsory, of course, and many composers did perform their own music) and it allowed the musical work to have a life and an existence of its own, not wholly dependent on the individual performer to remember or elaborate a given template. A piece was frozen in time on the page. However, with the advent of recorded sound, an improvised, un-notated performance on one night in one place *can* be preserved in time, it can and does become a Work of Art, a thing. Recording has been doing for non-Western 'ethnic' music and popular music what notation did for European classical music a thousand years ago: it has created fixed, definitive 'masters'. It is turning pop and jazz and blues and soul and techno and rap and reggae and Asian and Japanese and all the others into a living museum too. Where once a catchy, impulsive melody made up on the spot and enjoyed for an evening would die the next morning, never to be heard again, everything can now be captured for posterity. And attempts to discriminate between things that might be worth keeping and things that would be better off lost can be seen as patronising and presumptuous. At least 150 years ago, the very slowness of making a notated score of a piece of music meant that the creator had to live with it and think about it for a period of time before it was released to the world. Now a recording can be made instantaneously, even at the very point of creation.

What Thomas Alva Edison didn't predict was that his humble invention, when applied particularly to the unwritten music of African origin, was to change utterly the course of music history itself. As soon as portable recording machines became available, around 1900, intrepid engineers set off across the globe to capture the strange and wonderful sounds of music from other cultures. The aim may have been to widen the musical horizons of record and radio listeners, but this process also broadened the minds and triggered the imaginations of composers. Before the invention of recorded sound, if you wanted to hear a Magyar Folk Ensemble or a Raga band

David Fanshawe records the Luo tribe, Kenya

you'd have had to travel to Hungary or India to do so. After Edison's phonograph you could listen to the world's music in your own living room. In addition, composers and musicologists could analyse music in detail that had never been notated.

During the early 1900s, the Hungarian composer Béla Bartók took a phonograph and recorded the folk music of his native country as well as that of the Mediterranean and North Africa. He analysed these sources in great depth both for historical interest and as the starting point for many of his new compositions. It was, he said, like examining musical objects under a microscope. 'Classical' composers like Bartók learnt many things from the study of ethnic music through recording, not least of which were ways of treating the musical language itself that were less bound by the old rules of harmony, rhythm and melody. All composers started to 'hear' music differently.

Over the course of the century, one form of music above all others came to exert its influence on European music. The rhythm, soul and energy of African music, as carried across to the Americas by two million slaves, gave birth to wave after wave of new musical forms and styles. From African roots came ragtime, gospel, blues, jazz, bebop, rock & roll, rhythm & blues, soul, and more recently hip-hop, house, garage, rap and jungle. Recording took the music of black America out of tiny clubs and bars, out of remote neighbourhood churches, out of deprived ghettos and into the homes and lives of the rest of the planet. It did the same to the magical, sensuous rhythms of Latin America. The music of the poorest people on earth became big business. Sooner or later, composers were going to succumb to the power of ethnic music. Notwithstanding some half-hearted jazz pastiche in the 1920s and 30s by Stravinsky and Ravel, the true impact of this revolution has only really been felt in the last thirty years.

The English composer David Fanshawe toured Africa, the Middle East and the Pacific extensively in the 1970s, compiling a vast library of tapes of tribal music, much of which will no longer exist within one or two generations. There is an archival purpose here, but also a creative one: his *African Sanctus* mixes Western and African music openly, combining his tapes with live instruments and singers. Other contemporary composers have been affected more subtly. The work of Philip Glass and Michael Nyman is unthinkable without the rhythmic energy and the simpler harmonies of popular music. However, the influence has not been totally one-way. Cross-fertilisation between the two traditions had already begun in the 1960s.

A much larger constituency of African-American musicians had had 'classical' training than it was customary to admit until relatively recently. From Fats Waller and Duke Ellington to Aretha Franklin and Stevie Wonder the harmonic language and keyboard conventions of old-fashioned European music can be clearly heard. Stevie Wonder's landmark double album *Songs in the Key of Life* is a superb example of the interplay between these traditions. One moment we are riveted by the hypnotic dance pulse of 'I wish', the next being lilted from side to side by the keyboard strings of 'Village Ghetto Land' as if Joseph Haydn himself were at the Yamaha CS-80 (another writer, 'Byrd' is credited in this track though I don't know if it's the sixteenth-century English composer William Byrd or someone else). White artists like Frank Zappa, Brian Eno, Mike Oldfield and Keith Emerson used the structures and sounds of classical music to inspire their albums. Even the Beatles tapped into this well for their influential *Sergeant Pepper's Lonely Hearts Club Band.*

Meanwhile, avant-garde composers from a classical background were engaged in experiments with sound and technology that were to have an equally profound effect on popular music. In the 1950s and 60s, John Cage and Steve Reich in America, Luciano Berio in Italy, Pierre Boulez in France and Karlheinz Stockhausen in West Germany pioneered the introduction of electronic music, of synthesisers, and perhaps most crucially of all, of sampling. They probably don't know it, but all the DJs in the world are now mixing dance music with the help of these techniques.

Digital sampling is the lovechild of recording and music. Few composers have been as intrigued by its possibilities and as key to its development as the brilliant New Yorker, Steve Reich. His seminal piece *It's Gonna Rain* of 1969 uses tape samples of spoken phrases again and again against a musical background. The rhythmic repetition of the speech makes one think of contemporary black dance music, in particular rap, and yet Reich's piece pre-dates the arrival of these techniques in pop by nearly twenty years. For me the most important and moving work to attempt the blend of speech, tape and live performance is his 1988 masterwork, *Different Trains*, composed for the Kronos Quartet. Here the on-stage string quartet plays along with pre-recorded tapes of themselves which provide a rhythmic underscore, but in addition the musical material itself is derived directly from recordings of speech. That is, the musical phrases are composed by imitating the patterns and rhythms of people talking. You hear the voice speaking, then the string instruments responding.

In the first movement, the sampled voices are those relating to train journeys Reich made as a child in the early 1940s,

Steve Reich in his Broadway studio, New York, 1992

travelling by train from New York to Los Angeles between his two separated parents on either coast. We hear his governess reminiscing about the journeys and a retired Pullman porter working the same line. In the second movement, we hear the voices of Holocaust survivors talking of their very different experiences on the appalling train journeys they were forced to make in Europe at the same time during the Second World War. The third and final movement of *Different Trains*, 'After the War', is an attempt to reconcile the painful memories of the past with the present. Few contemporary composers have managed as effectively to marry such ideas with musical techniques so full of originality and promise, defying the old musical boundaries.

Reich himself talks of electronic music as the urban folk music of our time. He believes that music is returning to its original condition – one in which the divisions between 'classical' and 'popular' music did not exist. In recent years, record companies have paid lip service to the notion of 'crossover' music. What they mean, though, is one artist symbolically crossing the floor of the record store to plunder the audience of another artist. Kennedy playing Hendrix, Vanessa Mae playing Bach with a drum machine, symphony orchestras playing Queen songs, tenors pretending to be football stars, and so on. They do not mean crossover in the Steve Reich sense, that is, the true collaboration of idea A with style B to create form C. Reich is engaged in a creative – not commercial – crossover. Reich's vision of an urban contemporary music that knows no boundaries is not shared by all classical music lovers, but it is a hell of a sight more challenging and plausible than the marketing efforts of ailing record companies.

Even as I write, the tradition of European classical music that we've been following in this book is being absorbed into a much bigger mainstream – one that is overwhelmingly dominated by popular music. Music historians of the future might describe this as the Age of Convergence. Western European classical music isn't dead, but like a cleverly mutating DNA gene, it is transforming itself and cross-fertilising with other forms right in front of our eyes. What we are witnessing is the meltdown of previously rigid musical compartments and styles, a process we owe principally to Edison's big bang – the invention of recorded sound.

AN EPILOGUE

Alles muss sich ändern

(Everything must change)

Moving from one century or millennium to another has put us in a mood of appraisal and prediction. The appraisal bit is relatively easy. I am an enthusiastic admirer of ethnic – 'world' – music, indeed I sit on the board of Folkworks, an organisation devoted to promoting the traditional music of the British Isles – but it's hard not to see Western classical music as a wider, and even richer inheritance. No other culture has an equivalent to the constantly evolving, sophisticated, notated tradition that stretches from the first harmony in around AD 1000 to John Adams in AD 2000. No other culture has attempted anything like the extended, multi-layered architectural structures in the symphonies of, say, Haydn or Sibelius, or the operas of Wagner or Janáček. No other culture has spent over a thousand years adding to, refining, modifying and enlarging its stock of musical instruments, nor found ways of recording itself. No other culture has cracked the seemingly impossible task of building an interlocking tuning system for all instruments to play in all keys.

All these things make this cultural bequest unique. This is an historical matter, not a qualitative one. Classical music is not 'better' than popular music, but it has been developing from its raw state for much longer and it has been more ambitious in its goals. Indeed, most contemporary popular music in the West owes as much to a classical heritage as it does to African roots. First there are songs that engage in a kind of pastiche of classical style for effect, like Björk's 'It's Oh So

Quiet', the Verve's 'Bitter Sweet Symphony', Sinéad O'Connor's cover version of 'success has made a failure of our home', Embrace's 'All You Good Good People', the Beatles' 'Eleanor Rigby,' Queen's 'Bohemian Rhapsody', Sting's 'An Englishman in New York' or Stevie Wonder's 'Village Ghetto Land'. Then there are direct collaborations between classical and popular artists, such as Elvis Costello's project with the Brodsky Quartet, *The Juliet Letters*. In the 1970s there was a fashion for 'epic' rock concept albums from bands like Yes, Emerson, Lake & Palmer and Pink Floyd, all of which betrayed classical training and inspiration in their arrangements. Alongside this trend can be placed Rick Wakeman's grandiose efforts for multiple keyboards, such as *Journey to the Centre of the Earth* and (I'm afraid) *The Six Wives of Henry the VIII*, Mike Oldfield's hugely successful quasi-orchestral *Tubular Bells*, and the concept comeback album of the 1980s, Jeff Wayne's *The War of the Worlds*.

While these examples demonstrate an overt allegiance to classical scale, style and orchestration, they are as nothing compared to the impact on the rock catalogue of the harmonies and melodic shapes of European concert and sacred music. If you analyse the melody and harmony of a pop song written in the period 1960–2000 and cross-check it against a song written by Mozart or Schubert, there isn't a chord or phrase that would shock or alarm these two songwriters. Once you strip away the contemporary production values – the electronic instruments and drum patterns – the average pop song, at the piano or guitar, is not that different in its choice of chords and melodies from an aria of the eighteenth century. The fashion for ornamentation and the singing style has changed, but the predictable Intro-Verse-Chorus-Verse-Chorus (repeated)-Coda form of the songs is similar if not identical. While some twentieth-century *classical* music would give Mozart or Schubert a nervous breakdown (because it has developed away from their style so much as to be almost unrecognisable as orchestral music as they would have understood it), the majority of *popular* songs would pose no difficulty. This is partly to do with issues of 'tonality'

– whether or not the music still obeys the comfortable old rules of key and note-organisation (like all popular music does, slavishly) or whether it has broken away with the avant-garde to redefine the nature of sound altogether.

It is possible to see parallels here with modern art: 'serious', museum and gallery art spent much of the twentieth century reinventing painting and sculpture to challenge the accepted notion of what a piece of art might be. By contrast, popular art in magazines, newspapers, books, on street corners, on the Internet, on TV, video and film has continued relentlessly to obey all the old rules of figurative and representational art. The newer form of photography, like the newer form of pop music, more often than not conforms to conservative values in its choice of subject and framing.

Right now, at the cutting-edge of dance music, there is a movement to deconstruct the familiar sounds and forms of music, to employ 'non-musical' sounds as a basis for rhythmic or even melodic patterns – a trend that saw its first manifestation among avant-garde classical composers of the 1950s and 60s (Stockhausen, Berio, Cage and Boulez in particular). But this dance music itself is on the fringe: the mainstream is still firmly anchored in old-fashioned Western 'tonality' – indeed, one of pop music's most remarkable features is its obsessive curling back on itself. In the 1990s, Oasis quite self-consciously re-created the style of the Beatles, down to minute details of sound and instrumentation. Their 1960s borrowing was mirrored by many other groups and this fad was followed, not surprisingly, with a rediscovery of the disco music of the 1970s, particularly the soundtrack of the movie *Saturday Night Fever*.

The single biggest contribution to the traffic between the classical tradition and twentieth-century popular music, though, has been through hymns: hymns and religious songs that travelled the world with European colonialism for 400 years, carrying their Lutheran harmonies with them wherever they went. At the very source of the rivers Pop, Rock and Soul lies the 12-bar Blues, whose chord patterns (moving between the basic I-IV-V triads) derive in roughly equal measure from

African tribal call-and-response chants and the simple triadic chords of missionary hymns. I believe that the marriage of the two traditions, African and European, that takes place in popular music is something to celebrate. That the hideous inhumanity of slavery should have been turned by African and Caribbean peoples – with typical generosity of spirit – into a magnificent cultural gift can only leave Europeans like myself feeling humbled. Even the missionary hymns – our contribution to the recipe – came laden with intolerance, bigotry and compulsion, however well-meaning the initial motivation was, whereas the tribal songs came out of an impulse of hope and redemption.

The canon of classical music we are bequeathing to the next millennium is impressive. If we listen to Mozart's or Verdi's *Requiems*, Monteverdi's or Rachmaninoff's *Vespers*, Vivaldi's or Poulenc's *Glorias*, Beethoven's or Mahler's Ninth Symphonies, Tchaikovsky's or Sibelius's Violin Concertos, Dvořák's or Elgar's Cello Concertos, Schumann's or Khachaturian's Piano Concertos, Pergolesi's or Szymanowski's *Stabat Maters*, it is hard to believe that this was the same civilisation responsible for the Inquisition, the Somme and the Nazi Holocaust. Yet if all the above masterpieces were somehow suddenly lost, Western music could invent itself anew within hours thanks to the brilliance and logic of its systems of notation, tuning, harmony, instrumentation and structure.

Looking at what happens next is a much tougher assignment.

The most pressing problem is what to do about live performance. Since the advent of easily available CDs and high-quality digital broadcasting, the case for going to a live orchestral concert on the grounds of richness of sound has been terminally undermined. Though it is undoubtedly exciting to hear the wondrous fullness of a symphony orchestra in the flesh, at most concert venues the sound is quieter and gentler than on home audio systems or personal stereos. Furthermore, at a live concert the poor orchestra is competing with a hubbub of bronchitic, unmuffled coughing, fidgeting, rustling and murmuring.

A modern audience enters a concert hall with quite different expectations from their Victorian predecessors. With no television or cinema, a shorter working day (for the middle classes), a lower ambient level of urban noise, an education obsessed with concentration, discipline and attention, a Victorian audience might settle down to a concert lasting four or five hours. A higher proportion of the people there would have had a basic musical training and a piano at home that they actually played. Their concert halls reflected the importance attached to culture – huge, grand, confident buildings that provided decorative, palatial surroundings. The modern music lover, on the other hand, often enters a concert hall in a rush. We have lamentably short attention spans, we are impatient and restless. Our greater height and girth makes regimented seating with minimum legroom uncomfortable, and we have been spoilt by TV and film close-ups so that we want to be able to see the faces of our performers. Yet despite these social changes, the classical concert continues blindly as before. Orchestras shuffle on stage, apparently oblivious to the audience, sporting drab blacks and tuxedos, reminding us that once upon a time at the Esterházy Palace musicians wore the same uniforms as the waiters and porters.

Even some of us who *did* grow up being introduced to the glories of classical music find live concerts devoid of the energy, urgency, passion or wit found in other cultural pursuits. If movie-goers were expected to see films in the same way as their 1900 predecessors – with poor or no sound, flickering black and white images, and subjects that addressed the concerns of the 1890s, they too might not go to the cinema in the numbers they do.

Modern concert halls need to be less like airport lounges, devoid of atmosphere, charm or humanity, and more like somewhere you would choose to spend an evening. No wonder people prefer concerts by candlelight in churches or at stately homes with firework displays: at least they have an interest and value to offer the eye. The truth is that audiences do not care one iota who a symphony orchestra's oboe or cello players are, but they will pay good money to see a star soloist,

'He'll be a riot at the Queen's Hall.'
Cartoon from *Night and Day*, London

a star conductor or a star singer. And you know what? They're right. They're right to want star quality, because that way the concert experience might be transformed by personal charisma, and the music allowed to burn its way into our heads. The fact of being in a room with 2,000 people and a world-class celebrity quickens the pulse of an audience. It is an event, a one-off, an evening to remember, a moment to have been *there*. Students wouldn't stay up all night queuing for tickets, use up their precious beer money or suffer the indignity of being squashed cattle-like into some hideous hangar of a venue to see 'some musicians' playing the hits of Pulp – they do it to see Pulp *themselves*, to be in the room with Jarvis Cocker and tell their mates afterwards what it was like. This is the modern experience of live culture. It is a shared event or it is nothing.

Classical music is not a compulsory part of our growth as people, it is a wonderful bonus, and it is high time classical musicians woke up to the reality that they are a sector of the entertainment industry. The beauty and value of the music is beyond question: what is being challenged is the stagnation in live performance of the classical repertoire. What is the point of London having four subsidised symphony orchestras all playing the same nineteenth- and early twentieth-century pieces again and again? Why have so few performing groups responded to the initiatives so effectively presented by the Californian string quartet Kronos? Kronos dress to perform and sometimes change outfits during a concert to suit a changed mood, they use lighting effects and colours, they play music from every conceivable genre and make it their own, they commission new works and promote them enthusiastically around the world like a rock band might do with new material. Kronos rearrange music, setting pieces side by side for effect that have never been linked before, and they surf the world's music for quirky ideas and fresh ways of approaching their programmes. They do not patronise their listeners by assuming they are familiar with the 'great' chamber works of 'great' composers, they are irreverent and cheeky, they take liberties with the repertoire and seem to enjoy what they do enormously. They talk to their audience in a relaxed, friendly way, engaging with the people who have come to hear them as if the interaction between players and listeners really matters. All these things are straightforward, undramatic improvements to the performance of classical music, yet hardly anyone else has seen fit to adopt such methods. When promoters try to bring new listeners to orchestral or operatic music, enhancing the experience with PA systems, open-air picnic concerts, themed programmes or unfamiliar, unusual venues they are often seen as cheapening or dumbing-down the content, as if the 'family' concert were some kind of gimmick.

Why, when one goes to a concert, are there so few surprises? Surely one reason the BBC's annual Promenade Festival at the Albert Hall is so successful is because so many unexpected things have taken place at Prom concerts over the years that audiences don't know what will happen next. Someone may get sick at the last minute and a member of the audience may take their part; a famous foreign orchestra with a great reputation may turn out to be not as gripping as the National Youth Orchestra who played the night before. Revelations and discoveries are made every year, accumulating a library of reminiscence, gossip, myth, legend and anecdote that belong not to the music but to the people who are experiencing it. In short, the audience has a real role to play. They are visible, vocal, opinionated, volatile and committed. Like fans at a rock show they are truly interacting with and making a difference to the musical performance. They have a status denied most audiences in classical music.

Yet even the Proms are trapped in a time warp that assumes when we say 'music' we mean 'classical music of the European tradition'. The repertoire – admittedly more eclectic than anything else on offer – is nevertheless largely made up of the 'great' pillars of the romantic era interspersed with the kind of 'contemporary' music (by white men in middle age) that only specialists in the field (white middle-aged music critics) have identified as important.

Classical music is now a part of the overall picture, not its centre; it has become a highly specialised branch of the mainstream of popular Western music. Its power and drama are part of the scenery of our lives – in films, commercials, television programmes and trailers classical music is used to great effect, especially when the mood is one of gravitas, high passion or suspense. There are ways classical music moves and excites us that popular music still cannot provide.

I was educated as a chorister in New College Choir, Oxford. The choir school environment is singular to say the least. I was surrounded by other musical, well-motivated, bright children who like me sang every night of the week – to a frighteningly high standard – 500 years' worth of sacred choral music as if it was the most ordinary pursuit in the world. Very few people who have had this experience either forget or regret it: our childhood was saturated by music and a sense of historical continuity. In some English cathedrals the uninterrupted tradition of choral singing is 800 years old. This tradition has few counterparts elsewhere in the world.

There are vestiges of the old way in isolated pockets of Europe, like in the Lutheran Thomaskirche in Leipzig, Bach's church, where the choir school was maintained even during the days of the DDR (though the boys were removed from the service when not actually singing Bach's Masses and motets lest they become brainwashed by the opiate of Christianity). In Protestant Scandinavia and North America, the choral tradition has been modified to suit modernised democracies (adult mixed-voice choirs generally replacing single-gender choirs with children), and though these communities often vigorously support their many excellent choirs, few would dispute the seniority of the English tradition.

And yet the English tradition is gradually fading away. One reason given for its slow demise – the introduction of girls – may cause controversy and alarm within the church-music world but is a red herring. The truth is that parents no longer want to hand over their seven- or eight-year-old children to someone else to educate and discipline; the choir school ethos is powerful and mysterious and many modern parents find it threatening and strange. Boys of ten nowadays are not used to the kind of concentration required to read at sight – without a mistake – a Mass by Palestrina at ten o'clock on a Sunday morning, and many parents have decided (perhaps understandably) that this is too intense and pressurised a lifestyle for their children. Another pressure is the general shift amongst boys away from artistic, sensitive occupations like music. In Western society all children are encouraged to have the tastes, hobbies, musical preferences and attitudes of urban adolescents. In such an atmosphere, a twelve-year-old boy marching off to choir practice feels vulnerable and marginalised. How can the choir school phenomenon survive that kind of battering?

It has survived for 800 years thus far. Is it going to fail, now, at the last fence? I believe it is of sufficient worth, that the best choirs are of such a world-class standard, that it could indeed soldier on against the tide of the majority culture. But even with changes in attitude to the development of young boys that would allow them to pursue non-macho activities with impunity, there is still one outstanding threat: the possibility that those remaining corners of the Anglican Church where the old-fashioned cathedral choral style is still tolerated might abandon it in favour of a pop-based, participatory style of sung worship. Or in the pejorative slang, go happy-clappy. Cathedral choirs with their own schools attached are expensive, and while their gorgeous singing may lure music lovers and tourists into the congregation, they don't bring in true converts and young believers. This style of singing, so the argument goes, has no evangelical or missionary purpose to it. The old-style Anglican choirs sometimes sing music in Latin, some of which is inherited from the Catholic past, they sing complex, multi-layered Renaissance anthems and sophisticated settings of the psalms and canticles that do not invite audience participation. They give the impression of putting on a concert as performers, not sharing God's Word as communicants.

This view prevailed in Catholic France in the middle of the twentieth century and to some extent everywhere in the Roman Church in the century before. In France, the dismemberment of the cathedral choir tradition has been complete: it has vanished without trace. Despite the celebrated choristers at the Abbey of Montserrat in Catalonia, one or two exempted foundations in England, and some fine children's choirs in Poland and the Czech Republic, the Catholic Church in Europe has abandoned its ancient choral style, replacing it with either no music at all or music of droning banality. This fate awaits the choral tradition in Britain, should the view of Anglican modernisers prevail.

The urge to do away with old-style choirs is understandable, indicative of a cultural movement away from the esoteric, refined style that produced the turbulent geniuses of Palestrina, Bach, Handel and Mozart, and towards a more inclusive music that carries none of the baggage and heaviness of the classical repertoire. This conflict between populist and traditionalist is one that runs right through the twentieth century like a *leitmotif.*

I have bemoaned the *lack* of populism and modernisation in the performance of the concert repertoire, yet defend – by implication – the right of church musicians to continue their old-fashioned ways, resisting modernisation. How do I answer this apparent contradiction?

I think that every time classical musicians convene on a stage in front of an audience they should treat it as a special event. There should be ceremony and ritual, a visual feast to accompany the ear, colour, light and warmth and a priority given to addressing the people sitting there with them. This is the experience of opera at the beginning of the twenty-first century, and we can see how full and successful opera houses are. Demand vastly outstrips supply for great swathes of any opera house's season. These are exhilarating affairs – people look forward to them enormously, booking well in advance and making a special evening of it – going to the opera is a real *treat*, and no one expects to go every night of the week or even every week of the year. You cannot replicate the live experience at home by listening to the sound only through your stereo. It is unlike the cinema, more audacious in scale than the theatre and, with its darkened auditorium and suspended reality, more involving than a concert. Opera is full of surprises. The world has changed so much since, say, Handel wrote his operas and oratorios, but the music he wrote for them is as beautiful and accessible now as it was in the eighteenth century. Each generation should find for itself the antiques in the attic: in opera, pieces can be rediscovered by inventive or unexpected staging, tailored to the tastes and sensibilities of a different era. There is no danger whatever that the music will wither and die; on the contrary, more music by more composers of greater diversity is available now than ever before. This is how it should be – classical music must continue to grow and change and breathe. But just as opera has benefited from enlightened and provocative staging, a way has to be found for symphonic concert music to rediscover the live performance. The renewed interest in opera teaches us, despite its expense and despite the cinematic alternative, that modern audiences want their night out to be distinctive and different. They want to be swept off their feet by something so demanding of attention, so visually arresting

The choir of Christ Church, Oxford, performing Howard Goodall's
Missa Aedis Christi, 1993

and so sure of its own power that they leave the building
changed. An opera, a rock concert or a film is a memorable,
pulse-quickening event designed to stimulate the eye as well as
the ear. This is also true of the ancient ritual of a great cathedral choir performing Evensong or Sunday Mass. Here too is
ceremony, symbolism and drama.

The sheer complexity of the music sung by the thirty young
men and children would be enough to capture one's imagination, even if it were not in the setting of a darkened, hushed,
medieval cathedral with candles lighting the faces of the
singers. They proceed through the ancient liturgy with weird
ease and concentration, giving voice to music written when
religion was the dominating cultural force for an entire continent. Giovanni Palestrina, the Vatican's most brilliant musical
mind, charged with laying down the musical vocabulary of

the Counter-Reformation, can be heard side by side with William Byrd or Thomas Tallis, torn but inspired composers of the new, excommunicated English Church. Bach, the unparalleled master of the Lutheran revolution, heard side by side with Samuel Sebastian Wesley, great-nephew of the founder of Methodism, whose grandiose, tuneful anthems were the staple of every English cathedral of the Victorian age. The music may not have the sweep and romantic abandon of Beethoven, or of Tchaikovsky's symphonies, nor the singing have the power and range of the nineteenth-century orchestra, but a musical drama is unfolding nonetheless. Most of all, the layperson's reaction to the passion of sacred music is that it is an unfathomable mystery. It is beautiful, distant and ethereal, yet it is occurring in front of one's very eyes, metres away, coming (expertly) out of the mouths of children. A mystery.

I want choral music like this to continue to be performed because I believe it to be spiritually powerful and emotionally engaging. Its relative inaccessibility is part of its strength – great sacred music is attempting to fathom and express the supernatural and divine. Likewise I believe that the immense catalogue of secular classical music we are handing on to the next century is of inestimable value because the power of Mozart's or Stravinsky's or Adams's music is one of the few things we have left in our culture which cannot adequately be explained. There are no easy answers to account for being moved to tears by notes on a page, or of being stirred to anger and action, or being comforted in our loneliness. It is a mystery how Rachmaninoff's flowing melodies and ripe harmonies make people feel romantic and amorous, or how Ravel's *Boléro* conjures up sexiness. It is a mystery the way Shostakovich manages to express all Russia's Stalinist agony without losing the essentially unbreakable spirit of his people at the same time. It is a mystery why Elgar's 'Nimrod' move-ment from the *Enigma Variations* makes one think of England when he was writing to articulate his love for a German friend, or why Tippett's use of Negro spirituals in his 1945 secular oratorio *A Child of Our Time* so perfectly captures the desper-ation of the victims of Nazism in the Second World War.

This sense in which music seems to come from beyond the frontiers of our knowledge and understanding is key to its place in our lives. If musicians are able to remind themselves of this truth when they perform the music of the last 1,000 years, then there is an important role for classical music in the cacophonous musical highway that lies ahead. It can and should be an alternative, a precious reminder of what we were before we plugged in and turned the volume up, before we switched on the TV and became part of a noisy, global party. When we *don't* feel like dancing, speeding down the *autoroute* or white-water rafting, all this thoughtful, miraculous music will be waiting patiently there for us.

'A Musician's Dress', a 'grotesquerie' by Larmessin, showing a range of now obsolete instruments including the tall one-stringed fiddle called a trompette marine, and the serpent.

ACKNOWLEDGEMENTS
AND FURTHER READING

First I would like to thank the indefatigable team with whom I made the TV series *Howard Goodall's Big Bangs*: producer Paul Sommers; four brilliant directors: David Jeffcock, Rupert Edwards, Justine Kershaw and Alex Marengo; and the extraordinarily talented Sarah Spencer, Associate Producer. The impact of her research in particular is felt throughout this book. The series was commissioned by Helen Sprott, shepherded elegantly by Janey Walker and seen to conclusion by Jan Younghusband at Channel 4. Veterans of the TV series also include Caroline Bourne, Colin Case, and my excellent personal assistant Ali Whitehouse. The director of music at Christ Church, Oxford, Stephen Darlington, was a constant source of expertise and enthusiasm, and Ros Rigby and Alastair Anderson at Folkworks kept me on the World Music straight and narrow. A special mention should go to my icon, John Adams, who gave his time and intelligence in equally generous measure.

My total lack of experience in the book-writing field has been plastered over superbly by the book's editor, Jenny Uglow, who has always been gentle when rough would have sufficed, and Alison Samuel's enthusiasm and commitment for the project has been thoroughly inspiring.

When I travelled France looking for places to compose, more often than not I would end up as a guest of the embarrassingly hospitable Anthony, Kathy and Oscar Pye-Jeary. I did much of the fair copy of my *Missa Aedis Christi* as gatecrasher on their family holiday. Jo Laurie gave me a lifelong respect for Jewish tradition and history, and my dad Geoffrey's piano-playing gave me a love of 78s and Fats Waller. The teachers who inspired my first compositions were Paul Drayton, David Stone, David Gatehouse and Robin Nelson; the choirmaster who made me into a chorister was David Lumsden. Thanks also to Stewart Pollens, Courtney Pine, Steve Reich, David Fanshawe, Simon Lole, Norman White, Gary Thomas, Oliver Taplin, Paula Bezzutti, Andrew Olleson, Barry Makin, Karl Schmuki, Orazio Occhialini, Padre Alessandro Barbari, Bodil Bundgaard Rasmussen, Simon Preston, Melvyn Bragg, Charles Hart, Dominic Combe, Geoff Smith, Susanne Lundeng, Cat Ledger, Stuart Williams, Peter Bennett-Jones and Caroline Chignell.

In the course of a year making a TV series and book on a big subject like this I have read and referred to hundreds of books, but a few stand out which I will list for both further reading and acknowledgement.

GENERAL
The New Grove Dictionary of Music and Musicians
Music: A Very Short Introduction by Nicholas Cook, Oxford University Press, 1998
The Rough Guide to Classical Music, London, 1998
The Rough Guide to World Music, London, 1994
A History of Western Music by Donald J. Grout and Claude V. Palisca, 5th edition, W. W. Norton & Co., London and New York, 1996
The Hutchinson Concise Dictionary of Music (Open University), ed. Barrie Jones, 1998

NOTATION
Man & Music: Antiquity and the Middle Ages, ed. James McKinnon, Macmillan Press, 1990
Gregorian Chant and the Carolingians by Kenneth Levy, Princeton University Press, 1998

Strunk's Source Readings in Music History Volume 2: The Early Christian Period and the Latin Middle Ages, ed. James McKinnon, W. W. Norton & Co., London and New York, 1998

OPERA

Viva la Libertà! by Anthony Arblaster, Verso, London, 1992

Opera and the Culture of Fascism by Jeremy Tambling, Oxford University Press, 1996

Claudio Monteverdi: Orfeo by John Whenham, Cambridge University Press, 1986

The Rough Guide to Opera, London, 1997

The definitive and scholarly edition of the music of *Orfeo* and the 1610 *Vespers* we used was that of Clifford Bartlett.

EQUAL TEMPERAMENT

Internet articles:

'An Introduction to Historical Tunings' by Kyle Gann, 1997: Kgann@earthlink.net

'Temperament: A Beginner's Guide' by Stephen Bicknell: http://www.users.dircon.co.uk/~oneskull

'The Well or Equal Tempered Clavier?' by Gordon Rumson Madison, Wisconsin, April 1993

'Essays on Music Theory: Pitch, Tuning, and the Physics of Musical Tone' by Gilbert Hock van Dijke, Rotterdam 1997: Hoekvandijke@bnt.fgg.eur.nl

'Pythagorean Tuning and Medieval Polyphony' by Margo Schulter, June 1998: mschulter@value.net

'Mathematics and Music' by Christoph J. Scriba, reproduced in *Mathematical Review* (American Mathematical Society), 1990, online at MathSciNet.

PIANO

The Pianoforte in the Classical Era by Michael Cole, Clarendon Press, Oxford, 1998

The Early Pianoforte by Stewart Pollens, Cambridge University Press, 1995

The Cambridge Companion to the Piano, ed. David Rowland, Cambridge University Press, 1998

The Oxford Companion to Musical Instruments by Anthony Baines, Oxford University Press, 1992

Musical Instruments and Their Decoration by Christoph Rueger, David & Charles (Edition Leipzig), 1982 and 1986

Pleasures for Both Eye and Ear by Eszter Fontana & Birgot Heise, translated by A. C. Johnson, Musikinstrumenten-Museum der Universität Leipzig, 1998

The Letters of Mozart and his Family, ed. Emily Anderson, Macmillan Press, 1989

Selected Letters of Gustav Mahler, ed. Knud Martner, Faber & Faber, London, 1979

CHOSEN PEOPLE

Europe: A History by Norman Davies, Oxford University Press, 1998

Jews: The Essence and Character of a People by Arthur Hertzberg and Aron Hirt-Manheimer, HarperCollins, New York, 1998

Great Jews in Music by Darryl Lyman, Jonathan David Publishers Inc., New York, 1986

Mahler: A Documentary Study by Kurt Blaukopf, Thames & Hudson Ltd, London, 1976

RECORDED SOUND

From Tinfoil to Stereo: The Acoustic Years of the Recording Industry 1877–1929 by Walter L. Welch and Leah Brodbeck-Stenzel-Burt, University Press of Florida, 1994

Enrico Caruso: My Father and My Family by Enrico Caruso Jnr and Andrew Furkas, Amadeus Press, 1990

RECORDINGS

Allegri 'Miserere', Choir of Westminster Abbey, ARCHIV 415 517-2

Goodall Choral Works, Choir of Christ Church Cathedral, Oxford, ASV CD DCA 1028

Monteverdi 'L'Orfeo', conducted by John Eliot Gardiner, ARCHIV 419 250-2

Adams 'Nixon in China' ELEKTRA-NONESUCH 979 177-2

Mahler 'Ich bin der Welt abhanden gekommen', sung by Anne Sofie von Otter DEUTSCHE GRAMMOPHON 439 928-2

Mahler 'Kindertotenlieder' sung by Kathleen Ferrier, EMI GOM5669112

Reich 'Different Trains' Kronos Quartet ELEKTRA NONE-SUCH 979 176-2

The author and publishers would like to thank the following for permission to reproduce illustrative material:

Judith Becker, *Traditional Music in Modern Java*, University of Hawaii Press, 1981, 162–3; Bibliothèque Nationale, Paris, ix; Bibliothèque Royale Albert I, Brussels, 72; The British Library, 16; The British Museum, 57; Fanshawe One-World Music, 207; Houston Grand Opera/Jim Caldwell, 82; The Lebrecht Collection, 26, 30, 32, 123, 124, 149, 157, 192, 210; Lianne Henscher/Bruce Hyman/Above The Title Productions, 223; Library of Congress, Washington, 69; Granet Museum, Aix-en-Provence, 146; Musée de Bourges, 113, 141; Royal Opera House Archives, 197; Richard H. Smith, 96; Paul Sommers, frontispiece; Tom Uglow, 108; US Department of the Interior/Edison National Historic Site, 181; Mark Williams, 5.

INDEX